MOMOTARO

XANDER AND THE DREAM THIEF

MARGARET DILLOWAY

with illustrations by Choong Yoon

DISNEY · HYPERION

Los Angeles   New York

First Hardcover Edition, April 2017
First Paperback Edition, April 2018
1 3 5 7 9 10 8 6 4 2
FAC-025438-18047
Printed in the United States of America

This book is set in Penumbra Sans/Fontspring; Fournier/Monotype.
Designed by Joann Hill

Library of Congress Cataloging-in-Publication Control
Number for Hardcover Edition: 2016010073
ISBN 978-1-4847-9007-6

Visit www.DisneyBooks.com

SUSTAINABLE
FORESTRY
INITIATIVE

Certified Chain of Custody
Promoting Sustainable Forestry

www.sfiprogram.org
SFI-01054
The SFI label applies to the text stock

For Keith, who makes all my dreams come true

"If you wish to control others, you must first control yourself."

—Musashi Miyamoto,

The Book of Five Rings, 1645

No matter how many hours pass, the right moment never comes. Is there ever a good time to interfere? the pale old man wonders. In the past, he was always so sure he was right. Now he doubts everything.

His stooped form hovers in the doorway of the sleeping boy's room, not quite inside and not quite outside. His silvery shoulder blades stick into the hallway with its clusters of family photos; his transparent chest faces the hand-drawn pictures tacked to the boy's walls; the rest of his body is squarely in the center of the hollow door. Such flimsy things, the old man muses. These doors could not block a licking flame, or even subdue a shout. He wishes he could tell his son, Akira, to replace them with solid wood. He sighs, thinking of all the things he wants to tell his only child but cannot.

The boy has been thrashing in his tangled sheets all night, and perspiration is making his silver hair stick to his scalp. It looks like strands of tinsel on a Christmas tree. Poor Xander. The pale old man inhales sharply. I could appear in his dreams, make things easier for my grandson.

No, the old man decides reluctantly. He mustn't. Xander has to learn on his own how to deal with his new abilities, no matter how painful it may be to observe his struggles. The old man had treated Akira the same way. When, as a boy, Akira was beaten up by the local bullies, the old man had not stepped in. Instead, he had watched from inside their house, cringing at every blow to his helpless son, praying that Akira would summon his warrior strength. And then there were all those times he had forced Akira to practice his sword work over and over, never accepting less than perfection, even when his son had cried and begged to stop, even when his hands had blistered. The oni won't care if you cry, he had told the boy. Blisters turn into calluses.

But maybe he'd been wrong about it all. Perhaps what his wife had said was true: he'd been too hard on his son—too gruff, too unbending. He should have shown him more kindness. Then Akira wouldn't have moved to America, far away from the father he believed had the soul of a glacier. If only he knew, thought the old man, how much that had hurt me. His own heart had turned into a callus in the end.

He tightens his obi belt around his waist and adjusts his kimono collar, which had slipped down uncomfortably. You'd think that a ghost wouldn't be bothered by things like clothing anymore.

The dog sleeping at Xander's feet sighs and rolls over onto his back, his large golden paws splayed apart, his tongue flopping out of his mouth. Inu, wake up Xander! the old man thinks at him. One big dark eye opens halfway, unseeing, before the dog covers it with his leg. The old man can't help but smile, remembering the feel of Inu's great-great-grandfather's soft curls under his fingertips.

Now Xander's fists fly out at invisible opponents, flailing in the darkness. A strangled groan escapes his throat as beads of sweat pop out on his face. His grandfather wavers, disappearing into the fake wood paneling of the door for a moment. Forget it. He will help Xander. He can't stand watching this struggle. He won't make the same mistake he did with Akira.

He thinks of Ozuno, the head of the oni, monsters determined to kill the Momotaro and the entire human race. He envisions Ozuno's mocking eyes trained on his only grandson. Xander must prepare, before it is too late. . . .

Then he remembers how Xander won his first important battle, despite knowing little about his powers. His grandson has already demonstrated that he can be the greatest Momotaro ever, the one who may finally defeat Ozuno once and for all. His strength must be allowed to grow on its own.

Now isn't the time. Later, perhaps, but not now.

Reluctantly, the old man backs away, through the door, into the stillness of the hall. He can't watch this struggle anymore. He'll go downstairs to check on his ancient wife.

But maybe there's one thing he can do. The old man lifts a picture and lets it bang against the wall, waking the boy from his slumber.

CHAPTER ONE

My feet thud against the pine-needled forest floor. My arms feel rubbery; my toes are smashing against the ends of my red Converse. In the shivery mountain air, my breath mists into a cloud. My lungs burn, and I hack.

Welcome to Dad's physical fitness day.

The golden sunlight streaming through the trees glitters with dust motes and gnats. It's completely silent, unless you count my cough, which makes me sound like a howler monkey with the flu.

"Quiet! Your enemies will hear you. Don't slow down!" my father shouts from someplace above me. "Move those toothpicks you call arms!"

"Trying," I manage to squeak out. I'm getting light-headed, and my ears are buzzing. Then suddenly I'm lying facedown, as if I'd been shoved, though I didn't feel anything on my back. My palms are on the ground, arms tensed into a push-up position. With my weak stomach muscles trembling from the effort, I try to keep my body stick-straight as I lower my chest to the imaginary tennis ball below. Farther, farther, farther, I will myself. If I don't get low enough, the push-up doesn't count, and Dad will make me start all over again.

Something heavy slams against my spine. "Extra weight." Dad's standing above me now. Is that his foot? This is a new torture. "Keep going. One hundred fifty."

"But I've only ever done twenty." My body quivers like a feather, then gives out. "I can't."

Dad's foot drives my stomach straight into the ground. I can't breathe. "I'm sick of your excuses!" He leans down, puts his face right next to mine. His breath reeks of old coffee and partially digested eggs. I wrinkle my nose, try not to gag.

"Get off me," I pant.

"You need to learn, Xander!" Dad's voice sounds almost . . . gleeful. Is he *enjoying* this? What's wrong with him?

Anger roils up into my midsection like a great coiled python. "I don't want to."

"You will." Dad releases the pressure, and I flip over.

I get unsteadily to my feet, feeling my lip curl into a sneer. If he's going to be so mean, I'm not going to stick around. "I'm done. You can't make me do this." I turn to head for home.

"You're not done until I say you're done." Dad digs his fingers into my shoulder. *Ouch.*

I turn, shove him without looking. "Leave me alone!"

My palm sinks into his flesh, which is as mushy as moldy bread. I gasp and look at my hand, expecting to see it covered with goop, but it's clean. "What—?"

A voice comes from up above. "Xander, why don't you ever listen to your father?"

I slowly lift my head toward the treetops.

Dad floats in the air as if lifted by invisible threads. His hair hangs in a silver curtain around his face, hiding it.

He's floating because he has no feet.

"Dad?" My voice sounds like the peep of a baby chick.

He doesn't answer, just swivels in a slow circle, up in the air. All casual, like this happens every day.

Uh-oh.

I have a fairly good suspicion that this most definitely is *not* my father.

Time to use my Momotaro power.

I take a step back and try to lapse into the relaxed half-dreaming state I need to be in for my powers to work. *Disappear!*

Nothing happens.

The wraith thing moves its hair enough for me to see a silver eye, the color of a tarnished knife, glaring out of its nothing face.

————

I wake up choking, like a goldfish too long out of its bowl. I try to orient myself.

I take a big breath and enjoy the oxygen. My alarm clock blinks 5:30 A.M. in big red letters. A whole half hour before I need to get up. Inu, my big Goldendoodle, snores at my feet, sounding like a rooting pig.

I breathe a deep sigh of pure relief.

I should've known it was a dream when Dad called my arms "toothpicks." He'd never say something so mean in real life. I rub the sleep crust out of my blurry eyes, fluff my pillow, and flop around, trying to find a comfortable position. Let's see . . . that makes nightmare number four tonight.

First I dreamed that I got held back in sixth grade—and Mr. Stedman, who won the Most Boring Teacher of the Year Award (a secret award given by me and my best friend, Peyton), was going to teach all my classes. I'd woken up so sweaty, I was afraid I'd wet the bed.

Then I dreamed that I'd failed as Momotaro, and everyone I loved had been killed by oni. I shudder thinking of that one. I'd woken with tears streaming down my face, scream-sobbing so loud that Dad had run in to see what was wrong. That's when he told Inu to get on my bed and stay there.

The third I can't recall. I just know it was a nightmare because I woke up thrashing, with Inu whining anxiously and licking my face to wake me.

Will I never have a good night's sleep again? The nightmares have been bothering me ever since we got back from that island of monsters.

I can't take any more of this baloney.

I sit up, my mouth feeling as sticky as a movie theater floor. My water glass is all the way across my room, on the desk.

I extend my hand toward the glass and envision it flying through the air.

Smack! I feel the cold glass hit my palm.

I smile as a small surge of victory goes through me. At least I can still do this, make things happen with my imagination. I gulp down the water and wipe my mouth with the back of my hand, trying not to feel guilty.

Dad told me not to go around using my powers all the time. "There's a cost to our magic, Xander," he had said. "For me, it's terrible headaches—something like the flu. For you, we're not sure yet."

I've been doing stuff like this for the past two months, ever since I found out I'm the Momotaro. Once, I thought Momotaro was only a Japanese legend, about a boy warrior who fought the oni, the monsters responsible for all the bad things—wars, natural disasters— that go on in the human world. But when the oni took my father, I suddenly discovered that Momotaro wasn't a legend after all.

Momotaro is me.

And my father before me, and my grandfather before that, and so on and so on, going all the way back to the original peach boy (yes, that's what his name means—the warrior was found inside a giant peach). And every Momotaro basically had the same kind of powers, until I came along.

I'm different. I'm half-Japanese and half-Irish, and my father isn't quite sure how this will affect me. Hopefully, it'll all be for the better. Dad acts like I might accidentally cause the house to explode, but I control my powers with my imagination, and my imagination is always under control. So I'm perfectly fine. Better than fine, in fact. I'm like Xander 2.0, the beta version. I'm super-booted, and all my bugs have been fixed.

I just don't let Dad see me doing it. It's easier this way.

Besides, how am I ever going to find out what all my powers are like if I never get to use them? Nobody knows when the oni will try something again. And if I'm not ready, maybe next time I won't be able to defeat them.

The way I won last time was just plain dumb luck. Me fumbling around, trying to figure out my new abilities. Plus, I had the help of my friends: Jinx, Peyton, and Inu.

What I haven't told my father, or anyone, is how really, really not heroic I feel about the possibility of tangling with the oni again. Battling monsters from the underworld or wherever isn't as much fun as it seems in the movies. Part of me wants to just hide in this bedroom forever so I don't have to deal with any of it. I wonder how easy it would be to build a fortress around this house.

I glance at the clock again, then decide it's not worth going back to sleep. This morning, we're going to actually do the mountain training I was failing in my dream. Hopefully, Dad won't turn into a drill-sergeant-wraith in the middle of it, though.

I free my legs from the tangled sheets. We've been getting up early to do some form of training every day since school let out for the summer two weeks ago. We do physical activity in the morning, while the weather's still cool. In the afternoons, we sit around in my un-air-conditioned house, sweatily reading ultra-boring books written by samurai who lived six hundred years ago.

We won't get to the good part—sword training—until the middle of July. I sigh noisily. Longest. Summer. Ever. And not in a good way. Maybe I wouldn't be having so many nightmares if I were having some actual fun.

Inu opens one large brown eye and chuffs at me like a tiger.

"Wanna get up, buddy?" I swing my legs out of bed.

He shuts his eye and grunts ruefully.

No doubt Inu's tired from my waking him multiple times in the night. He probably thinks I'm crazy for not staying in bed. But the sweet, delicious, greasy-salty scent of bacon is wafting up the stairs. I can hear it sizzling in the pan down in the kitchen. My stomach rumbles. Maybe my nightmares just didn't want me to miss the yumminess.

I hold on to that thought and hop out of bed. Inu yawns loudly, and then, his nails clattering on the hardwood, he slowly follows me downstairs.

CHAPTER TWO

My mother stands in front of the stove, using the cast-iron skillet that's older than my father and me put together. She shrieks and dances back as hot bacon grease spatters. "Ack! I should've worn my welding mask," she says. A chipper smile flashes in my direction, but I don't return it. Inu sits down next to her to watch the bacon as intently as a cat watches a bird.

"Time to do your business, Inu." I open the back door, temporarily sweeping aside the dried beans that line the doorway. The beans, called *"fuku mame,"* are supposed to keep out the oni. In some places in Japan, people still participate in bean-throwing festivals. To them, it's just an ancient tradition. To my family, the beans are the real thing. Anyone who visits us wonders why we have them all over our floors. It's a good thing we're practically hermits.

Dad says the fuku mame are a kind of insurance, to buy us a little time. They wouldn't protect us from an army of oni camped outside the house, but they're better than nothing.

Inu ignores me. I sit in a tattered lawn chair that has seen better days. When two people were suddenly added to our family, we had to call our outside chairs into service in the kitchen. I slap my thigh. "Come here, Inu. Stop begging." But he just sort of nods his big golden curly head and continues to watch my mother. There's no distracting him when it comes to bacon.

"You're up early, *mo chroí*." This is Irish for *my heart*. You don't even want to know what she calls my father. "How did you sleep? Better, I hope." My mother, her wild red hair tamed by a blue bandanna, wearing oversize sweats and one of my father's old T-shirts, swivels to smile radiantly at me again. The sapphire wedding ring that my dad saved for her glints on her finger.

"I slept okay," I lie, not wanting her to fly into her *oh-my-love-I'm-so-worried-about-you* mode. You know how mothers are—you tell them ONE THING and then they make such a fuss that you wish you'd kept your big mouth shut. I trace a scar on the table from a hot-glue-gun project gone wrong.

Mother.

I'm still not used to thinking that word. To seeing her in our kitchen, cooking breakfast. As if she hadn't been MIA for eight long years. Almost my whole childhood.

Shea, I call her. Not Mom.

It's been two months since Shea returned.

She was waiting at home when we—Dad, Peyton, my sort-of friend Jinx, and Inu—all came back from the island of monsters. Where I had tried out my Momotaro oni-fighting skills.

If it weren't for the silver hair I ended up with, I might have doubted that the whole adventure actually happened. That it wasn't some dream I'd had while battling the flu.

Anyway, when we arrived home that day, we expected to see the house still wrecked from the earthquake and tsunami that had happened a few days earlier. But everything looked to be in good shape. Instead, something else was waiting for us.

Shea stood in the kitchen, chatting with my grandmother. Both of them were laughing as if she'd gone out for milk and, I don't know, gotten stuck in traffic for a few minutes. Like it was not a big deal.

All the joy I'd felt at saving my father from the demons (not to mention the world, too, ahem) drained out of me in a big, practically audible *whoosh*, like air escaping a slashed tire.

I stared at the woman, not knowing who she was at first. Or—if I'm being honest—knowing who she was and wishing I didn't.

My father let out a *whoop*, swept her into his arms, and smooched her like they were on the cover of one of those gag-worthy romance novels. Minus the shirtlessness, thank goodness. "Shea!" he cried.

I just stood there like I was playing freeze tag. *Who is this?* my head asked over and over again. *Does not compute. Fatal error. Fatal error.*

Your mother, my gut answered, but I didn't want to believe my gut. It didn't seem real. I stared at her some more. A gale-force wind couldn't have blown me over.

When my parents finished their clinch, Shea turned to me with a wide smile. "Xander."

My nose began running as if someone had turned on a spigot, and my eyes burned with salty tears. I felt my lips quivering and my throat shaking like a maraca. I wanted to run away and I wanted to hug her at the same time.

"Xander," Shea repeated. "Baby. *Mo chroí.* I cannot believe it. My little lad, all grown up." She took a step toward me, holding out her hands. Her long white fingers looked as delicate as a porcelain doll's. And about as realistic.

I opened my mouth to say something. Anything. *Hi. Long time no see. What the heck are you doing here? Why did you leave me?*

Maybe even *Don't you know how much you hurt me?*

But my vocal cords wouldn't work. Instead, a garbled noise, the sort of sound you make before you're going to be sick, burbled out. I clapped a hand over my mouth.

She reached me in a single step and wrapped her arms around my shoulders.

I stiffened. It might as well have been a random woman off the street hugging me. Then I inhaled her scent—a mix of flowers and green grass and orange slices—and I knew, without a doubt, who she was.

It was my mother, all right. And I wanted nothing to do with her. I shoved her away. "No." It came out of my mouth like a moan. "No. Where were you? Where have you been? I thought you were dead!"

Dad stepped toward me. "Xander, let us explain."

"No." I held out my hand, and both of my parents stood still. "How dare you?" My voice was low and steady now. I pointed at Shea. "What makes you think we want you back? That you can just walk in here like nothing's happened? I've got news for you. We've been fine this whole time."

"Xander!" Dad's voice dropped an octave.

"We don't need you!" I continued. "In fact, maybe you did us a favor."

Dad glared at me. "Do not speak to your mother like that."

Shea touched him on the shoulder. "It's all right," she murmured in her sonorous Irish accent. "Let him have some time."

"I don't need time. What I needed"—I blinked back my tears—"was a mother when I was growing up. In the past!"

Her face crumpled as if I'd hit her with a brick. Good. I turned and ran upstairs to my bedroom before I could start feeling bad about it.

They'd given me an hour to calm down before my father knocked on my door. I lay on my bed staring up at the ceiling, trying to figure out how all this had happened. How I'd become Momotaro and fought demons and gotten silver hair and my mother back, all in one fell swoop.

Before that, life had been so boring. I kind of missed boring.

"Xander?" Dad tiptoed into the room. His face was both wrinkled with worry and full of joy. A happiness I hadn't seen in him since forever. "Son, this is a good thing, your mother coming home. Believe it or not."

I swiveled away from my father, staring at the wall.

Dad sat on my bed and patted my back. "Xander, I couldn't tell you this before." He drew in a breath. "There's a lot to the story you don't know."

"What?" I wiped my nose on my sleeve. "Did you do something bad to her to make her leave?" I said it, but I didn't believe it for one second.

"Of course not," Dad confirmed. "Your mother had to leave for your safety."

"What's that supposed to mean?" I moved away from Dad's hand. "Was she in the witness protection program or something?"

He hesitated. "In a way. You see, your mother—she has this . . . well, this light about her. A glow."

"Ew." I rolled my eyes. "I saw you guys kiss. I don't need to know about that. Please."

"No." Dad laughs a little bit. "I mean your mother has a literal light. One the oni can spot."

I rolled over so I could stare at him with my best poker face. What on earth did he mean?

Dad fiddled with the blanket. "You know how I'm a Momotaro? *Was*, I mean? You're the Momotaro now because there can only be one at a time."

During our journey, Dad had explained that his powers were gradually transferring to me. As mine grew stronger, his would fade away.

"Yeah." A surge of pride went through me. *Momotaro*. The one who had bested those monsters—the snow woman, the kappa, the oni eggs, and, of course, Jinx's dad.

Dad nodded. "Well, your mother's not exactly normal, either, Xander." He seemed to be having trouble figuring out the words he wanted to use. "She's a fairy."

"What?" I bolted upright, almost jumping clear off the bed. My head must have looked like it was about to spin off its axis. "A fairy fairy? Like Tinker Bell?"

Dad laughed and pushed his glasses up his nose. "Not the teeny-tiny kind. No, Shea's part of the tall folk, who traditionally protect Irish land." Dad cocked his head at me. "Before you were born, your mother only glowed when she was using her powers. She could control it. But after you came, her glow became stronger. Brighter every year. She had no control over it anymore. By the time you were four, it was becoming a real problem."

I sat down next to him.

"The oni can see this glow, Xander. We were worried she was becoming a beacon. So she left. To protect you. So they wouldn't find you before you were ready."

I considered this, turning it over and over in my head like a coin. "But why did her glow appear only after I was born?"

Dad's shoulders moved up and down. "We don't know, Xander. Some connection to her baby? The joy of motherhood? It hadn't happened to her other relatives, though. We think it may have something to do with the Momotaro powers interacting with hers."

"But didn't the oni already know where you were, Dad?" I raked my fingers through my hair. I wasn't sure this was making sense. Maybe it never would.

Dad's mouth flickered into a smile. "I'd stopped fighting oni before I even met your mother, Xander. They no longer cared about me."

I grabbed Dad's arm. "But now they know *me*. Is she still glowing? Could they find us now?"

Dad nodded. "Yes, but they already know where we are. You have your powers. You can protect yourself, and we can help." He put his hand on my shoulder. "We were going to wait until you turned thirteen to tell you. But it didn't go as we'd hoped."

I snorted. "Understatement of the millennium."

Dad sighed. "I know, son. We did our best." He swallowed audibly. "We managed to buy you some time, at least."

I looked at Dad's creased face, and I couldn't help but gulp, too.

"So does this mean the oni will never stop coming after me? My whole life?"

He hesitated, as if he was thinking about the best way to break the news to me. "Correct," he said at last.

My stomach already knew the truth. I clenched my hands against the knot under my belly button. "What are they going to do—form an army and march up to the house?"

"Well," Dad said slowly, "they might just continue their work in the human world. Cause World War Three, more global warming. And hope you don't do anything about it." Dad lowered his eyes for a moment. "I'm afraid that's what happened with me, Xander. I wasn't a strong Momotaro. You see, I thought there was another way. That I could find better, more permanent answers in the lore, buried somewhere in the stories." He took off his glasses and rubbed his eyes. "As a result, things got out of hand. Perhaps I should have been more on the offensive."

I understood then why Dad had become a professor of folklore, so he could immerse himself in fairy tales and stories. My stomach hurt even worse. "What you're saying is you expect me to go out there and launch some kind of war against the oni?"

His mouth twisted. "You will have to defeat their king, Ozuno. Eventually," he added hastily, as if that would make me feel any better. "First we must train you and see what powers you have."

I drew my knees up to my chest. "And what'll happen if I don't? Will the world end?"

"The oni have spent many years growing in strength and number," my father answered. "If this continues, the world won't end. But it won't be the same." He drew in a shuddering breath. "They feed on discord and suffering, Xander."

It was like every single fear I'd ever had had gotten tangled into one huge knot. I wanted to hide under my bed and explode at the same time. I grabbed Dad's arm. "If all this is true, then what difference would it have made if Mom had been here the whole time?"

"A big one. You might not be here, talking to me. Had they known about you before now, they would have tried to take you out before you discovered your powers." Dad pressed his forehead against mine so I could see my eyes reflected in his, light blue inside light blue. "Xander, please don't blame your mother for all this. I know it's a shock, especially after our whole adventure. You need time, that's all."

I reached up to rub my eyes and realized my hands were wet. Look at that, crying and I didn't even know it. "It's just . . ." I faltered, trying to figure out *what* I was feeling. Nothing, I decided. Though I was crying, I felt numb inside. "She's a stranger, Dad. I don't know that woman. What if she's changed? You have, and I sure as heck have. Everybody except Obāchan has. What if she doesn't . . ." I couldn't continue.

"I'm sure you have nothing to worry about. Give her a chance." Dad wiped my tears away with his thumb. It felt rough, like a cat's tongue. "For me."

CHAPTER THREE

So I've been trying, for Dad's sake. Really I have. But whenever I see Shea, I don't just see the lady standing before me. I see every mother-son event at school when I had to go with my grandma instead. I see way more nights than I want to remember when I cried myself to sleep because my mother wasn't there to sing to me. I see me waiting for the mail carrier every day, and his small pitying shake of the head when he didn't have a letter from her.

Letters aren't beacons. They're paper. She could've sent something. A postcard. A carrier pigeon. A message in a bottle. A telepathic message—what good is being a fairy if you can't send something super cool like that?

But, oh no, she never bothered. Instead, she traipsed back to Ireland and was the veterinarian on her family's horse farm, birthing foals, blacksmithing horseshoes, and taking care of the land the tall folk are supposed to protect. I would have liked to have visited, to meet the grandparents and aunts and uncles I hardly know anything about.

And judging from the looks of her, from how completely not sorry and unaffected she is, wrinkle-free and glowing, she had a grand old time without the burden of her son and husband weighing her down. She was like the Irish Beyoncé doing her single ladies dance across the pond.

"Xander." My mother's voice is sharp.

I blink and shake myself out of my thoughts.

Shea is holding out a plate of bacon and eggs at my eye level. "Are you hungry, love?" She puts the dish on the table, and I say nothing, just lift my fork and shovel a mouthful in. "A thank-you would be nice." Her accent grows thicker with each word.

"Arigato goʒaimasu." I bow my head so low my forehead smacks the table. She flinches. "Thank you. I am most appreciative of this wonderful breakfast you prepared with the food that my father has paid for."

She inhales noisily, annoyance rising off her like steam from a fresh-baked cake, then turns back to the stove and cracks two more eggs into the frying pan.

Good. If she can feel just a tenth as bad—or even a twentieth as bad—as I felt all those years, then maybe, just maybe, we'll be even.

I take a piece of bacon and shove it into my mouth. It's

overcooked, dry, too salty. I spit it into my hand and throw it at Inu, who catches it more surely than a major league outfielder.

I regard the rest of the bacon on the plate, and my stomach flips. Obāchan's bacon is always perfect. I open my mouth to tell Shea that she ought to take cooking lessons from my grandmother.

"Xander." As if on cue, Obāchan shuffles into the kitchen, shooting her warning evil eye my way. "Look at all this work your mother has done. I hope you appreciate it. Good morning, Shea."

I clamp my mouth shut and nod.

"Good morning, Aya." Shea is the only one who calls my grandmother by her first name. My mother turns off the burner under the bacon pan and wipes her hands on a kitchen towel. "It's no trouble at all. Happy to do it." She gives us a smile. "I'm going to go wake up your dad." Shea disappears.

Obāchan shakes her head at me, and I know she's heard everything I said. "She's really trying, you know."

I shrug. Inu leaps over to Obāchan, his whole body wiggling as if he hasn't seen her in thirty years. "Sit," she commands, and she waits until he does before she pets him. "Good boy." She settles into a regular dining chair with a sigh and a grimace. "These old bones are feeling mighty old these days."

I hop up and go to the cupboard where we keep the medicine. Obāchan's got at least five dozen different bottles and tubes that nearly spill out when I open it, but I find her Tiger Balm for sore muscles. "You want this, Obāchan?"

"Thank you." She smiles at me, her face oddly smooth even though she's older than any grandparent I've ever met. Meaning she won't tell me how old she is.

I make sure my mom's not coming back into the room and lower my voice. "So, tell me, did you and Ojīchan welcome my mother into the family? You weren't worried about Dad marrying a fairy?"

She laughs. "Your father never asked for our opinion. He didn't tell us until they'd been married for half a year." Obāchan takes a paper napkin from the center of the table and folds it absently as she speaks. "I trusted your father to pick a good woman. Ojīchan was worried, of course, not knowing how a fairy would affect a Momotaro. . . ." She bites her lip, lost in some sad memory. When she looks up, her eyes are bright. "Shea was the best thing that ever happened to your father. She was the one who convinced him to call us. Before that, he and your grandfather hadn't spoken to each other for years. They never did make up. . . ." Obāchan blows out a breath. "Ah. What's done is done." She crumples the napkin and throws it at me playfully, then changes the subject. "You are up awfully early. Still having nightmares, eh?"

"Yup." I eat a tasteless piece of bacon. My head feels like it's full of lead. "All I want to do is crawl back into bed. How am I ever going to finish Dad's training if I can never get a full night's rest?" My eyes fill with tears. That's another thing. Not sleeping makes me way more emotional than usual. Now I can see why keeping people awake is a method of torture.

"Your father will understand, Xander." Obāchan scratches under Inu's chin, and he closes his eyes in bliss.

A shuddering sigh escapes me. "Obāchan, I don't know if I can deal with this whole hero thing. How will I ever be able to sleep, knowing the oni could be coming after me at any second?" This is the first time I've spoken the fear out loud. Instead of dispelling it, though, it makes it worse.

Obāchan puts her hand on top of mine. "I know it's scary. But you cannot worry about the oni bothering you any more than you can worry about a wildfire or getting hit by a car."

Great. More things to be anxious about. "Gee, thanks."

"Xander, anything could happen at any time, oni or no oni. You're as safe as you ever were. The difference now is that you know about the oni. And you have powers to use against them."

I stick my fingers into my hair, making it stand up. "Obāchan, I know you think you're helping, but you're not, actually." I wonder if I could move someplace else. Like Canada. Or Antarctica. Some new place to hide.

Obāchan blinks at me several times. "I'm going to do something for you, Xander. You grandfather would tell me not to interfere, but I didn't interfere with your father and it made things worse."

"You mean the whole oni-growing-stronger thing?" I wipe my tears away, hoping she hasn't noticed them. "Yeah, I kind of agree." If my dad or grandfather had defeated the oni, I wouldn't have to deal with any of this.

She mutters something to herself in Japanese, then reaches into the neckline of her kimono and takes off a red string hanging around her neck. A green pendant dangles from it. "I dug this out of my closet for you, Xander. A *baku* charm. It's jade."

It looks like an elephant, except it has no big ears. Maybe an anteater with a long nose. "What is it? An oni?"

"No. More like a *yōkai*. A supernatural creature, not a demon."

"What's it do?" In stories, yōkai aren't necessarily bad. Many are benign, or playful.

"Put it under your pillow," Obāchan says, taking a piece of dry bacon. "When you have a bad dream, call to it: *Baku, baku, come eat my dream*. Then you won't have another nightmare that night."

Sounds easy enough. "Okay, thanks." The jade is cold and heavy in my palm. "Will the baku literally come into my room, or what?"

"Or what," Obāchan says. "She will come into your dreams. Don't worry, she's not scary." She smiles at me. "I used the baku charm when I was your age."

"Oh." I grin at her. "So it's super old."

She laughs, then gets serious. "But remember"—she puts her hand on my arm—"only use it as needed. Do you understand? Otherwise the baku will get impatient with you."

I put the string around my neck, feeling the cold jade thump against my chest. "I will use the baku responsibly."

Inu appears at my leg, drool already coming out of his mouth, sticking to the fur of his beard. *Woof,* he says, and puts one huge paw on my thigh.

Obāchan stands, pushing her chair away from the table. "I'm going to put this Tiger Balm on."

"Maybe you can make breakfast tomorrow?" I catch hold of her hand. It's smaller than mine but quite possibly a lot stronger, like sparrow bones made of steel.

Obāchan grins. "Okay. How about some fish-head soup, salted salmon, and fermented soybeans?"

I drop her hand. "Sure," I say with as much false bravery as I can muster. "Yum."

"Be careful what you wish for, Xander-chan." She pats my head before shuffling away with her tube of Tiger Balm clutched to her chest.

Inu slaps my leg with his paw again, and I throw him a piece of bacon. He catches it neatly.

"Don't feed the dog at the table," Shea says as she comes back into the kitchen.

"He's not a regular old dog." I pat Inu's soft head. With his golden curls and expressive brown eyes, he resembles a gigantic living teddy bear. With hidden sharp teeth. "He saved my life."

"Still, you don't want him doing that to guests, do you?"

"Nobody comes over but Peyton. Who cares?" I push my eggs around with my fork. They're too runny, the whites like snot. I put the plate down rather noisily on the floor for Inu, then brace myself for a lecture.

Instead, Shea shrugs and pours herself a cup of coffee. "You'll be hungry in half an hour. But suit yourself."

"I will." I stomp away. For some reason, her blasé response makes me even angrier. When I get to my bedroom, I slam the door hard enough to wake the rest of the neighborhood.

CHAPTER FOUR

n my room, I sit and stare at all the pictures covering the walls; images of Pokémon and superheroes and monsters flap in the breeze. I should tear them all down. They're old and no good. I'm so over drawing.

The last time I was really into it, I made pictures without even knowing I was doing it, as though I had temporary amnesia. I drew a whole comic book about the tale of Momotaro, I created a picture of the demon that was coming after me, and—worst of all, in terms of getting into real-world trouble—I drew a really mean caricature of a girl from school.

Maybe if I don't draw anymore, nothing bad will happen. Or at least I won't have to worry about it ahead of time. Drawing things that become real is like a being a fortune-teller who can predict how he's going to die. Who wants to think about that?

I get up and start pulling down the pictures. They're mostly pretty bad. I think I traced some of these superheroes. I don't know why I ever thought I was any good.

The room looks strange when it's bare. I'd forgotten I had beige walls. I tear off a piece of Scotch tape still stuck to the wall. I could repaint, but I don't even know what my favorite color is anymore.

I shove the drawings into a desk drawer, smooshing them down so they fit, and sit on my bed. My stomach grumbles. Maybe I could create in a different way. . . . I imagine a plate of French toast, buttery and covered in real maple syrup, sitting on my lap. I relax and close my eyes.

Sure enough, suddenly there's a small weight on top of my thighs. I open my eyes and grin.

French toast on a platter! Happiness washes over me like a shaken-up soda.

"Who's the best at magic? *Xander*. Who can make whatever he wants? *Xander*." I snap my fingers at an imaginary crowd. "Let's give it up for Xander! Yeah!"

Unfortunately, I forgot to imagine a fork, so I have to use my fingers. I don't care. I suck off the syrup and wipe some of it on my bedspread. A little stickiness never hurt anybody. Mmm. It is, literally, magically delicious. Hey, maybe I'm part leprechaun, too. I chuckle to myself.

I know the stuff I conjured is about as substantial as cotton candy, but it doesn't matter. I can create more food while we're on the hike. I'll just go off into the bushes, pretending I have to answer a call of nature, and then imagine myself a big sandwich. I'll get by.

When I finish, I put the plate on my desk, knocking a pile of papers onto the floor. Ugh. This room's a mess. Dirty clothes cover the floor. Comics and books are strewn all over the place. In fact, it looks sort of like it did after that earthquake hit.

And Dad told me I had to clean it by suppertime.

The problem is, my room's way too small. I need more space. A place where I can play video games with Peyton. A spot for us to hang out. Maybe a bunk bed.

Why not do more? a voice whispers in my head. *If you can imagine it, why not?*

Before I fully think it out, the room shimmers. A bunk bed materializes under me. The room expands to twice its size, complete with a small couch and a big flat-screen TV. A desk against a wall holds three brand-new computers and state-of-the-art gaming equipment.

It is glorious.

"Whoa," I breathe. My whole body tingles, and my heart thunders as if I've just won first prize in a contest. I get up and pick up a game remote. A brand-new PlayStation. Of course, Dad will never pay for a subscription in a million years. I could try to play, though. Maybe my Momotaro powers can access the network for free.

What else can I do with my powers?

A pounding at my door startles me. Jinx yells, "Leaving in ten. Your dad says not to dillydally!"

And just like that, the room evaporates. I see a sharp flash of red out of the corner of my eye—probably anger descending over me like a cloak. "The world's not going to end if we're late," I mutter. "It's just a stupid hike!"

"*You're* stupid!" Jinx pounds the door again.

I lick some extra syrup off my fingers. "Takes one to know one," I call back.

"That doesn't even make any sense!" she responds before she stomps away.

Jinx and I haven't exactly ended up as best buds since she moved in. I guess that shouldn't be a surprise, given how annoying she has always been.

When I first met Jinx, she was living in a jungle. Well, technically she was imprisoned by a snow witch, but her natural habitat was in the trees. She was rude and could climb really well. So I called her the monkey girl.

It's not an insult. According to the legend, Momotaro originally had three companions—a monkey, a bird, and a dog. Peyton, my best friend, had actually sprouted wings on our adventure, so he played the bird role. Inu was a magically strong supercanine in the other world. And Jinx was my monkey friend. A half-demon monkey friend who betrayed me initially, but it all turned out okay. Even if she does still annoy me sometimes.

After we returned home, we couldn't exactly send Jinx back to live alone in the enchanted jungle again. And Dad realized that Jinx's mom was from our world, and she was a friend of Shea's. That's another thing Jinx and I have in common: mothers who took off.

Her mother had had serious problems. Exactly what they were, Jinx never told me. But I do know that her mom ended up giving her ex full custody. And her ex just happened to be an oni named Gozu.

Since Gozu could take whatever form he felt like, I couldn't really blame Jinx's mom for being fooled by him. Gozu was the one who had taken Jinx to the island of monsters and used her against me.

Anyway, now Jinx's mother was nowhere to be found. Dad had decreed that Jinx would live with us for as long as she needed. Which, realistically, will probably be forever.

We turned Dad's office into her bedroom. She painted it black and hung dark blue curtains over the windows, so it now looks like an undersea cave where horrible creatures lurk. Very cheerful. Dad even got her an iPod and speakers, so her mournful emo music pipes through the house day and night, people wailing about how sad they are because the world's against them specifically.

The first thing Dad had wanted to do after we got settled in was to register Jinx for school.

"It's the end of the year!" Jinx had complained. "What's the point?"

I'd agreed. What would happen at school when Jinx, the wild monkey woman of the jungle, with her crazy Medusa-like hair and rude mouth, showed up? Not to mention me, with my silver hair?

"It's better than Jinx sitting around doing nothing at home," Dad had pointed out.

"She needs to reintegrate into society first," I had argued for her. I saw a documentary about that once. "Like a soldier coming back from war." Then I thought of something else. "Oh! Maybe Peyton and I should take the rest of the year off, too."

"If you do, you'll repeat sixth grade," Dad had said drily.

So Jinx got enrolled in my grade, though she's a full year older than me and really ought to be in seventh grade. Dad had remembered which city she said she was born in (Honolulu), and he got a copy of her birth certificate. On the father line it says *unknown*. Just as well. Who would want to remember that their father was a demonic oni?

The day we went back to Oak Grove Lower after spring break, the school, naturally, went crazy. Here I was, showing up with silver hair, as though I'd gotten the shock of my life (and honestly, finding out you're Momotaro should qualify as the shock of anyone's life, so the whole silver hair thing makes total sense). Peyton looked like he'd aged five years overnight, his body all buffed out like a secret body builder's. Then there was Jinx. Though her hair was secured in a ponytail and her face was freshly scrubbed, she looked nothing like the other girls, with her muscular frame, suspicious eyes, and angry eyebrows. And in fact she *is* nothing like the other girls—not after living alone in the oni jungle for who knows how long.

We were sort of like celebrities.

"What happened to you?" Lovey, our resident mean girl, pretty as a pop star but as venomous as a rattlesnake, looked me up and down as we sat in Mr. Stedman's social studies class. "Why's your hair all gray?"

"I dunno. I looked at your picture and then *poof*!" I widened my eyes at her.

Lovey grunted, pursing her lips. "Who's your new girlfriend?"

I shuddered. "*Not* girlfriend. More like a cousin."

Mr. Stedman was not pleased to receive a new student so late in the year. He didn't have an extra textbook. "I see I'm going to have to use my own funds to order one," he muttered to himself.

I raised my hand. "I'll be happy to lend Jinx my book, Mr. Stedman. Just give me a free pass for the rest of the year." I smiled angelically.

Mr. Stedman shook his head. "If you know what's good for you, Mr. Miyamoto, you'll keep your mouth closed for the rest of the year."

Jinx sat by Lovey's best friend, Clarissa. Who was also my friend, though I'll never understand in a billion years how anyone could like Lovey. "I'll share with her, Mr. Stedman," Clarissa said, tossing her mop of black curls off her shoulders. Jinx and Clarissa exchanged smiles, and before long, they were chatting in whispers like they'd known each other for years.

My stomach soured with dread. Lovey was not going to like this. Sure enough, when I looked up, she was eyeing Jinx from across the room, no doubt trying to figure out how to create DOOM.

Clarissa ate lunch with Jinx, Peyton, and me that day instead of with Lovey and her clique. Lovey tried waving Clarissa over, then threw her the evil eye and even texted her, *Come sit here*, but Clarissa ignored it all.

"Why don't you sit with Lovey anymore?" I finally asked Clarissa the next week. "Not that I'm complaining . . ."

Clarissa shrugged. "I'm just sick of all her stuff." She wrinkled her nose. "It's always the Lovey Show, you know? Maybe she'll learn to appreciate me when I'm gone." She smiled and took another bite of sandwich.

"You need to watch out for Lovey," I told Jinx.

Jinx cast a disparaging look in Lovey's direction. "Her? After dealing with oni and that jungle, Lovey's about as scary as a kitten."

Lovey's attempted revenge on Jinx came soon enough. Lovey and her little coven took action on an afternoon when Peyton's mom picked him up early for a doctor's appointment, and when Clarissa wasn't around.

Jinx and I were walking home, arguing. A totally normal day for us. "Obviously, the oni are causing humans to act badly and thereby causing global warming," Jinx was saying as we threaded our way through the alley behind the school. "If you don't think so, you haven't learned anything."

"So nobody is in charge of themselves?" I asked. "Like, if I push you right now, is that because of an oni or because I just feel like pushing you?"

Jinx blinked rapidly at me. "Considering that it's you we're talking about, Xander, I think there's a pretty high likelihood that it's an oni."

I sputtered with laughter. But then I remembered the wraith from my dreams, and I wasn't so sure.

Just then, Lovey and her five minions popped out from behind the Dumpster. "Jinx, I want to talk to you."

"You already are." Jinx stopped and regarded her with a stillness I recognized from being on the monster island with her. She *looked* calm, but she was ready to spring into action.

Lovey sort of blanched, as if she'd taken a bite of something she'd expected to be sweet but was actually sour. Then she gathered her composure and spat out her premeditated speech. "You think you're all that? Well, you're not. You're just a little orphan girl who lives with old man Xander over here." She nodded in my direction, and the other girls snickered on cue.

I glowered my best mean look at Lovey, eyebrows together, gaze hopefully as steely as the hull of one of those ice-breaking ships. "Knock it off, Lovey." Nobody gets to say bad stuff to Jinx. Except maybe me and Peyton. But we don't really mean it, so it doesn't count.

"Or what, little old man?" Lovey sneered at me.

"I'll take action." I crossed my arms.

Lovey laughed. "You can't fight a girl. You'll get suspended."

"Lovey, you outweigh me by, like, twenty pounds," I pointed out. "I'm pretty sure you have the advantage here." *As long as you don't know about my Momotaro power, that is.*

Lovey turned back to Jinx. The muscles on her neck bulged. Jinx had really gotten to her, I realized. I wondered if Clarissa had unfriended Lovey. "This is an *AB* conversation, Xander, so *C* your way out," Lovey said.

"Ha-ha. I've never heard that one before." I took one step toward her. "Let's settle this like the two civil people we are."

Lovey blinked. "There are three of us talking, genius."

"Like I said, *the two civil people*." I wanted to distract her from Jinx.

"I'm handling this, Xander. Go on home." Jinx pulled her shoulder blades together and straightened her neck as if an invisible wire pulled it taut. She walked over to Lovey and stopped about a half inch away. Jinx was a good two inches shorter than Lovey, but she planted her hands on her hips and stared at the girl with that eerie calmness that made me want to tell Lovey to run. I mean, Jinx *is* half-oni. She's the toughest person I've ever met.

Lovey licked her lips. "So? We going to settle this?"

"Settle what?" Jinx cocked her head to the side. "You're right."

"What?!" Lovey and I chorused.

Jinx ticked off the points on her fingers. "Yes, I am an orphan. Yes, Xander does look like an old man with that ridiculous hair."

"Hey!" I piped up.

Jinx put her hands down. "Yes, I am different from you. Because, even though I may have done some mean things, I'll never be as mean as you are."

Lovey glared at her, the color rising into her cheeks.

Jinx looked back at her calmly and allowed herself a smirk. "Your best friend likes me better, and you hate me for it. As for me, I don't really care."

Lovey's hands flexed and unflexed, and her eyes widened, but she didn't move. "You don't care? You should care!" The other girls shifted uncomfortably at their leader's humiliation.

Jinx shrugged. "What are you going to do about it?"

Lovey opened her mouth and took a breath as if she was about to say something, but she ended up closing it.

"That's what I thought." Jinx whirled around on her heel. "We're done here. Come on, Xander, let's go." Jinx, her back to Lovey, began walking away.

Lovey grabbed her book bag, fat with twelve pounds' worth of textbooks, and swung it at the back of Jinx's head with a deep grunt.

No.

I stopped the book bag in the air, and as Lovey watched, horrified, it swung back in a circle and smacked her square in the face with a sickening crack.

She fell to the pavement, holding her bleeding nose. The other girls rushed to her like hawks to a fallen rabbit.

Oops.

A small sprout of triumph made me grin. Lovey had it coming. I was defending Jinx.

Jinx shot me an alarmed look, grabbed my arm, and pulled me away from them. *Did you do that?* she mouthed.

I hid a smile. "So what?"

"So what?" Jinx shook my arm. "So what? Xander, this is bad." Jinx dropped my arm and went to examine Lovey.

"Get away from me!" Lovey roared.

Then a shout rang through the alley. Who else could it be but Mr. Stedman? "Xander! Lovey! Jinx!" he shouted, striding into the fray. He looked at us as if he'd stumbled onto a bed of scorpions. "What's going on?"

Tell him we were helping you with homework, I think at Lovey.

"I just had a homework question, Mr. Stedman," Lovey said through the blood. "I tripped and fell."

"You should get her some ice, Mr. Stedman," I said innocently.

He looked at me like a little kid tricked into getting a shot at the doctor's office. "Come on, Lovey. You two go home."

I grabbed Jinx and pulled her away, managing to hold my laughter until we got around the corner.

Jinx punched me in the shoulder. "Xander! What's wrong with you?"

"What?" I rubbed the spot where she hit me. "I saved you. You should be thanking me."

"You could've just stopped the book bag," Jinx pointed out. "And I was going to duck. I'm faster than she is."

"She deserved what she got." Resentment billowed in me like fire in a clogged-up chimney. "Lovey's lucky I didn't do worse to her!"

"You shouldn't use your powers like that." Jinx sped up, walked ahead. "It's not good."

Seriously? Who was Jinx to tell me what was good or not? She was the daughter of an evil oni.

Sheesh. Some people never appreciated anything.

CHAPTER FIVE

So that's all the sorry school stuff that's happened since we got back from our adventure. Now that we're on summer vacation, I've managed to forget about Lovey and her nose. I've been too distracted by Dad's boot camp.

This morning, Shea, Dad, Jinx, and I arrive at the head of the hiking trail at ten-fifteen on the dot. The sky's cloaked in what we call "June Gloom," a thick cloud cover that will burn off by noon. There are only a couple of other cars parked nearby.

Peyton is already there, waiting for us, sitting on a boulder near the log fence that marks the trail entrance. His blond hair is sticking straight up in its usual hairstyle. He has one ankle crossed over his knee and a sketchbook balanced on top of it. A woodpecker is perched on the railing, staring at him with a beady black eye, and

Peyton stares back at the bird, his pencil moving rapidly over the paper. I grin, thinking that they look like cousins.

Peyton had been changed by our adventure on oni island, too. The magnificent wings he'd grown had disappeared when we returned home, but he remained bigger and stronger, both inside and out. Not only had his mom had to buy all new clothes for him ("Who gains ten pounds of muscle in two days?" she had moaned), but also Peyton had, no joke, told his dad that he was DONE with all the sports his dad wanted him to do.

So what did Peyton want to do instead?

Take art classes. Like me. Which I'd never known. But I guess, no matter how well you think you know someone, there are always things about people that will surprise you.

Peyton's super-strict sports-oriented dad, Mr. Phasis, had made him a deal. Peyton could take art as long as he also enrolled in a military-type boot camp for teens this summer.

And it turns out that Peyton's been harboring a secret talent.

He's way better at art than I am.

"Hey, Peyton," I call, but my mother puts out her hand to stop me.

"Shhh," she whispers. "Let him finish sketching the bird."

I dodge her hand to get to Peyton. I don't even know why she came along on this hike. I mean, she should find her own hobbies. This training is for me and my friends, not for her.

The woodpecker squawks and flies away. Peyton looks up at me. "Dude, could you be a little quieter next time?"

"What are you now, the bird whisperer?" I examine his sketchbook.

It looks like that Audubon guy drew it. Except better. The lines reverberate with life, as if the pencil has actual blood coursing through the lead.

But he drew it with teeth. As if it was a tiny dinosaur, not a bird.

I blink.

No. My mistake. There are no teeth.

I inhale, sharp and quick. Don't tell me that's going to start happening again, even if I'm not the one drawing. . . .

"You okay?" Peyton eyes me with concern. "You have that look."

"What look?" I step back, pretending everything's okay.

"The look like you ate a bad burrito and there's no bathroom nearby." Peyton shuts his sketchbook. "You know, your Momotaro look."

Great. And here I thought I looked like a superhero. "I'm just not sleeping well," I say, and this isn't a lie. Maybe my lack of sleep is making me hallucinate.

Dad and Jinx catch up to us. Inu barks a greeting to Peyton and jumps into his lap. "What a fine day for a long hike!" Dad says in his most cheerful tone. "Nice cloud cover. Fresh air."

Jinx, standing behind him, smells the air showily. "I love this weather."

"Me too. It reminds me of Ireland," Shea says. "Not as cold, though." She laughs.

Inu barks twice, wagging his tail and pulling on the leash.

I slouch. Why is everybody acting so cheerful, like they're about to break into song? Are we living in a musical? "Let's get this over with already."

Peyton sticks his book into his big waterproof backpack. "What are you so cranky about?"

"The question is, what is there to be so happy about?" I march off. I know they're all looking at one another, either shrugging or shaking their heads. *That Xander. So moody.*

Maybe I won't talk to anybody all day. We'll all be better off.

We start hiking. Our packs are crammed with plenty of supplies to act as weights—the highlight being a gallon jug of water. Did you know that a gallon of liquid weighs eight pounds? Yeah, neither did I. That's a fact I could've lived my whole life without knowing.

Dad makes us move at a pace reserved for those crazy speed walkers we see sometimes, with their arms pumping up and down. Peyton and I walk in front, me taking two steps for every one of Peyton's. It's hard going—the trail's covered with loose rocks, and I've tripped a few times already. But there's no way I'm going to let Peyton get ahead of me.

Maybe . . .

I have a thought, and I glance back at Dad to make sure he won't notice. He's pointing out birds to my mother. She pulls his face down and kisses him. Gross. But, yay, they're distracted.

Soon my shoes are sending out little invisible jet puffs, propelling me up the mountain just a teeny bit faster than I could normally go. I grin.

Being Momotaro is good.

Dad stops and yells, "Wait!"

I let my feet drop to the earth, my heart pounding. Uh-oh. I've been found out. "What's the problem?" I ask, as if I really don't know.

Dad points down at the trail, gesturing at the loose dirt and stones littering the path. "What do these rocks mean?"

We stand there and look. Nobody responds.

Dad bends and picks up one of the stones. It's round and smooth, blue-gray. "Round rocks means you're in a riverbed. A flash flood bed," Dad says. "The rocks are smooth and round because of the churning water. They're loose because they've been carried down and around. So, if you're on a trail like this and it starts raining hard, get out."

I stifle a yawn. It's June. There's no way on earth it's going to rain that hard here anytime soon. We get most of our rain in the winter. "Yeah, yeah, yeah. Good lecture, Dad." I give him the thumbs-up.

Dad tosses the rock down and exchanges a look with my mother. The *Xander's-got-an-attitude* look. Oh well. I'm almost thirteen. It's basically the law that I have an attitude.

The trail up the mountain goes through oak and cottonwood trees with washed-out green leaves. The treetops have grown together, branches intertwined, and soon we're plunged into darkness. It reminds me of the dream I had. I stop for a moment, a chill going through me.

The wraith's face. Or lack of a face.

"Who's read *The Art of War*?" Dad calls from behind us. "Favorite quote?"

Peyton raises his hand. *"Being unconquerable lies with yourself; being conquerable lies with your enemy."*

"Did you actually read it, or just memorize random quotes?" I say rather irritably, mostly because I'm panting.

He jostles me. "Dude, chill out."

Dad ignores this. "Now let's discuss what that means," he says. "Jinx?"

"It's obvious, isn't it?" Jinx doesn't sound the slightest bit out of breath. "You have to control what's within yourself so you don't lose."

"I think it means you can do anything if you put your mind to it," my mother says, panting like me. She's not used to doing all this stuff. "It's a good study motto for me."

"Oh! What are you studying?" Peyton asks.

"I have to take the veterinary boards here to transfer my license," my mother says.

Good. That should keep her busy. The last thing I want is my mother always breathing down my neck.

But I feel a little pang in my stomach. Just a little one.

Eh. I'm probably just hungry.

"Did you bring any Twinkies?" I ask Peyton under my breath. "Or anything good?"

"My dad helped me pack, so no," Peyton says. "He thinks this hike is the greatest thing ever. If he knew we were reading all these books, he'd be showing up every day, too."

I glance over my shoulder at my mother. My father has his arm wrapped around her waist, helping to propel her up the steep grade. Her cheeks are flushed, and she's smiling at him. "It's a bit crowded as it is," I say. "But maybe Shea will keep Dad distracted and we'll actually get a break."

"Speaking of breaks," Jinx pipes up, "did you know that Lovey's nose is broken and she has to go to a plastic surgeon?"

A spasm of guilt closes my throat, and I feel my shoulders stiffen. "That's too bad," I say in a neutral tone. *Shut up, Jinx!*

"Really?" Peyton adjusts the backpack on his shoulders. "What happened? Did someone finally get tired of her being so mean?"

Jinx and I go quiet. Jinx side-eyes me, and I feel my face go hot.

Peyton glances down at me quickly, his eyes widening as he grasps the nuance of everything. "Really?" he whispers.

"Xander." My mother suddenly materializes next to me, like smoke after a fire. All of us kids freeze. Shea puts her face about a centimeter away from mine, and I can smell her bacon-tinged breath. "What did you do?"

Mom's Spidey-senses sure are in full working order for somebody who wasn't here for most of her parenting life.

"Why do you automatically assume I did something bad?" My voice breaks on *bad*. I shoot a murderous look at Jinx. "This girl Lovey hit herself in the face with her own backpack, okay?"

Jinx stares at her feet, her eyebrows raised. She whistles.

I'll get even with her later.

"I know a guilty stance when I see one," my mother says evenly. "You cannot hide anything from your own mother, so best not to try."

Is she joking right now? I glance at my father, but his face is set in a mask of sternness.

"Tell me," Shea says softly.

"There's nothing to tell," I snap. I step away from the group. "Lovey was going to beat up Jinx, okay? She tried to hit her in the back of the head with her heavy backpack. It would have knocked Jinx out." My eyes well up at the injustice of it. "So I just made her hit herself, is all. The laws of motion. An object continues to move at a constant velocity unless acted upon by an external force. Well, that external force was her own head instead of Jinx's." I giggle to show that it's funny, but my parents look about as amused as gargoyles perched on a church.

"You could have just stopped the backpack," Jinx says quietly. Her cheeks are deep red. "I was handling it."

"Not well, obviously. And I couldn't stop it. I could only reverse it." I scuff at the orange-brown dirt with the toe of my hiking boot. "Why are you so hell-bent on getting me into trouble?"

"Because!" Jinx almost hisses. "Because you enjoyed it. You laughed afterward, Xander. And it reminded me . . ." She gulps.

"Of what?" I demand.

She chokes out the next words as if they taste like throw-up. "Of my father."

She might as well have broken *my* nose. I remind her of her awful, murderous oni father? I feel all the blood drain out of my face like water leaving a bathtub. "Take that back."

Jinx shakes her head, her amber eyes bright as gemstones. "No. It's true."

I take in a ragged breath, then another. I'm suffocating, a bug caught in a jar. It's bad enough that Jinx called me out in front of everybody. But now Peyton stares at me with a profoundly shocked expression. My father's is all caved-in disappointment. Even Inu looks serious, his mouth shut, staring with doggy disapproval as if I stole his last piece of bacon.

My mother glares at me. She grabs my arm and pulls me roughly to her, so I stumble on the loose rocks. Her hair seems to electrify, the curls rising of their own volition to stand above her scalp. "These powers are not to be toyed with!" she says. "Don't you know what danger you're playing at, *boyo*?"

"Ouch!" I protest, though it doesn't really hurt. I look to Dad for help, but his arms are crossed. So this is what it's like to have two parents. Two people in coalition against you, a tag team of disciplinary action. "I was helping Jinx."

"But you were drawn to hurt Lovey, weren't you?" Shea asks. "You liked it. Do you not see the problem in that?"

Now Dad adds his two cents. "You cannot go around hurting people because it feels good. Nor should you use the magic unless absolutely necessary! Xander, I told you already. That's like you driving a car without a license. You need practice and supervision."

Another lecture. This is so unfair. "If Lovey hadn't tried to hit Jinx, I wouldn't have done anything to her!" I yank my arm away and point at Jinx. "Traitor! I'll never help you again as long as I live."

Jinx kicks a rock away. "Whatever."

"Whatever yourself."

She sticks her tongue out.

And Peyton doesn't defend me. His head is bowed, his hand stroking Inu's back. My best friend can't even look at me.

"You'd think I killed someone!" I explode. Fine. I don't want to be here. They can't keep me prisoner. I turn to leave, and Shea tries to grab me again. Without even trying hard, I cause the dirt and rocks underneath her to roll like a conveyor belt. My mother's feet fly up, and she lands on her back with an *oof.*

Ha is my first thought.

Then, before another awful thought can wedge its way into my head, I run.

CHAPTER SIX

I run fast, no jet pack needed, off the trail to a place where Peyton
and I sometimes go. Mostly during the winter, when a waterfall
cascades down a jagged shelf of rocks. Next to the waterfall is an
outcropping of boulders where we can sit and look out onto a small
valley.

It's our secret spot. Nobody ever comes here, because it's in an
area marked STAY OUT: REFORESTATION.

Breathing hard, I get to the boulder pile and sit down. The
waterfall's barely a trickle right now, a slow drip into a slimy green
pond. I blink, feeling like there's sand in my eyes, and take a drink
from my water jug.

I replay the scene in my head. Shea falling, my father trying to catch her, and Inu leaping for her. Peyton's horrified face. Jinx jumping into the air.

My mother is all right. I know she is.

I hold my stomach. Mingled with the guilt churning in my belly is something else. And it isn't gas.

It's glee.

When I made those rocks move and she fell, my first instinct was not to help my own mother. It was to laugh with joy. Because my powers had worked.

Oh my gosh.

These Momotaro powers are turning me into a supervillain. Next thing you know, my silver hair will fall out and people will start calling me Lex.

I hang my head. Maybe that's why I've been having bad dreams. I actually AM a horrible person.

I close my hand around the baku charm my grandmother gave me, its weight cold and comforting against the base of my neck. Can I use it to make my bad thoughts go away, too? Can he eat those?

I wish I didn't have these stupid Momotaro powers at all. Not if they're going to make me feel this way. Why did I have to be born into this family? All I ever wanted was a normal life.

I lean back against the stones, putting my left hand behind me for balance. *Baku, come eat my dream*, I think.

Suddenly there's a sharp pinch on my wrist, then a burning pain.

I scream, shake my arm, and look down.

A red scorpion stares up at me from below, waving its lobster-like claws around, its stinger retracting. Oh crud. What kind is it? I peer closely at it, holding my injured wrist to my mouth instinctively. I think baby scorpions are the deadliest.

Instead of the usual alien-like face, I see a flat nose, rolling round eyes, and a smirking mouth. Human. Or humanoid.

An oni!

Quickly, with my right hand, I pick up a rock and hurl it at the scorpion as it tries to scuttle into a crack between the boulders. I got it, I think. I hope. I get up to see. I blink rapidly. I must have imagined that weird face. I have to find it, show it to Dad, so we can figure out how poisonous it is. Was it a desert scorpion, or a sawfinger? But this one was red. . . . My thoughts are jumbling. . . .

And then the world turns black, as though someone slapped a hood over my face.

CHAPTER SEVEN

When I open my eyes, my grandfather is sitting on the boulder next to me. His gnarled hands hold a knife and a piece of wood. Small chips whirl down as he whittles, humming tunelessly.

"Ojīchan?" I touch his arm, clad in a rough blue-gray cotton kimono. Man, my dreams sure are detailed. My grandfather died a long time ago, and I never met him. Not in real life, anyway.

"Musashi-chan." My grandfather calls me by my middle name. He puts down his carving. "You've been having trouble with your Momotaro powers."

I don't want to admit the mean and selfish things I've been doing. But Ojīchan looks at me with so much understanding that it's obvious he already knows. "Did you ever feel like that, too?" I ask. "Like you're out of control or something?"

"Yes, of course. We all do." He smiles at me, lines fanning around his mouth. "But with time and experience, you will learn control. What is appropriate and what is not. We are like doctors, the Momotaro. We say, *first, do no harm*."

"*First do no harm?*" I wrinkle my nose. "Um, isn't that kind of the opposite of what warriors do?"

"Ha. Do woodchoppers cut down every tree in the forest?" Ojīchan bends over and hands me the carving. "Take this."

I hold it in my hand, turn it over, and examine it.

It's a piece of burned tree. Carved into the blackened wood is a figure with a silver face, like a blade. Like the wraith version of my father from my nightmare.

The carving expands, blowing up like a balloon, until the figure looms above me again.

I gasp.

The scenery fades and changes. Above me is Shea's face, her eyebrows drawn together and her skin red with strain. Blue sky, trees blowing in the wind. Normal.

I look around with my eyeballs only because I can't move my head. I try to blink, try to talk, but nothing is working. Am I really that bad off? Finally, I manage to twitch my legs.

"You had us worried, Xander," Peyton says from someplace to my left. "Good thing I knew where to find you." Inu whines next to him, and he's probably licking my face, but I can't feel it.

"Look at these bite marks." Dad lifts my arm. *Auuugh!* It hurts like he's stabbed me. The people blur, the edges of my vision blacken again. I try to tell them about the scorpion and my symptoms, ask if they've called 911, but still no words will come out.

"He's really messed up," Jinx murmurs. "I mean physically now, too."

Thanks a lot, Jinx, I want to say.

"Oh, *mo chroí*, this is going to hurt." My mother presses my bitten wrist. Her hands feel hot-sharp on my tortured skin. Imagine a needle going into an open wound. My arm flinches automatically, trying to get away.

"Stay still," Dad says in such a commanding tone that I freeze. He sounds far away now. My ears are ringing the way they did after I went to a too-loud concert.

"Was it a rattler?" Peyton asks, his voice faint.

"A rattler shouldn't nearly kill you within two minutes," Dad says. "No, this is oni."

My mother's hand grows hotter and hotter. It feels like she's holding my flesh against a red-hot barbecue grill.

Don't they know how painful this is? I scream with every bit of air in my lungs, and nothing comes out.

Then my vision clears abruptly.

My mother's eyes are screwed shut, her face as white as sugar. Her hair billows about her head as though a hurricane is whipping up.

My dizziness vanishes. "Shea, stop! It hurts." My voice comes out like a bullhorn. Peyton and Jinx and Dad jump. Inu barks as though he's glad.

"Shea!" I yell again.

Something inside her seems to click, a lighter being flicked on.

She's glowing blue-white.

I look down at her hand.

It shines like one of those glow sticks kids carry on Halloween. Underneath her hand, my skin shimmers, red as a lobster in boiling water. The searing heat goes up my arm and into my spine.

Her teeth chatter, her eyes roll into her head.

I try to wrench away, but Shea holds on tight. "Stop!" I say, not so much because of my pain but because I'm afraid that this is killing my mother.

Dad clenches his jaw as he looks from my mother to me and back again. "One more minute, Xander. Can you take it?"

Okay, I want to say, but then the pain reaches my brain. It's like the worst ice cream headache I've ever had, times two thousand.

I scream again in answer, and everyone can hear it. Canada can probably hear it.

Dad taps my mother's shoulder. "Shea, it's too much." His face contorts. She doesn't move from me. Dad grabs both her shoulders, and now his fingers are glowing. With a shout of pain, he lets go, shaking his hands.

Her whole body trembles like a flag in a storm.

Oh my gosh, she's going to die. "Stop, Mom!"

At the sound of *Mom*, Shea releases me. She falls back onto the ground, Dad supporting her. Her skin is a horrible zombie-like blue.

"Mom?" I want to crawl to her, but I'm not strong enough. "Is she breathing, Dad?"

Dad lays his palm on her cheek. "Yes. Are *you* all right, Xander?"

"I think so," I croak. Peyton helps me sit up. Inu woofs and crawls into my lap. *Oof.* "Not really helping right now, Inu." I try shoving off his 140-pound body. Inu thinks he's the size of a teacup poodle, I swear. He whines and licks my face.

"Have some water." Peyton holds a bottle up to my lips. I gulp it down. "Dude, don't scare us like that. It's not even close to Halloween."

"Yeah, I did it on purpose," I manage.

I remember how I laughed when my mother got hurt, and I think about the wraith from my dreams. I'm sorry for it all. Sorry I even have these powers.

Jinx appears, clutching a limp piece of rope in her hand. I blink. No, it's a black-and-white snake. "Is this what bit you?" she asks. "I found it crushed between the boulders."

I shake my head. "It was a scorpion, not a snake."

"Those can't kill you," she says.

"This one had a face." I close my eyes again. "And a stinger and claws."

"Oni," Dad says. "Without a doubt."

The sick feeling drains from my body as quickly as it came in. I take the bottle from Peyton and finish it off, wiping my mouth.

"I'll go have a look for the thing that bit you," Peyton says.

"It's long gone, whatever it was." Jinx steps in front of him, blocking his way.

Peyton crosses his arms. "What's the matter, Jinx? You protecting that oni like you protected your father?"

Fire leaps into her eyes. "Go ahead and look all you want," she says tightly. "I'm done protecting any oni, Peyton."

He steps around her, but he doesn't go anywhere.

I slowly get to my feet. My mother is bent into a twisted *S* shape on Dad's lap, her mouth slack, her eyes glazed. Her skin is light green now, the color of bile.

Instantly, I understand. She drew the deadly poison into her own body, absorbed it all.

For me.

Warmth floods over my body, then icy fear.

Kneeling on the ground, I put my arms around her. Her skin is cold and inert, like a stone. "Mom?" My voice shakes, and I struggle to control it. "Are you okay?"

Barely, she manages to nod. "You called me Mom," she says in a low voice.

I feel like I've been caught sneaking a peek at a present. "Um. Well, yeah, you are, aren't you?"

"Forever and always." Her eyes refocus as she lifts her hand to touch my face. I let her wipe the sweat off my forehead. "I'll never leave you again. You have my word on that."

It is almost as though her own words give her strength. She begins to sit up, and Dad lets her lean into him.

"She'll be fine, Xander," he says. "It just takes a temporary toll." He strokes her hair.

Inu barks and pushes in between us to lick Mom's face. I pat her arm. "I'm sorry I pushed you down."

She smiles. "Oh, *mo chroí*, you didn't push me. I tripped."

That's not true, but I don't correct her. I stand up and brush myself off. Jinx looks at me, then glances away as if I've done something embarrassing. Or horrifying.

I don't meet her eyes.

CHAPTER EIGHT

When we get home, Mom immediately retreats to her bedroom, her color still not quite right, her limbs a bit rubbery. I, on the other hand, feel back to normal, for the most part.

"How was your hike?" Obāchan asks from her easy chair, where she's working on a ridiculous green Christmas sweater for my father, with a goofy-looking reindeer stitched in the middle. She makes these every year. She doesn't think they're goofy, so we wear them without complaint.

"Not great." I tell her what happened.

Obāchan makes a *tsk*ing noise. "Be thankful your mother was there."

I sink into the couch. "Obāchan, you're acting like I sprained my ankle. It was an oni. Don't we need to do something? Go hunt it down, at least?" I'm more than a little freaked out by the idea that various monsters could be hiding anyplace. One might be under my mattress next time.

She flaps her hand at me. "Let's not get too excited, Xander. The oni will periodically want to test you. Consider it a lesson." Obāchan yanks out another length of yarn from her basket. Inu settles against her stockinged feet with a great sigh. "You want some chicken soup?" she asks. "I have a Crock-Pot ready. Help yourself."

I traipse into the kitchen, where Jinx is already getting out two bowls. I ladle soup into them.

"You know you're lucky, right?" Jinx picks up her bowl too violently, sloshing out liquid.

I take out two spoons and hand her one. "Yeah, yeah. I could have died."

"No." Jinx ignores the spoon and slurps out of the bowl. "You're lucky because your mother loves you enough to sacrifice herself."

I open my mouth to tell her I know that, thank you very much, but before I can speak, Jinx turns and runs up to her room. The door slams.

Yes, I'm lucky. And I do know that now.

Before my mother helped me today, I'd never seen her fairy-ness. I had no idea how powerful and special it is. That she really *is* some kind of beacon the oni could have spotted when I was a defenseless little kid.

I wonder if I'm a beacon, too. Or if I can heal people like she can. Next time someone gets hurt, I'll try it out.

Or maybe I got absolutely nothing from her.

Neither my mother nor my father is a good artist. The best they can do is draw stick figures with eyelashes. Maybe their DNA combined in some completely new way to make my talents.

I go into the living room and sit gingerly on the couch, being careful not to spill.

Obāchan mutes *Wheel of Fortune*. "What happened to Jinx?"

"Nothing happened to *her*, but *I* got bit by an oni. I don't know why Jinx is so upset," I say. "I didn't do anything to her."

"She's not mad at you." Obāchan takes a sip of coffee from her mug. "She's feeling hurt because her mother did what was easy, not what was right."

"That's not my fault." I spoon up a juicy chunk of chicken. Inu's face appears next to my bowl, drooling. He watches me greedily. "Back up, Inu." I push at his chest, but he doesn't budge.

"You'd better feed him dinner," Obāchan says.

I get up and go into the kitchen to mix up Inu's canned food and dry kibble. He waits by his eating spot. As I bend to put his dish on the floor, I realize that I don't even have a headache, which is pretty amazing, considering that I was poisoned earlier.

"Xander?" Obāchan calls to me. "Think of what it's like for Jinx, living here. Being the outsider. An orphan."

"I do," I mutter. I clap my hands twice, and Inu sticks his nose into the bowl, chomping down. I go back into the living room. "She's not an orphan, is she?"

Obāchan's needles clink as she shrugs. "Who knows? She might as well be."

Hmmm. That may be true, but Jinx doesn't have to worry—she has us now. Inu reappears at my side and paws my leg. "You're done already? Fine." I throw him a piece of chicken. "I know I'm lucky," I say to my grandmother, finishing my soup. "I don't need Jinx to tell me."

"Don't you?"

"I'm going to take that as a rhetorical question, Obāchan." I sit back against the couch, watching the lady on TV touch the letters as she trots across the stage, and I stifle a pretty grand burp. "Thanks for the soup."

"You're welcome." Obāchan shakes out the sweater over her lap. "Ahhh. The reindeer's eyes should be big, don't you think?"

"Bigger than his head," I tell her.

That night, before I go to bed, I use the baku charm. If ever a bad dream was going to show up, it would be tonight, after my near-death experience with that scorpion. I clench the charm tightly and say what my grandmother taught me. "Baku, come eat my dreams. Baku, come eat my dreams."

Once in my bed, I toss and turn, worrying about my mother. I hadn't seen her again this evening—she'd gone into a deep sleep.

What if she doesn't fully recover, all because of me? If only I hadn't used my power on Lovey. Then Jinx wouldn't have confronted me, and I wouldn't have run off. . . .

The next thing I know, I'm walking into a field of purple-tubed flowers, thousands of them hanging from green stems. The horizon is sunset pink. Pretty. This doesn't look like a bad dream at all. I relax.

Peyton sits on the ground a few hundred feet in front of me. The flowers are growing across his lap, covering him. His wings are back—those grand feathery things, more than six feet across, iridescent and golden, with greens and blues mixed in as highlights. He's eating the blossoms like popcorn, throwing one after another into his mouth and crunching down. "Want one?" he asks me between bites.

Then I realize what they are. Nightshade. Poisonous.

"Stop, Peyton!" I try to run to him.

He laughs, gets up, and flies to me. "You want one, Xander?" He shoves a handful into my mouth and down my throat, choking me.

I push him back, and he shoots off like a Ping-Pong ball, landing hard on the ground on his back with a sickening crack, as if a dozen eggs had dropped onto a tile floor.

Peyton! I cry without sound, and my dinner rises in my throat. I try to reach him, to reverse this dream, but I'm running in slow motion and can't get to him.

I stop trying. My fear and sadness disappear. My mouth tastes like I just ate a handful of my favorite jelly beans.

I stand there watching my best friend writhe in pain, and I feel . . . I feel *happy* about it.

A laugh comes out of me, the surprised delight of a little kid watching a magic trick.

Oh no. I'm disgusting! I've never hated myself—or anyone—so much.

The wraith appears before me. I look up at its blank silvery head. "You again?" I ask. "Why don't you just do something to me and get it over with? I'm sick of this."

The ghost creature angles itself so its face is directly across from mine.

I see me. A reflection in a dull mirror, my bedhead hair standing straight up, my eyes bloodshot, my teeth yellow and mossy from forgetting to brush tonight.

My breathing goes haywire. I try to run, but of course, because this is one of *those* dreams, my feet are stuck, my muscles as cooperative as tangled marionette strings.

Baku! I cry. *Where are you?*

Suddenly a four-legged creature lumbers over the horizon. It's smaller than Inu, with a long trunk that dusts the ground. An anteater—or maybe not exactly an anteater. For one thing, it's got green fur—a color that definitely doesn't exist in our current mammal kingdom. There are yellow whiskers over its eyes, and two short tusks coming out of its mouth on either side of its trunk. A mane of curly golden fur falls from its head over its short-haired back.

It looks right at me, its eyes warm and kind, but I know I shouldn't move, just like you shouldn't move when a doctor's stitching you up.

It waves its trunk over Peyton with a noise like air getting sucked through a tube. As in a cartoon, Peyton folds in on himself soundlessly, and he vanishes into the trunk like sand into a vacuum.

The baku sucks in the deadly flowers, and then the rest of the landscape, everything falling apart and away like dust. The creature continues around and around until it reaches me, and its trunk touches my face as softly as a cotton ball. Then there's just darkness. I fall into a deep, peaceful, dreamless sleep.

CHAPTER NINE

The next morning, I race downstairs. For the first time since I came back from the island of monsters, I feel energized. Like a new person.

My grandmother sits at the kitchen table with a bowl of oatmeal in front of her. "And how is my favorite grandson today?" She smiles.

"Wow, Obāchan, that baku charm worked great!" I slide across the tile and throw my leg over the top of the chair. "I'm as good as new. And you're right, the baku's not scary at all. I'm going to use it again tonight."

"Xander, you should only call the baku when absolutely necessary," Obāchan tells me, stirring brown sugar into her bowl. "Don't use it *until* you're having the bad dream. Not before. Otherwise she could take all your dreams."

"Okay, okay. I'm not stupid, Obāchan." I get up and pour myself a bowl of cereal. Last night, the baku took all my dreams, and I slept super well. I'd rather have dreamless sleep than nightmares. Her way makes absolutely no sense. That's like telling someone with a bad heart to wait to take their heart medication until they're in the middle of a heart attack. No way would a doctor do that.

"I know you're not stupid." Obāchan blows on her breakfast. "But you don't always think things through."

Luckily, I don't have to argue any further because there's a knock at the door. I run to answer it, but Jinx already has, though she's still in her heart-printed pink pajamas. I laughed when I first saw those—they're so not Jinx. She said she only got them because Target didn't have any black ones.

"Hold up. What's the password?" She blocks the person's entry by splaying her arm and leg across the door frame.

"I'm bigger than you. That's the password," comes Peyton's deep voice, and I see the looming shadow of his broad shoulders in the morning light. Peyton's spending the day here and staying overnight. The day after tomorrow he'll be leaving for that boot camp, where he'll be for two whole weeks, so we're hanging out as much as possible.

"For the love of Pete, let him in already!" I nudge Jinx out of the way as Inu races in and jumps on Peyton like he's been away at war.

Peyton scratches Inu's armpits as Inu tries to lick his face. "I'm here. Now the party can get started."

Jinx yawns dramatically, ruffling up her sleep-mussed hair. "It's too early for a party. If you need me, I'll be sleeping in." She runs off, climbing up the stairs on all fours.

"Monkey girl," I whisper.

"I heard that!" Jinx yells.

"How's your mom?" Peyton asks as I shut the door behind him.

I shrug. "I haven't seen her yet." A small tickle of fear pokes me. What if Mom isn't fine and I haven't even bothered to check on her?

"She's better, thanks, Peyton." Dad appears at the top of the stairs, looking somewhat worn out. "She should rest in bed today."

"I'm fine!" Mom bellows from their bedroom.

"Chill out, Shea! I'll bring you some eggs," my father calls back. He grins. "She's already bored. You guys have fun today. Try not to get into too much trouble."

We go upstairs so we can begin our action-packed day of hanging out, eating chips, and playing computer games. Along with his laptop, Peyton brought along a giant book about Impressionist painters from his art teacher's library, and we sit on my bed, flipping through the extra-large pages. I recognize some of the images from puzzles and things. Lots of water lilies. A night sky.

"You're super into this art business, aren't you?" I ask him. I reach for Peyton's sketchbook and check it out. My heart drops a little bit. He's so good. As though he's a professional and I'm a preschooler. I close the book and slide it across the bed to him, trying not to wish that Peyton wasn't so *fantastic* at absolutely everything he tries. It leaves only crumbs for the rest of us.

Peyton blushes a bit, smiling. "I don't know, Xander. I might have found my calling."

Ah. I still disgust myself. I shouldn't be jealous of him. "I thought you wanted to be a pro baseball player."

Peyton shrugs. "Who says you can't be two things? People can't play baseball forever. Hey, I know what: we'll be artists together. Like Gauguin and Van Gogh. This book says they were friends."

"You sure you want to do that?" I point to a paragraph about Van Gogh. "Because they think Gauguin cut off Van Gogh's ear."

Peyton caws his most raucous laugh, which echoes through the house. One thing about him: when he's happy, everybody in the neighborhood knows. "If I did that, it'd be because you deserved it."

I roll my eyes, and then, remembering my dream, I repress a shudder. "I'd never do that to you," I say a little too vehemently.

"Dude"—Peyton gives me a funny look—"I'm only kidding around. You okay?"

I shrug and consider telling him everything, just so I don't have to feel so alone. I haven't told Dad—or anyone—the extent of my nightmares or how bad I feel about myself sometimes. I don't need them to dislike me the way they did when we were hiking.

I don't want Peyton to know what a horrible person I might be deep down inside. What if he picks up his art book, says, *You're disgusting, Xander,* and takes off forever?

Just then, the door opens and in walks Jinx. She's changed into jeans and her MISFITS shirt, but her hair's still wild. "What are you guys doing?"

I throw a dirty sock at her. She dodges it nimbly. "How many times do I have to tell you not to barge in like that?" I say. "I could be asleep or naked for all you know."

"Yeah, right. I heard this cacklebox"—she points at Peyton—"going full-force. Ain't nobody going to sleep through that." Jinx sits on the bed next to us.

Peyton shuts the art book. "I don't believe you were invited in."

"I'm half-oni, remember? We come and go as we please." Jinx reaches for the book. "More art? I thought we were supposed to be reading about war." She produces a paperback of *The Bushido, the Warrior's Way*, from her back pocket. "I mean, the next time an oni scorpion ambushes Xander, what good is Monet going to be?"

I don't even have to look at Peyton to feel him tense up. I frown at her. "Art is how I found out about my power in the first place."

"At least we have talents, Jinx." Peyton leaps to my defense, his hair sticking up like a vengeful rooster's comb. "What's yours?"

She curls her arm and pops out her bicep. "Muscle."

Peyton snorts. "Let me get out my magnifying glass."

Jinx gets into a sumo wrestler pose, half squatting, lifting up one foot and then another. "Oh yeah? Try to knock me over."

"Please." Peyton waves her off. "I could knock you over with a feather. I'm not going to dignify that with a response."

"That *was* a response." Jinx jumps onto the footboard, her toes gripping the wood, and her arms dangling like a chimp's. "Or do you want to maybe run the mile again?" She smirks at him.

Peyton's expression darkens. Before Jinx showed up, nobody at school had ever beaten his mile time of five and a half minutes. Which is, like, elite-level good for our age. And then Jinx ran it in four minutes, ten seconds, and I don't think she was even trying particularly hard. He smiles at her. "Is that in the air or on the ground? Because if I could fly, I'd beat you."

She sniffs. "You're never getting your wings back in this world, Peyton. Might as well get used to it." She points at him with her big toe. "Here, you're as average as anybody else. But I'm half-oni no matter where I am."

Peyton's face goes blotchy. He stares hard at the art book.

I intervene. "You know what your talent is, Jinx? Getting under people's skin." I hit her with a pillow. "Seriously, Jinx, what do you even want to be when you grow up?"

She shrugs, bending to dodge my next pillow attack. "I do things the Zen way, baby. Worry about the present only."

"Yeah. That's how every president got to be president," Peyton scoffs.

She thumbs her nose at us. "Speaking of talents, where are all your drawings, anyway?" Jinx points at the blank walls.

"Yeah." Peyton looks at the walls, too, as if he's just noticing this. Which he probably is. "You didn't tear them up, did you? Some of those were really good."

"Whatever." He's being nice. I shrug. "I got tired of looking at them, so I stuck them in my desk."

Peyton frowns. He puts his sketchbook in front of me and a pencil in my hand. "Draw."

I stare at the book like I'm a little kid who doesn't want to eat his broccoli. "I don't want to."

"Just do it." He opens it to a blank page.

"What are you, some kind of art pusher?" Reluctantly, I hover my pencil over the paper.

What should I draw? Maybe a portrait of Jinx as a monkey and Peyton as a real bird. Nope. Not going to do it. I put the pencil down and look up at Peyton. He and Jinx are at my desk now, arguing about a YouTube video. How'd they'd move over there so fast? I hand the book to Peyton. "I'm not in the mood."

"What are you talking about?" Peyton points to the page. "You've been drawing for a half hour."

Oh crud.

I can barely bring my eyes to the page, but I do. There's a picture of me and my dad and my grandfather on a cliff above a raging ocean where a serpent slithers on the bottom. Above us is a cloud-like black shape, huge and threatening. Is it some kind of oni? It has no face, but just looking at it fills me with dread. Worse even than a math test I haven't studied for.

In the picture, my grandfather is lying down. Dead? He is in real life, so that's not surprising. But my father's on his hands and knees, trying to crawl away from the dark shape, moving right toward the cliff.

And what am I doing?

I'm holding the sword that I found on my adventure. The Sword of Yumenushi, the Sword of Dreamers. The Momotaro sword that can slay monsters. But I'm kneeling, my head bent, and the sword is on the ground. My other hand is up, shielding my face from the oni.

I'm cowering.

Peyton wrinkles his nose. "Well, that can't be good, can it?"

I shut the book so hard Peyton's hair ruffles in the wind. "I told you I didn't want to draw!" This is worse than I'd feared. Is this the future? Me, being all cowardly and scared while my father goes to his doom?

"But what does it mean?" Peyton opens the page to the drawing again. "Your grandfather's dead. Your dad's trying to get away. And you're just looking scared."

"Thanks for the recap." I shiver.

Jinx sits next to me and puts her arm around my shoulder. It's oddly comforting. "Xander, just because you draw it doesn't mean it'll come true. I mean, Lovey did not literally turn into an ape, did she?" She's referring to the cartoon I drew of Lovey, where I depicted her as a rather unfortunate orangutan.

"No, she didn't." I look at the cloud again. "But that thing is an oni. I can feel it. This isn't the same."

Jinx blows out hard through her nose. "Okay, maybe you really *did* draw the future, and you're going to wimp out on your dad and everybody else and get killed by some lame, vaguely threatening cloud. Is that what you want to hear?"

"Don't talk to him that way." Peyton's hair practically stands on end as he leans into Jinx's face. "Can't you see how terrified he is?"

"I'm talking sense into him!" Jinx doesn't budge.

"Is that how your father gave you pep talks?" Peyton asks. "Because that didn't work too well, if you remember."

Jinx's eyes narrow. "I suggest you stop bringing up my father!"

Just then, Inu busts in and throws himself between Jinx and Peyton. *Woof woof woof!* he barks sharply, pushing his great paws against Peyton's chest, then throwing his body against Jinx's. Inu hates it when people fight. Even play fighting upsets him.

"Hey! I can speak for myself. I am not terrified, Peyton." I pat Inu's hindquarters, making him sit. "Everybody calm down and let me think for a minute!" My mind is racing, my heart is pounding, and I feel like crying. Again. "I am never picking up a pencil again as long as I live." I gulp.

"Don't worry about it, Xander. I've got your back." Peyton rips the drawing out of the book and shreds it with his long fingers. He sticks a piece into his mouth and chews. "See? All gone."

"Save some for me." Jinx grabs a big handful out of Peyton's hand and stuffs it into her mouth. "Your scary drawings are deli-cious," she says, a piece of pulp flying out of her mouth and landing squarely on Peyton's cheek.

At this I have to laugh.

We spend the day playing computer games and watching TV. Nobody mentions the drawing again. Peyton keeps his sketchbook in his backpack.

Although nobody talks about it, the picture is all I can think about. I knew that would happen if I tried to create something. I'm going to have the worst nightmares ever tonight.

I'm definitely going to use the baku.

At bedtime, Jinx knocks on my door and sticks her head in before I can answer. "Good night, children. Don't let the bedbugs bite."

I throw another sock at her. "Again, WAIT before you come in here."

She sticks her tongue out. "You have an endless supply of dirty socks. You really need to do laundry." She shuts the door, and I hear her running down the hall.

"Ewww." Peyton swoops off the bed, lifts up the corner of his sleeping bag to check the floor underneath. "You don't actually have bedbugs, do you?"

"Couldn't you just eat them if I did? You're a bird." I get under the covers of my bed.

Peyton crawls into the sleeping bag. "I'm not much of a bird these days." Peyton lowers his voice. "You know, after we got back from the island, I actually tried eating an earthworm."

"No!" I pull the blankets up over my mouth. "Peyton, that's gross!"

"It wasn't too bad. Like slimy chicken mixed with dirt." He makes a gagging noise. "I'm joking. It was tremendously awful."

"I bet that's what the worm said about your breath," Jinx calls through the door.

I throw my shoe at it, knocking loose a poster. "Jinx! No eavesdropping."

"You better get to sleep. Tomorrow, training starts again." Her voice drifts down the hallway as she heads down to her room.

Peyton shakes his head. "Truly, I don't know how you stand her."

I think about this. Jinx isn't exactly like the other kids. Obviously—she's half-demon, for goodness' sake. But also, she's a year older than everyone else.

The other day, I asked Jinx if she wanted to play *Craftworlds* with me, and she said that thirteen-year-olds didn't play that game.

"Sorry," I'd said, "I didn't know you were so sophisticated."

Jinx had sighed. "Do you have any idea how much older thirteen is than twelve?"

"Four years?" I had answered dryly.

"Ten percent of my life. I have ten percent more experience than everybody else." Jinx had frowned at me. "I'm a freak at school."

"You're a freak everywhere," I'd muttered. "You could *try* to get along."

"*Do or do not. There is no try,*" she'd responded. "And I'm *doing not.*"

"Okay, Yoda." I'd gone into my room to play *Craftworlds* by myself.

So I shrug at Peyton, who's waiting for my answer. "I'm a saint. Plain and simple." I frame my face with my hands. "Look for this on a medal very soon: *Xander, First Prize for Putting Up with Annoyance.*"

I burrow down in my bed, covering myself so only my face is exposed. It's so comfy. Dad changed the sheets for me, so they're nice and crisp. I can dimly hear my parents watching television downstairs and laughing. Inu flops around on my bedspread, his front paws moving as he emits little yips of joy. I bet he's dreaming about chasing rabbits. Maybe this time he'll catch one.

Below me, Peyton's already breathing slowly and evenly.

I should have a good-dream night.

But still, maybe I won't.

I inhale and take out my baku. I had better use it, just in case.

If Obāchan knew how I was feeling, she'd understand.

Baku, baku, come eat my dreams.

I fall asleep.

CHAPTER TEN

When I wake, I don't remember a single thing about my dreams. That's good, right?

I stretch, feeling energy coursing through me. I want to get up and do stuff. I leap out of bed.

On the floor, Peyton yawns. I kick his sleeping bag semi-gently. "Hey, Peyton, let's make pancakes."

"Pancakes?" He stares at me like I've got a horn growing out of my forehead. "That's a lot of work. Can't somebody else make them?"

"It's a mix. Come on, it's easy." I start out the door.

"You go ahead. I'll be there soon." Peyton doesn't move.

Whatever. Maybe *he* needed the baku.

———

Downstairs, my parents are slouched over the table, tucking into heaping bowls of sugary cereal. Several boxes do a conga line across the table. Chocolate. Marshmallow. Chocolate and marshmallow. Fruity. "Where'd all this come from?" We never have stuff like this.

Dad shrugs. "I had a craving."

"Well, I'm not complaining." I grab the biggest cereal bowl I can find and fill it up.

We crunch away in silence. My parents seem particularly tired, barely blinking. Usually they're so chipper they could give those annoying TV morning-show hosts a run for their money. They're all like, *Xander, what are your plans? Today we're going to run a marathon and paint the living room and then make strawberry jam!* and I'm just like, *Ughhhh.* Too much ambition.

But maybe Mom's still not one hundred percent, and Dad's tired from taking care of her.

"I'm ready for archery. Should I set up the targets outside?"

Crunch, crunch, crunch.

They stare off into space.

Dad slurps the last of the milk out of his bowl. "Nah. It's too much trouble. Let's take today off."

"Really?" I look at my mother. She pours herself more Frosted Sugar Crunch. "Where's Obāchan?"

"Still asleep," Mom says through a mouthful of cereal. "She's got a cold or something. Let her rest."

Peyton stumbles downstairs, his hank of hair looking even crazier than usual. He stares blankly at the scene in front of him.

"Hey, Peyton," I say. "Ready for archery?"

He makes a face. "Can we watch it on TV?"

"Good idea," Dad drawls. "Netflix has its new movies loaded. Like the robot movie."

"The robot suit–wearing guy, or the robot who takes over the world?" my mother asks.

"Guy," Dad says.

"You mean *Iron Man*?" I ask. Why are they acting so dumb?

"Cool," Peyton says.

I glance outside. It's seventy degrees and sunny. I feel a weird, unfamiliar longing to get out there and do something. "All we have to do is set up the targets outside. I could do it."

They ignore me.

"I'll practice with you, Xander." Jinx comes downstairs. "Oh boy, Count Chocula!" She pours herself a big bowl, then runs water over it. Jinx doesn't drink milk.

I stare with worry at my friend. "You sure you're okay, Peyton?"

He nods with a mouthful of cereal.

"What am I, chopped liver?" Jinx kicks my knee softly. "I said I'd go."

When Jinx and I come back inside, Dad and Shea and Peyton and Inu are all slumped on the couch in the darkness, watching some reality show where little girls with spackled-on makeup compete in a beauty pageant as if their parents' lives are at stake.

"Who do you think will take it? My money's on Little Zazzy Zoo Zoo." Peyton has a bag of fun-size candy bars on his lap. Wrappers litter the floor by his feet.

Shea takes a slurp from a giant cup of soda. "Nah. Yolanda the Yodeler's got this one. Did you hear her lungs?"

"Is this all you've been doing all day?" I stride to the curtains, pull them open. "Mom, isn't your test tonight?" I point at her stack of books.

She waves her hand. "Eh. I didn't have time to study today. I'll take it later."

Later? "But you can't practice medicine until you pass." I try to hand her a book. "And I know you already paid for the exam."

Mom takes the book, then slides it under the couch. "There. Now it won't bother anybody."

I shake my head. What a completely weirdo thing to do. Like something a little kid would pull. "Whatever, Mom." I figure she's still not quite healthy. She can take it next month, or next year for all I care.

My father rips open a cellophane package of Twinkies. "I believe Little Zazzy Zoo Zoo's got the right combination of energy and talent. In her tap dance, she was like a young Gene Kelly."

"Don't you mean Shirley Temple?" Mom throws some M&M'S into her mouth. "Gene Kelly was a man."

"No. I mean the athletic grace of Gene Kelly, actually." Dad gobbles a Twinkie, its filling oozing out between his lips. He saves a small piece and tosses it to the dog. Inu makes a halfhearted attempt to catch it, but it bounces off his face, leaving a trail of yellow sponge cake crumbs. He licks the remains off the floor.

I blink. Wait a second here. Dad with Twinkies? All of them watching trashy TV? My mouth drops open. "What happened to the robot movie?"

"Oh, it was too hard to get it to load." Mom shrugs. "So we just watched regular TV."

Dad points at the remote. "Too many buttons."

This is just about the lamest thing I've ever heard in my life. Even including Mr. Stedman's class.

"But . . ." I grab the control, hit INPUT, select the Netflix box, then pull up the robot movie.

"Nooooo. Go back. Takes too long." Peyton hangs his head backward. "Uhhhhh. Pass me another Twinkie, somebody."

Dad throws one at him. Peyton doesn't even raise his hand high enough to catch it. It hits him in the chest.

I turn off the TV and whirl to face them. "WHAT IS WRONG WITH ALL OF YOU?"

I look at Jinx, who has joined Peyton on the couch, her shoes kicked off. She shrugs and holds up a package of Twinkies. "Come on, Xander. You know you want one."

I waver for a second. But only for a second. Then I, too, take a seat.

CHAPTER ELEVEN

My grandmother used to tell me that if I sat on the couch too long, I'd turn into Daruma, this wise man from Japanese folktales who has no arms or legs. You might have seen the dolls—they look like red balls with an angry face. You're supposed to make a wish and color in one of his eyes. When your wish is granted, you color in the other eye. But that's where Daruma comes from, some person who lost his limbs because he sat in the forest for too long, thinking his thoughts or looking at birds or whatever.

Well, everyone's acting like Daruma today.

A half hour of Little Zazzy Zoo Zoo is all I can take. "Let's do something else!" I suggest and reach for the remote, but Dad sticks it under a couch cushion.

"Uh-uh." Dad waves me away. "This good part. Leave 'lone."

What, he's a caveman now, too?

Jinx and I exchange a glance, the old *our-parents-are-completely-cuckoo* glance that I had missed out on when I was an only child. Jinx plucks my mother's laptop off the coffee table. "I've been researching monkeys and birds, you guys. Did you know that some birds actually have a good sense of smell? They can follow scents left on the wind."

I read the digital article over Jinx's shoulder. "I thought they only had good eyesight." I glance at Peyton, waiting for a comment.

Nothing.

"What about monkeys?" I ask Jinx.

"Let me find out." Her fingers fly over the keyboard. "The *New York Times* says here that monkeys actually have a great sense of smell, because they don't see as many colors as humans. So they need that to compensate."

I glance at her curiously. "You see colors, though, right?"

She gives me a half grin. "You're always saying I must be color-blind, based on how I dress."

"Peyton." I reach over and nudge his leg. "Did you hear that? Jinx is color-blind."

Peyton laughs, displaying a mouthful of half-chewed Twinkie. "Little Zazzy Zoo Zoo. That's funny."

I glance at the clock. Almost lunchtime. "Peyton, you'd better get going. You have art class today," I remind him, as though I'm his father. "You don't want to be late, or your dad will be mad."

He waves at me. "'S fine."

I pick up his arm and pull him. "It is *not* fine. Get out of here."

He resists me, but finally I tug hard enough and, with a groan, he launches himself up. "Okay. Later." Peyton slouches out the front door, leaving behind his sleeping bag and yesterday's clothes.

I blow out hard and shake my head at Jinx. *What's wrong with them?* I mouth.

She shrugs, then picks up another package of Twinkies from the coffee table with her toes. "I don't know. It's like an idiot virus has infected your house."

"It's your house, too," I remind her, but she just wrinkles her nose. Huh. Maybe Jinx doesn't want to live here after all.

I push that thought from my mind. Instead, I, too, try to pick up Twinkies in my special way—with my Momotaro powers. Yes, Dad's sitting right here, but I figure one of two things will happen: (a) he won't notice, or (b) he'll finally snap out of this weirdo mood.

I stare at the Twinkies, letting my mind slip into the state I need to be in, halfway between sleep and consciousness.

But the Twinkies just sit there. The wrapper doesn't even crinkle.

Finally, I just lean forward and grab the package before Jinx can touch this one with her gross toes. No sense in missing out.

My parents don't budge from the couch all afternoon. As they binge-watch every *Little Zazzy Zoo Zoo* episode ever made, Jinx and I go out and practice more archery. We bake cookies. We look up more facts about birds and monkeys. We read one of the samurai books and have an argument over Musashi Miyamoto, who used two swords versus one (Jinx is for two swords, I am against—mostly because it'd be a pain to carry around two swords, and also because they're harder to handle than you'd think).

At last, around six, I turn off the TV and stand in front of my parents. The living room stinks like old cheese, farts, and morning breath. "Anybody going to do anything about dinner?"

Dad blinks at me with bloodshot eyes. "I don't know. If anybody is you, then yes."

Mom laughs, showing a mouthful of Twinkie crumbs. "Good one, Akira."

"I give up." I go back into the kitchen.

Jinx gets out a box of mac and cheese and shakes it at me.

I nod and fill up a pot of water, set it on the stove. "Obāchan hates this stuff, though. We'll have to make her some rice."

"Where is Obāchan, anyway?" Jinx asks.

Uh-oh. Jinx and I stare at each other, our expressions growing more horrified as the realization dawns on us. No one ever checked on my grandmother!

I run to her bedroom and knock. No answer. I push open the door, sending a bag of yarn flying. Obāchan's room is full of stuff *we might need later*, according to her, but it's neatly organized for the most part. She wants to be ready for the end of the world. After what happened to us two months ago, I can't say I blame her.

My grandmother is asleep in her bed, pale and drawn. Alarmed,

I rush over to her side and shake her gently. "Obāchan?"

She licks her cracked lips, her eyelids fluttering. "Xander. Water."

I go fill up her empty glass and bring it back. "Are you ill?"

Obāchan shakes her head slightly. "Just . . . oh-so-tired."

A sick feeling comes up out of my stomach. "Obāchan, something weird is happening to everybody." I tell her about my parents and Peyton.

She barely opens one eye. "Yes. I am so ancient, maybe my dreams were the only thing keeping me alive." She laughs hoarsely.

"What do you mean?" The sick feeling gets stronger. I know what she's going to tell me.

Her dry, leathery hand clasps mine. "You used the baku too much, didn't you?" Her tone is gentle, as if I'd spilled a glass of water instead of, you know, completely ruining everyone's lives.

I swallow. Yes. No. "I . . . I don't think so."

"The baku has taken our dreams, Xander. The good dreams as well as the bad." She pats my hand. "Well, what's done is done."

I swallow. Taken our dreams? But we're awake. "I didn't know she'd take our, like, *goals*."

"Aren't goals dreams?" she asks in a soft voice.

I've really messed up this time. I hang my head. "I'm sorry, Obāchan."

"No need. You have turned out to be so much worthier than we ever thought." Obāchan pats at my shoulder. "I am, and always will be, proud of you."

Fear clogs my throat like a ball of grease in a pipe. "Why are you talking like that?" I ask sharply. "You're not going to die."

"Because I love you, Xander." Obāchan smiles at me. "Have you tried using your powers?"

My heart stops, thinking about how I tried to move the Twinkies, with no luck. "Oh no."

"Your subconscious fuels your Momotaro powers, Xander. It is where your imagination comes from. Without your dreams, the powers do not work. Lucky for you, you have more dreams to spare than most, so you aren't sick like the rest of us." Her breathing gets deeper as she begins drifting off. "You will have to find the baku. Get our dreams back."

"Where? How? Don't fall asleep!" Panicked, I shake her gently. This is bad. Very bad.

She breathes out a sigh. "Try asking the waterfall for answers."

"The waterfall? What waterfall?" I think. "You mean that trickle on the mountain?"

She barely nods. "Meditate under it."

"Under it?" I repeat dumbly.

"Under it," she says firmly, and then abruptly falls asleep, her face flattening out until it seems to be on the same plane as the pillow. I watch her for a minute to make sure she's still breathing.

I need to figure this out quickly.

Under the little waterfall. Okay, then. That's what we'll do.

CHAPTER TWELVE

Before dawn, Jinx and I get up and fill backpacks for us and Peyton with enough survival gear to make my grandmother proud. It's all the stuff my dad has been making us carry during his training sessions: a heat-saving waterproof blanket, tablets for purifying water, a nylon rope and hooks in case we need to climb rocks, packable down jackets in case it gets cold, some snacks, water, and canned drinks.

Most special of all are my octopus *netsuke* and monkey netsuke, which helped us on our last adventure. They are carved wooden figures with boxes dangling from them. The octopus's box holds salt, which can melt oni, at least temporarily. The monkey's box holds magic rice. I open the rice box and throw a grain into my mouth. It blooms into *onigiri*, a rice cake stuffed with various foods. This one has scrambled egg. "These still work," I tell Jinx.

Jinx is wearing the gold cuff bracelet that I found at the kappa's lair and gave to her. The last time I saw it, she'd thrown it across a room. That was right before she betrayed us all to her father, Gozu. I guess she didn't leave the bracelet behind after all. I frown at it. "You sure you want to take that? What if it gets lost?"

"I'm hoping it's good for something." Jinx tightens it around her wrist. "After all, nobody gave me wings or even a sword."

Good point.

My parents are still on the couch, fast asleep. Nobody gets up, not even Inu. I wish we could take him, but in his current condition, he's better off here. I scrawl my parents a note of explanation. By that I mean I tell them we'll be back soon, not getting into lots of detail. At the end, I add *DON'T FORGET OBĀCHAN!* Just in case, I leave saltines and Gatorade on her nightstand. She doesn't stir, but her chest still rises and falls. Even if we took her to the hospital, it would be no good. There's nothing I can do except go get her dreams back.

Jinx and I sneak over to Peyton's house, going the back way, up the steep hill instead of using the driveway. Luckily, they don't have a dog to alert anybody.

We creep around the side of the house to the front. A big camouflage-pattern duffel bag sits on the porch. PEYTON PHASIS, the tag says.

I swallow audibly. Peyton can't go to boot camp now. Not if he's going to act as lazy as he did yesterday. I hope I can convince him to get out of bed and join us.

"What?" Jinx whispers, too loud.

I put my finger to my lips. Mr. Phasis has pretty good hearing, and he's also the type of person who will go crazy first, ask questions second. I don't particularly feel like getting mistaken for a burglar so early in the morning. Or ever.

We climb up the trellis to get to Peyton's second-floor bedroom window and peer in through the curtains. He's lying on top of his bed, wearing the same clothes he left my house in. Weird.

I tap on the window. *Rat, tat, tat-a-tat.* Our special knock.

Peyton keeps sleeping.

I try again.

Nothing.

Jinx shoulders me aside. "Allow me." She removes the window screen, then slides the glass open. "Easy peasy, lemon squeezy," she whispers. Then she offers me her hand as a foothold. I put my sneaker on her palm, and she lifts me as though I'm a feather, almost launching me through the window. Luckily, his desk is right there, and I land on a pile of papers.

I climb down softly. "Peyton?" I go over to him and shake him. A cold fear penetrates me as I remember my grandmother. "Peyton?"

Eventually, he blinks, and I sag with relief. "It's not time for breakfast," he says. "But if it is, I'll take waffles."

"Peyton." I grab him by the T-shirt and haul him to a sitting pose. His hair stands in an impressive plume, fanning over the crown of his head. "You have to wake up. We have a mission to do."

He nods, rubbing his face. "Can't. Got kiddie boot camp." Peyton's eyes are oddly emotionless, as if he doesn't really care about this new development.

But I know he does. I swallow. The baku thing must still be affecting him, like it's affecting my parents.

"Peyton." I grab his hoodie, throw it at him. "Come with us. We've got to get you out of here."

Peyton lies back again. "What's the point?"

"You can't go to a military camp when you're like this," I say in a loud whisper. "You'll die. Like, literally. I think your heart might stop."

Peyton closes his eyes. "So what?"

"So don't you care?"

"Unngh." He rolls over.

Then Jinx is at my side, pulling at him, too. "You're coming with us, mister. No more monkeying around." She shoots a murderous glance at me. "And don't you make a joke!"

I grin. "Why should I? You already made it."

A knock at the door. Shoot. Peyton's dad heard us. Jinx and I immediately drop and roll under the bed from opposite sides, our shoulders colliding. *Please don't give us away*, I pray silently to Peyton. If my powers were working, I could *make* him do the right thing. But then, if my powers were working, we wouldn't be in this situation.

"Yeah?" Peyton grunts.

Mr. Phasis opens the door. "We're leaving in an hour. Get up."

"I'm sick," Peyton says, and he sounds convincing. Weak and hoarse. Jinx and I, shoulder to shoulder, hold our breath.

"The only thing you're sick with is a lack of motivation," Mr. Phasis says in his crisp voice. "Now go take a shower." He shuts the door again.

Jinx and I crawl out from under the bed. Because it's Peyton's room and his dad makes him clean it every night, we're not covered in dust the way we'd be if we'd been under my bed.

"You heard him," I whisper to Peyton. "Let's get you out of here."

Finally, Peyton manages a nod, his eyes still closed. I help Jinx push Peyton up, and he more or less cooperates in walking across the room. I go out the window first, somehow Jinx manages to shove Peyton through, and we practically drop him to the ground.

We don't use the road to get to the trail. Instead, we cut through people's yards and pastures, ducking under a couple of barbed-wire fences, and avoiding a cow that eyes us suspiciously. The dim light of the approaching dawn provides just enough illumination to prevent us from breaking our ankles on rocks or gopher holes.

Peyton moves much more slowly than usual. It's like he's getting over the flu, shuffling along, his hands lifelessly stuck in his pockets.

Jinx chews a wad of gum, blowing pink bubbles bigger than her head and popping them quickly.

"Catch any gnats with that?" I ask. I expect Peyton to laugh, but he doesn't respond.

"Yeah." She blows another bubble. "Extra protein."

I shift my backpack's weight. I might be carrying even more than Dad had us train with. And then there's my sword, too. If Mr. Phasis knew what we were doing, I bet he wouldn't have made Peyton go to that camp at all.

I squint against the bright morning sun. I forgot sunglasses and a hat. Oh well. Most of the time, the tall evergreens provide plenty of shade. "I wonder how long I have to meditate?"

Jinx gives me a side eye. "You never read what your dad gave us, did you?"

No point in lying. "Nope."

"Xander." Jinx sighs as dramatically as an actor onstage. "The book says that the warrior has to meditate for two weeks under the waterfall to achieve enlightenment."

I stop in my tracks. "You're joking. I don't have two weeks!"

Jinx shrugs. "I don't know what to tell you."

"But what will happen when I meditate?"

Jinx shrugs again, her shoulders popping. "How would I know?

You get enlightened, right?" She grins at me. "Whatever that means. Guess you're about to get pretty wise."

I kick a big rock off the path. "Dang it! I don't need enlightenment; I need results."

She blows another bubble. "Well, I'll do it, too, and maybe something will happen twice as fast."

I make a dismissive sound. "You're not the Momotaro. Who cares if you meditate?"

"I'm going to pretend like I never heard that." She strides ahead of me.

"How much farther?" Peyton's breathing kind of hard. "I think I might just rest here." He tries to sit down.

"You've been there before." I have the feeling that if Peyton sits down, it might be hard to get him moving again. "It's just a little bit farther, dude. Come on." I make him loop his arm through mine, and I yank him along the path.

The waterfall drips into that same pathetic puddle, covered with stagnant green algae that reeks of rotting plant life.

Jinx and I eye it doubtfully. There's a small niche in the rock behind the water. Not a cave—more like an indentation. Just big enough for one person to sit in, cross-legged.

"I guess it's you." She gestures. "Be my guest, O honored Momotaro-san."

I give her a sour look as I duck through the drip, which smells like a skunk took a bath in it someplace upstream. It's as warm as a shower, and I can't help imagining all the microbes and bacteria in it, now trying to leap into my bloodstream to sicken me. I shudder. No way will I last two weeks here. I might not even last two minutes. "Are you sure you'll be okay?" I ask Jinx.

"What, you think I can't survive without you? Remember, you don't have powers anymore." She leads Peyton over to a shady patch under a tree, where he lies down and she sits, taking a book out of her knapsack. "We'll be fine."

Thanks for reminding me, Jinx, that I'm helpless. "You look comfy. Enjoy yourselves! Don't let me keep you from having fun." I set my pack to one side, take off my sword, and lean it against the back wall. I try to get comfortable.

It's not easy. The granite's hard. A line of thirsty ants marches past me to the water. A few of them climb my legs, and I feel them bite me, their huge intruder. Ouch! I brush them off and scoot out of the way as best I can.

Some waterfall of knowledge.

I close my eyes and wait for something to happen.

CHAPTER THIRTEEN

Ugggggggh.

Meditation is so boring.

I can't understand why anybody in their right mind would want to do this. What's so fun about sitting still and trying not to think about anything? This is *impossible*. I'm always thinking about something, even when I don't want to. Like right now, I'm thinking about how I don't have any powers, and how heavy my sword gets when I'm hiking, and how not strong I am.

Stop it.

Okay. Let's try something different. I picture a blank piece of paper. Pure white, no words, no pictures.

I could draw that oni scorpion who attacked me. I try to imagine its humanoid head, its fangs. . . .

It's still out there. My heart flip-flops as I think of it. It could be living in those boulders right there, waiting for us.

Nope. That's not an empty mind, either.

I blow out a gust of air that wobbles the drips of the "waterfall." I can't do this much longer. I shift. The rock is making my bottom sore. Not exactly a La-Z-Boy recliner. My spine hurts.

I peer out at Jinx, who sits a distance away, reading her book. Next to her, Peyton lies under a tree, his face not visible from here. I wonder if his nap will do him any good. Maybe Jinx should be the one sitting under here. After all, she volunteered. Or maybe it should be Peyton, who is practically meditating all the time anyway.

Anger surfaces again like that green stuff sitting on top of the water. Why am I always responsible for everybody? How did I get to be *the one*?

You used the baku too much, and you lied about it, says a voice in my head. *That's how.*

Shut up, inner voice. Know-it-all.

I take a deep breath and think about my grandfather. Why can't he show up again and give me some more valuable advice? I've only had one dream about him since my big adventure, and that was a nightmare.

I'd told Obāchan about how her husband had helped me out during that strange journey. How he'd kept appearing in my dreams and giving me hints about what to do. "Was it really him?" I'd asked her. "Or was it just my mind making him up?"

She had nodded thoughtfully. "What you describe sounds like him. You used details that we never told you about, that you had no way of knowing." She'd shrugged. "But even if it was your mind, does it make a difference? Either way, he helped you."

Now I try to remember what my grandfather looked like. Silver hair. Same blue eyes as me and my father. The wrinkles between his brows and in the corners of his eyes. But somehow the whole image won't come together in one piece.

Side effect of the baku, I guess.

What would Ojīchan do if he were here?

But instead of my grandfather, Jinx flits into my head. Jinx, with her constant reading and butting in. Jinx, always trying to hang out with me and Peyton. Telling me how lucky I am. She should have her own friends. Like Clarissa.

My heart flutters.

Jinx likes Clarissa, but she's only invited Clarissa over once, and that was when Mom suggested it. Mom even called Clarissa's mother for her.

The two girls hung out in the yard—literally, since Jinx was up in a tree, dangling upside down from her knees. Clarissa sat on the branch next to her, reading aloud from a book. Jinx laughed from time to time, her face beet-red from the blood rushing into it.

Clarissa never came over again, and she'd never invited Jinx over to her house, either. Why? Could it be that Clarissa's parents knew that Jinx's dad was an oni? No, that was impossible. . . .

My temple throbs. Thinking about the social lives of girls makes my brain hurt.

Man, Jinx must be lonely. She doesn't fit in even worse than I don't fit in.

And there I was, resenting every second she was with me and Peyton. I might have to be nicer to her.

I don't know why this never occurred to me before. I stretch out my aching leg.

"Onamae-wa?" a voice beside me says.

I jump about a foot into the air and land hard on my tailbone. "What?"

Right next to me, coming up to about my armpit, sits a man. Or sort of a man. He is dressed in a cloak of deep orange-red. His white eyes stare sightlessly ahead of him. Two black eyebrows, as dark and wiggly as bristly caterpillars, work up and down like seesaws above his eyes. He doesn't really have a neck; his jaw seems to melt right into his chest. Below that, his stomach sticks out. He's kind of egg shaped, like if I touched him, he'd teeter back and forth.

"Onamae wa?" the man asks again.

Basic Japanese. *What's your name?*

Huh. Strange opening sentence. No *Good afternoon* or *How do you do?* No *not* trying to scare the living daylights out of me.

"Xander," I manage through a throat that feels like I just ate ten pieces of dry toast followed by fish bones. I cough heartily.

"I would pat you on the back, but you can see my problem." The

man chuckles as one arm stump moves beneath his cloak. He has no limbs.

I swivel myself around so I'm facing him. "Who are you?"

"I am Daruma." He blinks slowly at me. "You are in my cave."

Daruma. I look him up and down.

"Haven't you heard of me?" He wiggles his left eyebrow. "I am normally seen in airport shops and souvenir stores. Daruma. You know. Did your obāchan ever tell you not to sit around for too long, or your legs would shrivel away like mine did?"

"I know who you are," I say kind of brusquely. She had, but I didn't think it'd be polite to bring it up. "She might have mentioned that." I think of my parents back home on the couch and hope nothing worse happens to them—or to Obāchan. I need to get this over with as soon as possible. "I'm here because I'm looking for the baku. Do you know where I can find it?"

"Slow down there." Daruma's cloudy eyes roll toward me. "First things first. Your meditation brought me to you."

"Really?" I ask, feeling rather impressed with myself. "So *that* was good meditation. Huh. But I couldn't get rid of all my crazy thoughts."

"The point is not to get rid of your thoughts," Daruma says patiently, "but to watch them fall around you like snowflakes melting into warm ground."

Okay, whatever. "No need to get poetic on me," I mutter. All that matters is it worked. I slide toward him, eager to learn his information. "So, you can tell me where to go? What to do?"

He shakes his head slightly. I don't know how he turns it without a neck. "Not yet. First you must learn how to control your impatience and anger."

"What?" I scramble to my feet, almost hitting my head on the cave ceiling. "I don't have time to learn how to control my impatience and anger! I have a family to save! My grandmother might die because of me!" I bend over. "Please, Daruma, if you're going to help me, then help me. Don't give me weird advice riddles. I'm not in the mood." I hold out my hands, palms up. "I'll give you whatever you want. Like, anything." I look around for something. "My sword, even." I hold it out to him. "See? It's probably worth a lot."

Daruma sputters. "Pah! What need have I for a sword or money? I am helping you the only way you can be helped, *former* Momotaro-san." Daruma's wrinkled eyelids close, and he bows his head slightly. "It is best to keep one's head near one's body at all times, or else one's powers will be lost. Now, you can take my advice or you can leave my advice."

What the heck? "As far as I know, my head's still attached to the rest of me." I sit down.

Daruma ignores my comment. "Perhaps"—he clears his throat—"perhaps you could fetch me some water? It's been centuries since I last drank!"

I point at the pitiful stream trickling down in front of us. "This water?"

"Are you trying to kill me?" Daruma asks. "No, the water you have in your pack."

How can he see I have a pack? It's behind him. And how does he know there's water in it? "Sure." I pull a bottle from my knapsack and twist off the cap. I hold the bottle near his lips, trying not to let them touch the opening, but his head shoots forward and he gulps down half of the water before I can even blink.

Then he lets out a huge, cave-rattling belch. "Ahhh. Thank you."

I nod curtly.

"Now, as I was saying before you, ahem, lost your patience, you must learn how to control your anger and impatience, or else you will not be able to lure the baku to you." Daruma smirks as if impressed with his own wisdom.

I scowl. He's reminding me of my teacher Mr. Stedman. Which doesn't exactly make me want to turn cartwheels.

Daruma continues. "To do this, you must find Fudō-Myōō. He will show you."

"*Fu-do-me-yo-oh?*" I repeat dumbly. "How do I find him? What does he look like?"

Daruma closes his eyes. "Fudō-Myōō will not just appear to any old traveler. No. He is the Angry Lord of Light. He appears with a halo of flame around his head, and his mouth curled in a great sneer, ready to strike down demons and nonbelievers alike with his sword and rope."

"Angry Lord of what now?" I'm pretty sure I don't want to deal with anyone or anything with the name *Angry Lord*. Or with a halo of flame.

"Light," Daruma repeats. "And as I said, Fudō-Myōō will not appear for everyone or anything. No. Your cause must be worthy. You must prove yourself. You must call him so he hears."

By this time, I'm ready to kick Humpty Dumpty over and run out of this place. Which probably won't win me any worthiness points. I inhale and count to ten. "Do I just go around shouting, 'Fudō, hey, Fudō, come out, come out, wherever you are'?"

Daruma wobbles his head. "Not exactly. Did you bring him an offering?"

"An offering?" I have no idea what he's talking about. "Like a lamb? Are we going that medieval?"

He clucks impatiently. "Not a sacrifice. An offering."

I fiddle around in my backpack. "I don't know. I have a granola bar." I take it out.

He eyes it disdainfully. "Xander, I don't think you've heard anything I've said."

"I've heard everything you said." I thrust the granola bar into the backpack so hard it breaks in half. "I'm just waiting to hear something I can use. Otherwise, why'd you bother to appear? To taunt me?"

"Climb up the mountain. Through the gate. He's there. Somewhere." Daruma lets out a long breath. "That is all I know."

"This mountain? Really?" I doubt that. This is just a regular mountain, in San Diego County. It's not some mystical place where an Angry Lord of Light would be hiding out. Maybe some random angry person, like the guy they arrested last year for setting the forest on fire, but no actual angry lord. "I've been to the peak dozens of times, and I'm telling you, there's nothing special there." I pick up the bottle. "Maybe you need more water to help you remember?"

Daruma pushes his lips out in a pout. The caterpillar brows work up and down. Then he shimmers and disappears.

What? "Hey, come back here!" I shout. I kick the space where he used to be. "You're not done yet! ARRRRRRGH!!"

When the last *argggh* leaves my body, I inhale sharply.

I'm sitting down, and my eyes are still closed.

So that's what it's like to meditate? Well, that was somewhat more exciting than I thought it'd be. However, I still don't know exactly where and how to find this Fudō-Myōō character. Someplace on the mountain. That's real specific. This mountain's pretty darn big.

"Xander!" Jinx shrieks. "Get yourself and your sword out here pronto!"

Beyond the waterfall, I see a multicolored shape charge at Jinx.

CHAPTER FOURTEEN

A man in a flowing white robe paces back and forth in front of Jinx, an unearthly growl rolling out from his throat.

Um, I take that back.

A manlike thing on two legs with two arms and the *head of a dragon* paces back and forth in front of Jinx. A long, serpentine head, with green and red scales. Its body is as solid and muscular as a silverback gorilla's, and like an ape, its knuckles brush the ground.

Jinx stands still, her Leatherman knife at the ready as she eyes his movements. "You know what?" she says to me as I approach. "I super-duper need my own sword. This pocketknife just isn't cutting it."

"I don't know, I think a pocketknife cuts stuff pretty well." I stay back, trying to figure out what the dragon man's going to do, how dangerous he is. Dangerous enough, I decide.

"This isn't the time for jokes!" Jinx darts to one side, then the other. I realize she's not running up into a tree because she's protecting our friend. Peyton, amazingly, is still asleep on the ground behind her, his hands folded on his chest, snoring away as if he isn't about to get eaten by a ferocious oni.

The monster's head undulates on its body as it eyes Jinx, getting ready to strike.

She holds up her hands in the defensive stance my father recently taught us. "Hey, Christmas dragon! Don't make me use my moves on you!"

I break into a run, lifting my sword, which seems a lot heavier than the last time I used it in battle. He hasn't turned around yet. Good. For a person my size, the element of surprise is pretty much your best weapon.

But it's not enough of a surprise. The dragon turns and, without hesitation, leaps toward me.

And exhales blue smoke.

I wait until the creature is almost right on top of me, though I really, really don't want to. At the last possible second, I hop to the left and just barely escape him. His smoke crackles against my hair, and it feels like I just opened a freezer. I touch my hair. Icicles.

So he breathes cold, not fire? Okay.

The dragon whirls, coming at me again before I can react.

Jinx appears in front of me, waving a burning branch. "You want a piece of this?"

"Hey!" I say. "There are no fires allowed in this forest!" That's all we need, to set the whole mountain on fire before we find Fudō.

The oni hisses, *poof*ing away the fire.

Never mind, then.

I sprint toward the dragon and jab it with my sword, but he undulates his stomach to the side, dodging me. He spurts more ice-smoke at my face, and I brace myself to become a Popsicle.

Jinx's hand shoots in front of my eyes. The dragon's smoke bounces off her golden cuff and back into its face. He turns a blue-gray color as he freezes into stone. Or ice. Does it matter which?

But his claws can still move, and they grab Jinx around the waist. She yelps and squirms, but he holds her tight.

I squat and swing my sword in a wide arc from right to left, aiming at the thing's kneecaps. It's kind of a wild swing—I don't have much control in this position—and all I can do is hope.

The sword slices through him as easily as a hot knife in a stick of butter.

The oni's torso thuds into the dirt. The legs remain standing as if the feet are glued to the ground.

Not bad, Xander. Not bad at all, especially for feeling so clumsy. But still, I wish I were stronger. You'd think I'd be getting better at fighting, but I haven't improved any since our last adventure. I bend over for a second, getting my breath back.

"Hey." Jinx comes over and holds out her hand to help me up. "Good job finishing him. But otherwise, your sword work's really gone downhill."

I drop her hand and dust off my pants. "Jinx, can't you just say something nice and leave it at that? It's not like you're the ultimate ninja warrior."

She gives me a bemused look. "I'm saying your lack of powers is affecting your sword-fighting skills, Xander."

"Like I need you to tell me that." I bend over to examine the oni's legs. Scaly. I prod one with my toe. It's soft, as though it's a stuffed animal, not a real creature. "Jinx, do you know what this thing is?"

"Very good," comes a voice.

Jinx and I exchange a look of alarm. Then Jinx gathers herself and says, "Hello?" in a voice as calm as a telephone greeting, as if she's not completely freaked out by this turn of events.

"Who said that?" I hold my sword ready, turning in a circle, but all I see are a few birds flying here and there.

"I did."

Both of us look down. On the ground, the dragon head on the human torso morphs with a strange sucking sound. It turns into the face of an old man with long white hair.

As we stand there gaping, two human legs rapidly sprout out of the bottom of the torso. The old man waves his hand at us. "Help me up, children."

We take his hand—a human hand—and he stands, a bit unsteadily, on his twig-like limbs.

"*Arigato*." He bows, and we bow in return. "I am Daigon-gen. The protector of the mountain."

"Protector?" I jerk my head up. "Do you know Fudō-Myōō?"

"Of course." He shuffles over to a fallen log and lowers himself with a huff, like my grandmother always does, as if sitting takes a huge effort. "We have coffee every Tuesday." The protector shimmers like a mirage.

"Really?" I ask.

"No." Daigon-gen chuckles. "I cannot call him for you, either. He is not like a dentist's office that's open from nine to five." He shimmers again, fading from view for a moment. "But I'm here to help you now."

"What's a Fudō-Myōō?" Jinx says.

"I'll tell you later." I'm afraid the protector will disappear any second. "How can you help us? We'd be grateful for anything."

Daigon-gen peers up at me. "Where is the other?"

"Over there." I point at Peyton, who hasn't moved this whole time. Well, I guess sleeping that deeply can come in handy sometimes.

Daigon-gen's brows furrow, and he purses his lips. "Well, I suppose because the two of you did so well, he gets to come, too."

"Come where?" Peyton raises his head, blinking sleepily. "What'd I miss?"

"Through the arch." Daigon-gen gestures to a spot behind us. We turn.

A tall gate has appeared in the forest. It's a rectangular opening made out of logs too big to wrap your arms around, tall as a two-story house, and painted in lacquered red finish. Like the kind you would see in Japan.

I close my mouth, which I realize has been hanging open. I turn back to Daigon-gen, but there's nobody on the log now.

Of course there isn't.

"Thank you!" I say to the air, just in case, because Obāchan says good manners never hurt.

Jinx has gone over to help Peyton to his feet. "So we're walking through there?"

"Seems that way." I assist her. Peyton looks like he's been up for two weeks straight, with purple-blue circles under his eyes. "Dude, you look like you just lost a really bad fight."

He yawns. "I did. The sleep monster got me. But I'm good now." We chuckle at his little joke. "Ungh. Did you bring any candy?" he asks me. "I need sugar to keep going."

"Just walk, will you?" Jinx eyes the gate and swallows hard.

"What's the matter?" I ask.

She sucks in a breath. "It's a *torii*. Those are gates to the under-world, you know."

I nod as though I totally knew that. "Underworld, or other world?"

"Guess we'll find out." She runs her fingers through her tangled hair, which somehow makes it even messier. "I followed my father through a torii gate and ended up in that jungle by the snow woman's cave." Jinx pulls her mouth to one side. "It kind of . . . hurt. To go through it."

"Hurt? How much?" I ask sharply, but Jinx doesn't answer.

She faces the gate and bends her legs, bouncing as if she's in the Olympics and waiting for the starting gun of a race. "Only one way to do this. As quickly as possible." Her leg muscles clench and she takes off, bent over, sprinting toward the torii.

"Wait!" I don't even have my backpack on.

But it's too late. She's through.

She's gone. Nowhere to be seen.

Great.

I peer through the gate. It looks the same on the other side as it does here. Tall pine trees. A path covered by fallen needles, browned by summer sun.

I lean toward it. Just seems like a normal structure.

Peyton ambles up beside me and, without stopping, goes right on through the gate.

"Peyton!" I grab my backpack and lurch after him.

CHAPTER FIFTEEN

As I pass through the gate, I feel sharp, stinging pain all over, like a thousand burning matches flickering against my skin. Before I can react, the sensation evaporates as quickly as it started.

I slow to a walk. The landscape has completely changed.

Gone are the tall pines from the forest near my house. Instead, leafy trees stand branch to branch like soldiers lined up shoulder to shoulder. I gawk up at them. Their leaves, in varying shades of magenta, blue, and gray, form a vast, endless ceiling. I stop and pick up a cobalt-blue leaf that's perfectly round. Other leaves are the shapes of stars and moons.

Peyton slouches against an ashy gray trunk that looks like it's covered in lizard skin. It seems as though the tree is the only thing preventing gravity from crushing him against the ground. "Took you long enough," he croaks when I reach him. One side of his mouth twitches up in a weak, un-Peyton-like smile. He could use a bowl of hot chicken soup and some antibiotics. His eyes are crusty with sleep, and his cheeks are drawn. This is definitely not the Peyton who could normally pass as the lead singer of a boy band.

"What do you mean? I came in like two seconds after you did," I say. "Have you seen Jinx?"

He shakes his head. "No sign of her."

Great. Leave it to her to run off. "Jinx!" I shout. "Where are you?"

"Here!" she calls from someplace high above. Of course. She's the monkey girl.

Relief poofs out of me like air out of a balloon. Without her, there's no way Peyton and I would be able to make it. "Where? I can't see anything but forest."

She scrambles nimbly down a tree near us, as though the smooth trunk has invisible handholds. "Hey, slowpokes, I thought you guys were right behind me. I was up there forever."

"We *were* right behind you." I don't know what she's talking about. Talk about learning patience—these two could both use some.

Peyton rips off his hoodie and then his shirt with a burst of energy I haven't seen since the day before yesterday.

"What's the matter? Do you have ants on you?" I watch him with concern.

"My wings. I think they're back. Can you see them?" Peyton cranes his head over his shoulder.

"Hold still." I examine him. There are two flesh-colored lumps, like fists under his skin, on either side of his spine. I touch them, feeling the hard bone underneath. "They're trying to sprout, I think. Can you flap them?"

The nubs sort of twitch, like earthworms on concrete trying to find their way back to dirt. But that's it.

I hand him his shirt, hoping he won't be too disappointed. "Guess they're not growing back right now. Maybe they will later."

Peyton pulls his shirt on, not meeting my eyes. "I shouldn't have come. I'm a burden."

My throat closes. If he gives up now, we all might as well give up. "You wouldn't be a burden even if I had to carry you."

"You don't have to be nice to me." He pulls on his hoodie. "I'm going back. I'll see you on the other side of the gate thing." He turns and starts walking, but he can't move very fast.

"Peyton." Jinx bounces over to us. She reaches out to him. "Come on. If you guys could put up with me after the snow woman cave, we can put up with you being slightly slow."

He covers his forehead with his hood, screws his eyes shut, and frowns. I haven't seen that expression on him since we were seven years old and he got scared by a raggedy mall Santa. "I don't want to go."

I hate seeing Peyton like this. I'm so mad at myself for causing all this trouble that I could punch myself in the face. If I could go back in time, I never would have used that stupid baku charm. I would have just lived with my nightmares. "Peyton, Jinx is right. You'd help us if the situation were reversed."

His face contorts more, practically melting. "But I can actually carry you guys. Me, I'm too big for either of you."

Jinx and I exchange a glance. It's true. If he was healthy and I wasn't, he could easily throw me over his shoulder and cart me around.

"Xander and I will help you together, then," Jinx says. "You can't go back now. You might not even be able to."

He inhales and opens his eyes, eyeing her warily. "Why are you being so nice?"

Jinx crosses her arms. "I'm always nice."

Peyton and I both bark out a laugh at the same time.

"You guys aren't exactly Miss Congeniality to me, either," Jinx points out. "Come on. You know I'm good at this other-world stuff." She waves her hand around at the trees. "I'm more comfortable here than I am in the real world."

"She's right," I tell Peyton. "And I'm right. So let's go." I nudge him.

He nods, his face still screwed up, and shuffles forward as though he's a zombie.

That's a start.

We begin walking. "So you know where we're going, right, Xander?" Jinx prompts. "Exactly what did you learn?"

I think back to the cave. "Not that much, I guess." I repeat what the Daruma character said about Fudō-Myōō.

"Why didn't you tell me that *before* we went through the gate?" Jinx kicks a bunch of leaves out of the way, and they fly about in a confetti of colors. "I would've gone to the waterfall and asked Daruma myself."

"First, Daruma wouldn't have shown up for you. Second, you took off before I could tell you everything."

Jinx shakes her head. "Xander."

I shake my head back at her. "Jinx."

"Angry Lord of Light, huh? Sounds like a charmer," Peyton drawls, pulling the strings of his hood so it cinches even tighter around his face. "I don't feel afraid. But then, I don't feel anything."

"It doesn't matter if his name is the Angry Lord of Light or the Fearful Duke of Pooping—we just have to find him!" I look around the forest. I don't see anything but trees. And more trees. And then a few more after that. I kick a branch aside gently. "He could be any-where. In a tree, on top of the mountain . . ."

Jinx bares all her teeth as she gets in my face. "That's exactly the kind of information you were supposed to get from Daruma, Xander. Your interviewing skills need work."

I refuse to back away from her. "He wouldn't tell me."

"Did you ask?"

"Of course I asked. Stop second-guessing everything I do." I scowl at her. "Why don't you trust me?"

Jinx laughs bitterly. "Oh, I don't know. Maybe because you're the one who used the baku too much, and because you were using your powers when you weren't supposed to. Maybe it's because you created this whole mess in the first place!"

I swallow hard. "You wouldn't be talking like that if you were having my nightmares, Jinx."

She stomps on. "A nightmare is just a nightmare. It's your body's way of waking you up to go to the bathroom."

No. These were worse. *Way* worse. I think of that shadowy figure with the silver face. "Of course I don't expect you to understand."

"You guys." Peyton drags his feet forward. "If anybody should be mad at Xander, it's me. But I'm not."

"That's only because you're numb, Peyton." Jinx turns to deliver this line. "If you could feel, believe me, you'd be plenty furious right now. Enraged. Violent. Discombobulated."

"*Discombobulated?* Pretty sure that's not a synonym for anger." I keep walking.

Peyton yawns so wide I can see his tonsils. I take a can of iced green tea out of my backpack and offer it to him. "Here, this will help. Chock-full of antioxidants."

"Thanks." Peyton tries to flip up the tab on the can, but his fingers fumble. "Unnnnh."

"Give me that." Jinx grabs the can, cracks it open, and hands it back to Peyton.

"I would've gotten it," he says to her gruffly.

"I know," Jinx says. "I'm just helping."

"Can't you ever help without making someone feel bad about it?" I ask her.

"No. It's my job to make people feel bad. Totally my intention." She marches ahead. I can't tell if she was being sarcastic or not.

We continue on. The path winds downward, into a little mountain valley. My stomach growls, and I start dreaming about food. Real food, not just granola bars and beef jerky. I didn't eat properly before we left—I just grabbed a bag of chips. I should have had a bowl of oatmeal or something.

Turns out Dad was right about food being fuel and all that.

I hope he and Mom and Obāchan and Inu are all doing okay. They're at least as healthy as Peyton, I figure. Only my grandmother is in bad shape because she's super old. And she wouldn't have sent me on this quest if she thought she was going to die.

Would she?

I wonder if Mr. Phasis came over looking for Peyton, and what my parents said to him—I mean, they are currently pretty out of it. We'd left Peyton's parents a note saying we'd all gone camping, but I'm sure that hadn't made Mr. Phasis very happy.

"Peyton," I say, "do you think your dad will call the police?"

He shakes his head. "I don't care. He didn't listen when I said I was sick. I mean"—now he's breathing hard, trying to walk and talk at the same time—"can't he see how not right I am?"

"I thought your dad had, like, softened since spring break." A few months ago, Peyton couldn't do anything right as far as his father was concerned.

Peyton shrugs. "He's about as soft as a frozen stick of butter."

I take out my own green tea. It's warm, but that's okay. I drink it quickly and belch, the sound echoing through the forest.

Jinx cracks open another. "You call that a burp?" She belches, too, and pretty soon we're having a burping contest. Peyton even joins in for a second, and hope blooms in my chest. Maybe this place will make him better.

As we walk on, the trees change, getting shorter and squatter. Ripe fruit hangs heavy on some of the branches. Apples, I think. I jump, trying to get one, but my fingertips barely graze the plump sphere.

"Want me to climb up there?" Jinx offers. "You're a little short."

"No kidding." I hop again, determined to reach. "I've got it." My fingers close around a ruddy specimen, and I yank it off. "Success!" I polish it on my shirt, then lift it to my mouth.

Two white circles appear on the skin. The apple blinks at me.

I drop it and leap backward. "Ahhhhh!"

"What, did you find a worm?" Jinx asks.

The apple lies among the leaves. Black eyebrows seesaw above the eyes. *"Onamae-wa?"* it says.

Onamae-wa? That sounds like . . . "Daruma?" I bend down to it.

The apple giggles shrilly, the sound as loud and annoying as a preschooler after too many cupcakes.

"Xander." Jinx grabs my arm, pointing up.

All the apples have faces, and all of them are laughing at me. "Momotaro-san!" they jeer. "Going to pick another?"

"I volunteer!" one squeaks, causing the others to fall into helpless guffaws again.

"Oh no." I take a step back, not sure whether I want to run away or set all the face apples on fire. "This has officially gotten too weird. Even for me!"

"Momotaro-san!" the faces yell. "Momotaro-san!"

"Useless Momotaro-san!" one shouts in a deep voice.

"Powerless Momotaro-san!" another apple squeals.

"The Momotaro-san who will be defeated soundly by our master, Ozuno!" another apple says.

The hair on the back of my neck rises. I run over to a tree and chop at its trunk with my sword. "Ozuno?" I yell. "Is he here, too? Let him come out!"

My sword *clang*s uselessly, as if it's hitting a lamppost. Why won't it cut?

More laughter from the apples. "*Kawaiso* Momotaro-san! Poor little Momotaro-san!"

Grinding my teeth, I whack the tree again.

Jinx grabs my arm. "Sheesh, Xander, calm down!"

Then apples begin raining down on my head, pummeling me like softball-size hail. *"Kawaiso! Kawaiso!"* they hiss as they thud against me. The smell of rotting apples fills the air.

"Ewww!" I bat the fruit away, catching glimpses of grinning faces as they pass by. Trails of slime coat my skin where they touch.

I shield my head with my arms and start running through the orchard. The trail forks, and I take the left because the other way leads through more of those laughing trees. I can still hear them calling, "Momotaro-san! Come back!"

Um, no thank you. I speed up.

"Xander, wait!" Jinx yells from behind me.

CHAPTER SIXTEEN

I stop running but don't turn around. "I'm over here!" I yell to Jinx. I can't see her, but she can come to me. There's no way I'm walking back through a whole forest of apples with human faces that yell insults and throw themselves at me. I shudder. I'll take a haunted house over that any day.

Finally, my friends appear, Jinx supporting Peyton, the two moving as slowly as two elderly people with walkers.

"Xander, I know you don't eat a lot of fruit, but I didn't know you were *scared* of it," Peyton says with a glimmer of his old self.

I laugh and leap forward to help prop him up. "There's a first time for everything."

"Ah. Those were only *jinmenju*," Jinx says. Once I have a grip on Peyton, she extracts a packet of trail mix from her pack and rips it open. "If you didn't want to eat one of those, I would have given you some of this."

I make a face. "People actually *eat* those apple things? But they're alive! And not nice."

"I've heard they taste kind of like oranges." The corners of her mouth turn down. "I wouldn't know, though. Who wants to eat a moving face? But they're harmless—all talk. Literally. They have no powers."

"That one I saw looked like Daruma." I shudder again, just thinking of it.

As I lean Peyton against the tree, I think, *Onamae-wa?* If it was Daruma, why was he asking my name again? For a wise man, he doesn't seem so wise. I'm going to tell Obāchan to get rid of that ridiculous figure. He's not even worth the two dollars she probably paid for the souvenir.

Jinx looks around. "Well, now what? This trail ends right there." She points to where the path disappears into a dense thicket of low branches and bushes.

Now what indeed? I survey our surroundings, too. "You know, I bet we have a better chance of finding Fudō-Myōō if we go off the main path." I turn until I see an opening in the branches. "We could go through there."

Peyton holds out a hand for some of Jinx's trail mix. "I'd eat a talking apple if I had to. Especially if it tasted like an orange."

"Ew." Jinx makes a face.

"What? They're not actually people, are they?" Peyton pops the nuts and raisins into his mouth. "I mean, we have to be practical."

As I watch them eat, I decide I'm hungry enough to open my monkey netsuke box. I shake out a single grain of rice and put it into my mouth. It expands into an onigiri ball. I quickly bite down, eager to discover the filling. I blanch. This one's tuna.

Jinx grabs the monkey box. "Ooh, let me have one of those."

"Manners," I say, watching some precious rice fall to the ground. Jinx pops a grain into her mouth, then scoops up the ones that dropped and pockets them. I swallow. "What'd you get?"

Jinx wiggles her eyebrows. "Banana."

"Ew." That sounds worse than tuna.

"You're awfully finicky for a Momotaro hero," Jinx observes.

I shrug. "Some of us have taste buds." I hold out the box to Peyton, but he shakes his head. That's not like him. All he's had since we left the house was a little trail mix. "Are you sure?"

He nods.

Well, maybe later. I put the carved wooden figure back on my belt, the box swinging off its little rope, and I glance up at the sky. The sun is disappearing behind some mountain peak we still can't see because there are too many trees in the way. "We should get moving. We have to find shelter—or make it—before it gets dark."

"If only my wings were back." Peyton sniffles, drawing his hand under his long nose. "I could find us a place."

It definitely would be handy if we could search for Fudō from the air, but I don't say anything because I don't want to make Peyton feel worse.

"There should be a shrine someplace around here," Jinx says. "You would think."

"I would think," I agree.

We each take one of Peyton's arms and push our way through the bushes, following what might have been a trail once upon a time. The forest gets thicker as we go, and pretty soon it's as dim as a windowless bathroom with only a nightlight on. The branches grab at our legs. I'm glad we're all wearing jeans.

Oh wait. It's not dark because of the trees. "It's night." I cast around for somewhere we can camp. Who knows what's in these woods after sunset?

Jinx stops. "Great. I knew we should've gone back to the main path."

"If you knew, then why didn't you say anything until now?" I'm not in the mood to listen to Jinx's *shoulda-coulda-woulda* complaints. Despair floods me. How exactly are we supposed to find Mr. Angry Lord? He could be anywhere on this huge mountaintop. I shake my head.

Wait. *Mountaintop.*

"He must live up there!" I point upward, northeast, in the general direction of where I think the peak is. "All we have to do is keep going until we reach the top."

"*Who* lives up there?" Peyton sits heavily on the forest floor, unzipping his light backpack and taking out a bag of cheesy popcorn. He rips it open, spilling some neon-orange kernels.

"Angry Lord of Light. He's some kind of wise man, right? They always live on top of mountains, and people have to, like, pilgrimage up to see them."

"Maybe." Jinx helps herself to some of Peyton's popcorn. "But that doesn't help us right now. We need to find a safe spot."

I'm thinking Jinx is correct. I don't want to keep going deeper into an unfamiliar area in the dark. If worse comes to worst, we could sleep under those hideous apples. At least we know they're harmless. Still, I shiver a little. "I guess we should go back the way we came."

I start to turn around, but Jinx's hand clasps my shirt. "Check those out."

A ghostly wind whispers in my ears, tickling the small hairs there. Then every goose bump on my body prickles. I try to focus where Jinx is looking. "I don't see anything."

Peyton tugs on my pant leg. "Look at the beautiful lights!"

I shrug both of them off. "What?"

I finally see them. Three glowing circles hover in the air about a dozen feet away. They might be sparks—embers from a campfire. No, they're something else. They somersault and flip like juggling balls. They flit close to us, then fall back, then come close again, blowing a warm breeze on our faces with the scent of honeydew melon.

A memory flashes—me and Peyton sitting in a rope hammock

behind my house. An early summer evening, last year, right before the Fourth of July. Dad barbecuing, and the delicious smoke wafting over to us as Peyton and I play a new game on our handhelds. And me thinking, *This is the best evening of my life.*

Come with us, the lights seem to whisper to me now. *Come, we'll take you back to where you'll be happy again.*

And an overwhelming instinct wells up in me—as natural as breathing—to follow.

"No," I say out loud. Because my mother once told me about these. A long time ago, before she left. We were walking through the forest at night when I saw the same kind of little lights. "Fairies?" I'd asked her. (I was four at the time.)

She'd picked me up and held my face against her shoulder. "No, *mo chroí.* They're will-o'-the-wisps. Never follow them. If you see them, close your eyes, for they will try to call you to them."

"Will-o'-the-wisps?" I say aloud now, my voice ringing like a cowbell in the forest.

Jinx's eyes glow in the reflected light. She takes a step in their direction. "They're trying to lead us to something."

Peyton reaches out for one. "I want to catch it." He gets up and lumbers toward it.

"No, Peyton!" I grab for him, but he smacks my hand away. "Stop! You guys, it's a trap!"

The lights dance and flicker and zoom away, with Peyton in pursuit. It's the fastest I've seen him go all day.

I run after him, and Jinx follows me. Peyton skips like a little boy, giggling in a super-weird, high-pitched way, as if he just sucked in a bunch of helium. "Did they put a spell on him or what?" I huff at Jinx.

"I don't know. I just know I don't like this." Jinx frowns, and we redouble our speed.

Finally, we catch up with him, but only because the will-o'-the-wisps have stopped moving forward. We accidentally run into Peyton's back.

We're at the mouth of a cave.

CHAPTER SEVENTEEN

Ever since Peyton, Jinx, and I experienced the snow woman's cave of ice and doom, I haven't been eager to enter anything remotely similar. Unlike that cave, though, this one is large enough to drive a Mack truck into. We could get out of here in a hurry if we had to.

At least, that's what I tell myself because Peyton ducks inside and now I have no option but to go in after him. He pauses and looks back at me, the orbs swirling around his head like Saturn's rings. "They're showing us it's safe in here."

It is fully nighttime now. We do need someplace to sleep. But this cave gives me the creeps. Plus, I don't trust the will-o'-the-wisps. "I know I don't have my powers anymore, guys, but this place is *no bueno*. For real."

"Only one way to find out." Jinx steps into the interior. "Hello?" she shouts.

"Jinx!" I hold up my hands. As if that'll stop her. "Don't be a monkey's uncle."

"Gosh. I've never heard that one before." She waves a hand dismissively at me. "Don't worry. I'll go check it out. You can wait right here, safe and sound. Yup, just let ol' Jinx do all the dangerous work. Again."

I sigh. "Did I ask you to do anything? No. We all need to stay right here."

"Too late!" She scuttles into the cave. "If I'm not back in ten, come find me."

Gah. "Foiled again," I mutter. Now we have no choice but to wait. I'm not leaving Peyton alone. That Jinx.

I search through my pack for the headband that has a flashlight on it, fit it over my forehead, and turn it on. I shine it toward Peyton. He's sitting cross-legged, staring at the orbs with fascination, as entranced as a kitten by a feather on a string.

"Peyton! Earth to Peyton." I snap my fingers in front of his face. "Focus, buddy!"

Peyton wipes some drool from his chin. "Xander, you gotta watch these. They're better than TV!"

"Gah." I glare at the dancing orbs.

One pauses, just for a second, suspended in the darkness.

Just long enough for me to see the image of a skull inside the light.

Fear flashes through my spine, lightning fast. I grab my sword and stand up. "Peyton, run!" I bellow. "Get into the forest and hide! Anywhere!"

"Huh?" he says dumbly.

I slash at the orb with my blade. It dances nimbly away, flies up, the other two following. I chase. They mock me, flying close, then far away, out of the cave, disappearing into the navy-blue sky.

"Peyton, it's not safe here." I yank him to his feet. "Jinx!" I screech into the abyss. "Are you all right?"

I hear running footsteps, but there are too many, as though ten Jinxes are approaching. I shine the flashlight in.

Jinx comes barreling out past me, faster than I've ever seen her move. The whites of her eyes are huge. "Goooooooooooooo!" she screams.

And then I see what she's running from.

A spider thing as tall as an elephant scuttles after her, moving swiftly on its eight legs. Its body and head are striped like a tiger, and its face is that of a snarling feline. At least it doesn't have eight eyes.

I say a few words that I'm not allowed to use at home, then turn and grab Peyton, who's still staring at the empty space where the orbs were, and I start to run.

But, abruptly, something yanks at my hand, and Peyton's not in my grasp anymore. I look back. The spider has shot out a crimson web, which is twining around Peyton's ankles. Peyton falls to the ground and the tiger-spider drags its prey toward its open maw. Orange drool drips off its four great canines, each one as long as my sword. My headlight shines into an inner circle of jagged teeth, like a saw.

I leap backward. That image will be haunting me for, oh, the rest of my natural-born life.

"Don't stop for me!" Peyton shouts. "I'm dead meat. Go!"

Yeah, right. "Shut up and just keep breathing!" I try to figure out where to stab the creature. I run at it, but it smacks me away with one of its forelegs, sending me skittering across the cave floor.

Oof. The air's knocked out of me. I stare up at the tiger-spider, my sword clenched in my hands, hoping I can catch my breath before it eats one of us. The monster rocks back and throws its head to the sky, letting out a roar.

A roar that sounds more like a squeaky kitten.

"Really?" I get on my feet and run toward it again. "That's the best you can do?"

It roars a second time, its breath flattening my hair against my scalp in a wet pile.

Ew.

"I've got this, Xander." Jinx climbs up one of the tree-trunk-size hairy legs and gets on top of its body.

The tiger-spider hisses in the annoyed way a cat hisses at a dog. It shakes, flinging Jinx off its back. She lands with a thud.

I take advantage of the distraction. I leap forward and swing my sword upward, into the soft skin of its neck.

Purple blood squirts out. I dodge the stream, pull my sword back out, and the spider collapses like a boulder, shaking the whole mountain.

My ribs shudder with the effort of my heavy breathing. I lean over and clutch my thighs. Take that, spider.

"Xander!" Jinx screams. "Behind you!"

No time for a victory dance. I turn.

Three more spiders, these smaller than the first, scurry out of the forest.

Peyton lies facedown in a collapsed pile between them and me. His arms flop as though he's trying to get up and being really unsuccessful about it.

Great.

I race toward the spiders. No defense like a good offense, as my father would say. "If you see a threat coming at you," he said, "don't wait to strike! By then, it might be too late."

Whoosh. The sword sings through the air, chopping off a leg that's hairier than a kiwi fruit.

It hisses, and two of its other legs swivel about, knock me over, and pin me roughly to the ground, rattling my teeth and quite probably my brain against my skull. Spots swirl in front of my eyes.

"Jinx! Where are you?" I yelp, my face pressed hard against the dirt. "Take my sword!" I toss it blindly, hoping against hope that she'll get it.

"Xander!" Jinx shouts, and I manage to lift my head up enough to glimpse her, also pinned down by another tiger-spider, a few yards away.

My heart sinks like the *Titanic*. This is it. We're doomed for real this time. All the other times were practice. I screw my eyes shut and wait to feel razor-sharp teeth tear through my face. Man, what a sorry way to go. Eaten by a bug. Or possibly a mammal-bug. My parents' faces flash through my mind and I apologize to them, and to Peyton. I wanted to finish my quest. I really did. I brace myself for the final impact.

Then I hear the pounding of footsteps. Jinx? Did she escape?

"AWRRORRR!" a man's deep voice roars incomprehensibly, and two large man feet, clad in straw sandals with black straps, kick dust into my face. A light shines from someplace, suddenly illuminating the scene a lot more clearly than I would like.

I cough. Who on earth is that? It's definitely not Peyton.

More chopping noises, like knives going through watermelon. An arc of purple blood pours down, splashing me, and suddenly the pressure on my back is gone. *Whomp.* The spider hits the ground with a satisfying thud. I'm free! I roll away gratefully and look up to see who my savior is.

Two silver streaks fly through the air, attached to a man-shaped blur that attacks the other spider with a ferocity and speed I've only seen in an action movie.

That tiger-spider falls, too, with a *crunch* that sounds like a bunch of cereal being stepped on.

Then the man turns, and I see that he's not quite a man, but a teenager about sixteen or seventeen years old. He wears a short kimono jacket made of a sturdy blue-silver silken material with wide-legged gray samurai pants, the old style my grandfather would have worn. His hair is jet-black, tied in a topknot and shaved back at his forehead—the traditional samurai hairdo. In his right hand he holds a long, curving sword like mine. In his left, he holds a shorter sword, which he now sheathes with a metallic *twang*.

He bows deeply, folding himself in half, so I can see the shiny top of his head glinting in my flashlight. "Kintaro, at your service."

CHAPTER EIGHTEEN

stare at this newcomer dully. He remains bowed. Finally, I remember my manners and bow back. "Um, Xander. Also at your service. I guess."

Jinx gasps, getting up and coming toward us. She looks okay, except for her ultra-wild hair and the dirt and goop all over her. She smiles and attempts to wipe a smudge off her cheek, but she only succeeds in smearing it down to her chin. "Kintaro? *The* Kintaro?"

"*The* Kintaro?" I straighten up, scrolling through my brain data banks. Dad hasn't mentioned him. Maybe he was in one of those books I didn't read. "Who's Kintaro? Never heard of him."

"Kintaro. The Golden Boy. Surely Obāchan told you his story. He's a folk hero, like Paul Bunyan or Hercules." Jinx grins at him, puts her hands together, and bows. "Honorable Kintaro, I am glad to meet you. I am Jinx. This is Xander." She goes over to where Peyton is lying in a heap, like a pile of fall leaves, and grasps his wrist. "And Peyton. Come on, Peyton, on your feet."

"Unnnnh." Peyton resists Jinx's pull. She gives up, letting his wrist snap back toward the ground. His skin is the color of bleached socks, but he doesn't seem to be bleeding anywhere.

I swallow hard. I don't even want to think about how we can't move Peyton and how we're going to have to stay in this place overnight, where who knows how many more tiger-spiders will come out of their nooks and crannies. "Just let him rest for a second."

Kintaro bows again. "I am truly, deeply honored to make your acquaintances."

"You, too." I go over to Jinx and whisper, "Is he a folk hero like Momotaro?"

"Naw." Jinx smirks at me. "Momotaro was never considered to be that strong."

Ouch.

Kintaro swivels his head, searching the treetops and peering into the cave. "You need to leave this area. It's unsafe."

"My thoughts exactly." I turn to Peyton. "Come on, buddy, time to get going." Jinx takes hold of Peyton's wrist again. I grab the other.

Peyton is as cooperative as a sack of bricks. We can't budge him. "Too tired. Let me sleep, Mom."

"He's still asleep. Or hallucinating." I shake him. "You need to move."

"I okay." His eyelids flutter over the whites of his eyes. "I fine."

"What, the baku took his grammar, too?" Jinx squats over him, peering into his face.

"Your friend needs assistance." Kintaro's face looks like it's been chiseled out of one of the boulders dotting the mountainside. He's got that strong superhero jaw that would complement a Batman mask, and dark, deep-set eyes. They sweep over me and Jinx and Peyton like a security camera, and I see that he's assessing Peyton's condition and our ages and everything.

"I was out for my evening moonrise stroll when I heard the commotion," he continues. "Of course, I instantly ascertained that you required my skills."

He sheathes the longer sword, the katana, in the scabbard at his left hip. I recall the book we read (okay, Jinx read) by Musashi Miyamoto and how he went on and on about how two swords were better than one.

Now I see why.

"What were those creatures?" I ask him. Peyton's head flops to one side, onto some small rocks. I try to bunch his hood under his head to make him more comfortable. How are we going to get him out of here?

"*Tsuchigo*," Kintaro replies. "A tiger-spider. Those skull orbs lure people to the cave."

"Yeah. I figured that out."

"Interestingly, the orbs are the spirits of those who were eaten," Kintaro adds.

I shudder. "Now that's just plain creepy. You'd think they'd want to save people from the spiders."

"Things do not always work out in a just fashion," Kintaro says. "Particularly not in this world."

"Thank you for rescuing us, Kintaro." Jinx steps up to him with a brighter smile than I've ever seen on her.

He takes her hand very gently in his, as if he's holding an egg he doesn't want to break. "At your service." Then he lifts her hand to his lips and kisses it.

Oh barf. Really? He's, like, five years older than her. That's just gross.

"Thanks." I step forward and thrust out my hand for a shake. "You don't need to kiss me."

He shakes so firmly my knuckles crack, but I keep a grin on my face and don't let the pain show. At least I hope I don't.

"He's the Momotaro," Jinx says, nodding in my direction.

Kintaro squints at me, the corners of his mouth turning down. "Really? But you have no powers."

"Tell me something I don't know. It's a long story." I inhale.

Kintaro chuckles. "Well, little warrior, I don't know what you don't know, but I'll think of something to tell you. Come, I'll take you to my house so you can rest, and you can tell me your tale. But first, let me check your friend." Kintaro kneels and grabs Peyton's arm. He bends it, seemingly checking for broken bones. He runs his palm over the top of Peyton's tufted hair and looks back at me, his black eyes sharp. "Was this boy once a bird?"

"Once." Peyton opens one eye in a slit.

Kintaro shakes his head. "His dreams are gone. That is why he is so lethargic."

"Thanks, Sherlock." I plant my feet and cross my arms. While we sure needed the help with the spiders, the last thing we need is another know-it-all on this quest.

Kintaro flashes a smile. "I am Kintaro, not Sherlock."

I try to exchange a knowing glance with Jinx, but she won't look at me. Annoyance is rising off her like steam. What'd I do?

"We're trying to get to the Angry Lord of Light," I say to Kintaro, who has turned Peyton over and is examining the nubby stubs of flesh where his wings tried to grow. "He's supposed to be able to help us. Do you know how to reach him?"

"I do." Kintaro straightens Peyton's clothing, pulling his shirt over his back. He squats on his heels. "If you don't correct this malady, Momotaro-san, your bird friend will surely die."

"*Die?*" Jinx steps forward, her hands clasped at her chest. "Did you say *die?*"

I notice my arms are shaking. I hold them tighter to stop it. "Are you deaf?" I ask Jinx, mostly to make sure my mouth still works. Die? I thought Peyton would just act kind of lazy and sick for a while. Like my parents. Eating junk food and whatnot. I thought only my grandmother was in real danger.

Jinx punches my shoulder, not softly. Which maybe I deserve. "How long do we have, Kintaro?" she asks.

"I do not know for sure. You should not have brought him here. He is too weak." Kintaro takes hold of Peyton's arms and yanks him all the way to his feet, in one smooth move. "In this land, time passes more quickly. Every day here is like a week where you live. This boy is still on his world's time, so his symptoms are worsening."

Ohhhh. That explains why Peyton and Jinx thought I took so long to come after them when they vanished through the torii gate. What seemed like seconds to me was minutes for them.

My spine stiffens with fear. And here we are wandering around, lost in the woods. We've been in this world a half day at least. That's half a week gone in our world. "Let's take Peyton home and then come back."

"No," Jinx says sharply. "We've already come this far. We may not have time."

"The monkey girl is right." Kintaro lifts Peyton and deftly throws him over his shoulders in a firefighter's carry. "Complete your mission as soon as you can. It is your best and only hope."

Best and only hope. That sounds kind of melodramatic, yet it's probably true. My stomach gurgles in sickened response. I pick up Peyton's backpack. Luckily, it's not too heavy, since we drank those iced teas. "How far, Kintaro?"

"Not too far, but not too close," comes the answer.

Very helpful.

Kintaro left a lantern at the edge of the battle scene, which he now picks up as he leads us away from the cave and up another hill, out of the place I'm privately calling the Valley of Despair. Though he's carrying the 160 pounds or so of Peyton, he strolls like he has no extra weight at all. Jinx walks next to him, asking him about the trees and the bushes and probably each grain of sand on the ground. I'm not really listening.

Then Kintaro laughs, a melodious noise like a saxophone. Can't he at least have an annoying braying laugh like a donkey? "Ah, Jinx, I hope you don't bring as much bad luck as your name suggests!"

I scowl. How dare he make fun of her? Only Peyton and I are allowed to do that. "She doesn't."

He looks at me, his finely shaped eyebrows raised. "Oh, she is yours?"

"Mine?" I don't understand what he means.

"His?" Jinx casts a horrified glance back at me. "No way. Never."

Oh. He means like a girlfriend.

Heat rushes over my face, and I know I'm as red as a Valentine's heart. "First of all, Golden Boy, she's practically my sister. And secondly, even if she *was* my girlfriend, she wouldn't be *mine*, like property or something. What year do you think this is?"

"Calm down. It's only an expression." Jinx waves away my

concerns, even though I'm defending her. "Besides, I'm a lot older than you, Xander."

"Yeah, a whole year older." I scowl at Kintaro. "Don't even think about robbing this cradle."

"Shut. Up." Jinx shoves at me while continuing smiling demurely at Kintaro, fluttering her eyelashes in a way I only saw her do once, when she had a stomach flu and was about to barf.

"Jinx!" I tap her on the shoulder. "Do you need a bucket? You look a little green."

"I'm fine." She smooths down her hair, an uncharacteristic blush spreading from her collar into her face.

Kintaro studies her. "You do look a little worse for wear. I would carry you, but I'm otherwise occupied." He gestures at me. "Xander, could you?"

"Xander carry *me*? I could carry *him*." Jinx shakes her head. "Let's just get up to the house and forget this conversation ever happened." She grabs the lantern out of Kintaro's huge hand and moves forward.

Now it's Kintaro and I who exchange a glance. He grins and raises his eyebrows in a look I don't think I like. I hope this night is over soon.

CHAPTER NINETEEN

Kintaro's house is not located on the most accessible part of this mountain, unfortunately. First we climb a steep trail that zigzags among the trees. We hike for forty minutes in silence, except for the sounds of our breathing. The night air is cool, pressing down like an ice pack on my body. Occasionally the wind whips up and blasts through the leaves with a ghostly *oooooh* that doesn't help the creep factor go away.

Peyton doesn't make a single sound. A few times I run to catch up with Kintaro and touch my friend just to make sure he's still warm and breathing. How could I be so dumb, bringing him on this quest? I should have known that he, like Obāchan, would get the life sapped out of him. It had just taken longer with him because he's younger.

Are my parents and Inu as sick as Peyton is now? I swallow.

Maybe Jinx should have stayed home to take care of everyone. She would've argued about it, but that would've been the best thing.

I wish, just once, I knew the right thing to do *before* it happened, instead of afterward.

Most of the time, I follow Jinx's back. In her white shirt, she's the easiest thing to pick out in this forest. Kintaro's sure strides never hesitate, even when he has to hop over a huge log that Jinx and I bang our shins on. His long toes splay out with each step, his sandals leaving craters in the earth.

At last, Kintaro makes a forty-five-degree turn, and the landscape changes. Moonlight illuminates a gravel path, which crunches under my feet. The path is lined with tall bushes, so if there is a house nearby, I can't see it yet.

A low deep growl to my left makes me jump. I put my hand on my sword.

"It's all right, Xander." Kintaro speaks calmly. "Kuma, they are with me."

A black muzzle with sharp white teeth pokes out of the bushes with a snapping of twigs. "If you say so, Kintaro-san." Then the rest of the form comes crashing out.

I take a step back.

That muzzle is attached to a very large, very angry-looking bear. Without pausing, it lumbers toward me, its huge, wet nostrils quivering, its jet-black eyes narrowed.

I stop and stand as still as possible. That's what you're supposed to do in case of bear attack, right? Or is it lie on the ground in the fetal position? "Umm, it doesn't look like it's leaving us alone."

The bear shoves its snout into my belly and sniffs so hard my shirt flattens against its nostrils. It grunts, sounding like an old car trying to start, as it snuffles around my ribs. It tickles, and I giggle automatically.

"Kintaro," the bear says, "he smells too green to be a Momotaro."

This again. When will people—and bears—stop saying that? "Well, I am new to all this." I take a step back, squaring my shoulders. "But if I'm not Momotaro, explain this prematurely gray hair." I point to my head.

The bear stands up on its hind legs. I almost snap my neck looking up at him. It's approximately sixteen feet tall. "Maybe you dyed it," the bear says. "I understand it's all the rage now."

"It is," Jinx pipes up. "I would do it, except Xander already has gray hair, so I'd look like I was copying him."

"Hardy har har. I do not dye my hair." I cross my arms.

Kintaro continues up the path. "Kuma only means to say you smell green. Like grass." He rounds a sharp corner. "It is not a usual scent for a Momotaro."

"What do they usually smell like?" I ask.

Kuma snorts. "They smell sweet, like peaches. Spicy, like sandalwood. Never like grass."

"Xander sort of smells like his mother." Jinx falls into step beside Kintaro, matching his gait perfectly, despite her shorter legs.

I snort. "Jinx, why are you going around smelling my mother? That's creepy."

She shrugs. "I can't help it, Xander. If there's a Christmas tree in the house, I can smell it. If someone's baking cookies, I can smell it. If you and your mom are near me, I just happen to smell you."

"Still, if I smelled you, I'd never tell you about it." I hope we get to the house soon. Every single one of my muscles is twitching. My legs might fall off. "Yes, I'm not like the other Momotaro. But maybe I'm better."

"I know how you can prove yourself." The bear's front legs thud onto the ground. "We should wrestle."

"Um . . ." There are safer things I could do, like jump out of an airplane without a parachute. "I'll take a rain check." I start walking faster. "Hey, Jinx, wait up."

"Kuma, stop baiting Xander," Kintaro says without turning around. "That's how we met, Kuma and I. When I was very young and Kuma was but a cub, he and I wrestled."

Now the bear's face is right at my shoulder. "Kintaro beat me when he was smaller than you." His hot breath smells like fish that's been left in the sun. "I want to know if you can, too."

"Uh, yeah." I step away. "That's definitely not happening in this century. Or any."

Kuma sputters in disappointment. "You're no fun."

"I never said I was," I say rather sourly. I just hiked up a mountain that's a lot taller than I remember it being, fought off some tiger-spiders, and now they want me to wrestle a bear? If that last one is optional, then I choose to say no. "Listen, I just want to get some sleep."

"Understandable." Kintaro shifts Peyton's bulk around his shoulders. "Xander's still a little boy, Kuma. A regular little boy. Not one like me."

I roll my eyes. Whatever. If they get me to the house, I'll listen to any trash talk they hurl at me.

After what seems like another quarter mile, we finally step out from between the bushes into a wide-open yard. Dozens of hanging lanterns swing in the wind, lighting the way. The house is two stories tall, with a curved sloping roofline and statues of bears on its corners.

Oh, and it's completely covered in gold, as if a leprechaun melted down his pot of coins and poured it over the rooftop and walls. Even in the dim light from the lanterns, it shines as bright as a flashlight in a dark theater.

"Fancy," I say. I wonder what Kintaro would think of my house, and if living in this golden shack has totally ruined all other residences for him.

We head up a winding flagstone path toward the house. There is a large pond in front of the home, serving as both moat and decoration. Big flat rocks in the water lead to the porch. Kintaro steps across them. "Watch yourself. They can be slippery."

A gold-and-red koi fish the size of a small rabbit leaps out of the water, jumping through the air between Kintaro and me. I stop short so I don't run into it, and I lose my balance. I windmill my arms. "Whoa!"

The bear holds out his great arms to steady me, and his claws poke my back slightly. "The fish won't hurt you, little Momotaro," he booms.

"Huh. I know." I regain my footing, glad for the dim light so nobody can see me blushing. "If I were the fish, I'd be worried about you eating me."

Kuma blows more hot air out through his nose. "I don't touch the fish."

Kintaro clomps across the wooden porch, then slides off his sandals, still carrying Peyton as if my friend is a fashion accessory instead of an almost-grown human. "Welcome, treasured guests." He slides open the door. We follow his lead and kick off our shoes. The bear doesn't have shoes to remove, but he carefully wipes his big, clawed feet on the doormat.

Inside, more lanterns dot the space, glowing with energetic yellow light, but I doubt it is electricity. Tatami mats cover the floors. On one side is a low table spread out with lacquer boxes of food, a platter of fish, tangerines, and a bowl of hot rice.

Kintaro puts Peyton down on the tatami. He disappears into another room.

I sit down next to my friend. He's a strange pale color now, no longer whitish, but somewhere between blue and green. I touch his face. It feels like a Popsicle. "Peyton?"

His eyelids flutter, and blue-green irises focus on me like a slow-working camera. "Dude." He pats my cheek clumsily. "Thanks for getting me out of the forest." A smile wafts across his face. "I dreamed about a giant spider. Well, more like a nightmare, but it's a start."

My throat fills with a lump. No use telling him the truth. I have to find this Angry Lord person first thing in the morning. "Go back to sleep, Peyton. We're safe now. We have a climb tomorrow."

He doesn't have to be told twice.

I lean back with a groan. If we were on a street, we'd be standing on the corner of Desperation and Hopelessness. "How are we ever going to get him to walk on two feet, let alone up the rest of this mountain?" I ask Jinx.

Jinx eyes Peyton, her mouth working as if she's processing a whole bunch of emotions—sad, sulky, scared. Finally, she settles on determined. She crosses her arms. "We'll find a way, Xander. That's all."

At least one of us is optimistic. Somehow, I half believe her. Jinx isn't the kind of person to say that unless she was sure she could do it.

Kintaro appears with a round lacquered container. "You could leave Peyton here with me, if you like."

Jinx raises her head, a smile breaking her face. "Now that's an idea!"

"Wait." I hold up my hand. "What's the catch?"

"Why do you think there's a catch?" Jinx elbows me.

"There is no *catch*, as you say." Kintaro bends over Peyton, then meets my gaze. "But you must let me know before dawn."

I look at my friend. I don't want to leave him here, with this guy I just met a minute ago, but maybe there were worse things in the world. "I'll think about it. I guess."

What happened to never leaving your friend behind? Peyton and Dad wouldn't do it. Heck, I doubt Jinx would, either. Except she probably wants an excuse to return and visit Kintaro again.

Kintaro strides over to the table, puts down the container, and lifts the lid off. It holds small, steaming white towels. He picks one up with a pair of tongs and offers it to me. "To cleanse your filthy hands."

Nice of him to point out that my hands are filthy. I take one and almost drop it—it's scaldingly hot—but I manage to wipe my hands quickly.

Jinx is already kneeling at the table, dishing portions of rice into bowls. Even one for Peyton. Then she opens the lacquer boxes and, using a long pair of *hashi*—chopsticks—deftly serves their contents on square plates. Somehow, despite all the time she spent in the wilderness, she looks pretty darn clean and presentable. I consider waking Peyton but decide to save his food for later instead.

"Tell me about your life in the other world, Jinx," Kintaro says.

Jinx begins describing my house and Inu and my family. I

notice she says nothing about her own relatives, but why would she? Kintaro tosses his used towel into a basket across the room, so I do the same—except, of course, I miss. With a sigh, I get up to retrieve it.

A movement out the window catches my eye. I peer outside, trying to discern what it is.

Something dark slithers away over the pond. The way it moves reminds me of someone.

"Gozu?" I whisper.

Jinx looks up, the blood draining from her face. "Did you say *Gozu?*"

I nod, hoping against hope that I'm one hundred percent wrong. Gozu was the oni bounty hunter we killed—*I* killed. The demon who also happened to be Jinx's father.

Not that he ever acted like a father to her. He betrayed her to get to me.

But Gozu is dead. Gone forever.

Isn't he?

I think back to the moment when I defeated him. He'd just disappeared. *Poof.* Who knows what happened to him, really? A chill shoots up my arms. Maybe—maybe he wasn't dead after all. . . .

"It can't be." Jinx has gone rigid, her eyes wide. "Xander, you're seeing things."

"I hope so." I look out into the still, quiet garden. Not even a breeze stirs the plants. The lanterns cast golden shadows into the pond, reflecting off the golden house. The only creature I can see now is a large frog, iridescent green in the moonlight, that hops out of the water and onto a rock, where its gullet balloons and empties with a loud croak.

I must have imagined the oni.

I thought I couldn't imagine things anymore.

Kintaro comes to my side so quietly that I jump. "What do you see?" he asks.

"Just plants and a frog." I shrug. "I guess it was nothing."

"We must make sure." He claps, heads back to the table. "Kuma, please go and have a look."

Kuma, without further talk about wanting to wrestle, lumbers outside. His burly form roams swiftly over the garden as he sniffs the air. The bear is blacker than the darkest shadow, and he's certainly a lot bigger than anything that could be out there. I relax when I see Kuma bare his sharp, deadly teeth. We're safe here. Certainly safer than we'd be anywhere else on this mountain tonight.

"No sense in worrying," Kintaro's saying to Jinx as I watch the bear. He murmurs something to her I can't hear.

Outside, Kuma snuffles into the bushes. The sound of Jinx's laugh makes me turn toward the table. "That's hilarious," she says to Kintaro, as though her laugh hadn't already illustrated that fact. She eats a piece of pinkish fish.

Kintaro sits opposite her, smiling. "The salmon is my favorite. They come from the river in these very mountains. Every spring, when they spawn, Kuma and I stand at the waterfall and catch them as they try to go over."

Jinx takes a bite so delicate I'm not sure she's taken one at all. "Mmmmm. So buttery."

"Of course we only grab the ones that have the best flavor. They have a slight blue tinge right under the gills." Kintaro pantomimes grabbing a fish out of the air.

I take a piece of fish and put it in my mouth. Tastes like regular salmon to me. "I don't think that's possible. How can you have enough time to look at its gills as the fish is flying through the air?"

"Because, Xander, Kintaro isn't like anybody else." Jinx eats some rice, blinking at me rapidly in her patented *Shut-up-Xander* expression.

I shake my head in response. Sure, Kintaro saved our lives and is giving us some okay food. But does he have to sit there bragging about how great he is? We already know how great he is. He lives in a gold-plated house, for the love of Pete. I stretch my aching legs out to the side, ignoring Jinx's pointed look. I'm supposed to be sitting cross-legged or kneeling on the tatami, as is proper, but I don't care. "So, Kintaro, tell me about the old Angry Lord o' Light. He doesn't happen to have a phone number, does he?"

He pours a small amount of sake into a ceramic cup. "Phone number? Hmm. I don't think he has any numbers at all." Without asking her first, he pours some for Jinx, and then he moves toward my cup, but I clap my hand over it. No repeat of last time, when Tanuki, that badger-raccoon talking creature, got me drunk and captured. Actually, that was Jinx's fault. I take a sip of water instead—better safe than sorry.

Jinx laughs, throwing her head back like she just paid two hundred dollars to see Kintaro perform. "Oh, Xander. A phone? How would Kintaro know about that?" I watch disapprovingly as she takes a sip of the sake. She makes a face like she just drank battery acid before she puts down the cup. "Mmm, that's yummy," she says unconvincingly.

Kintaro watches Jinx with amusement, smiling smugly at his ability to make her giggle. I fight the urge to hurl my rice bowl at his face.

Why am I so mad about this guy? What do I care if he likes Jinx?

He throws back the contents of his cup with one swig. "For Fudō-Myōō to appear, you need two things. First, the purest, deepest anger of the heart."

"Got plenty of that." I select a bit of pickled seaweed and screw up my mouth before trying it. It tastes like salt and oil. "Ugh. If I have any more of this seaweed, I'll get the deepest anger of the heart, no problem. Or at least the deepest anger of my gut." I put down my hashi, feeling queasy. "Would you happen to have some plain food? Like crackers?"

Jinx glares at me. I scratch my head. Yeah, maybe that was a little rude, but Kintaro can take it. He's the Golden Boy.

"Our food is unsuitable for weaklings; it is true. Eat or do not eat; it is of no difference to me." Kintaro pours himself another help-ing of sake.

See? I knew he could take it. I sip some water, hoping to make my stomach feel better.

Jinx leans over and puts her hand on our host's tree trunk of an arm. "Kintaro, what was the other thing?"

"The other . . ." His brows knit. "Well, nobody knows."

I almost spit out my water. "What do you mean, *nobody knows*?"

"Nobody's ever seen Fudō-Myōō. At least, not since anyone was here to remember." Kintaro downs half his rice bowl.

Jinx and I look at each other.

"I thought you said you knew . . ." I say slowly.

"No. I said there were two things. I didn't know what the second one was."

To my immense satisfaction, Jinx rolls her eyes so hard I'm sur-prised her eyeballs stay in her skull. "All righty, then."

I take another bite of the ordinary fish. Now what?

Jinx shakes her head slightly, her golden eyes shifting to a darker, more brooding brown. "We'll figure it out, Xander."

Glad somebody's able to stay optimistic.

Kuma bursts in, startling me. He huffs and puffs with huge bear breaths. "Something *has* been here, Kintaro. Come tell me what you think."

CHAPTER TWENTY

We follow Kintaro and Kuma into the garden. Kuma stands on his hind legs, pointing up into a willow tree. "Here."

I peer upward. All I see are the vine-like branches of the tree, which we are stirring. "I don't see anything."

"Spirits live in willow trees." Kintaro stares up into the silvery-green branches as if he's searching.

"It's a spirit, all right." Kuma sniffs the air. "A vengeful one."

My stomach clenches. "Gozu? But how?"

Jinx sighs. "Sometimes, when oni are killed, they don't really die. They become something worse. A *reiki*. The ghost of a dead oni."

Wait. "Oni can become *ghosts*?" I almost yell. "Why didn't anyone tell me?" An oni is bad enough, but a vengeful, angry oni ghost . . . I can't even imagine.

"That could very well be it." Kintaro has the thoughtful, calm tone of a scholar. As if he's reading about an idea instead of facing something that could actually hurt us.

Even Jinx doesn't seem alarmed. I, on the other hand, don't feel calm at all. I want to run screaming back down the mountainside. "So what do we do about it? I can't just wait for him to find me. How do we get the spirit out of here?"

Kintaro laughs.

A flush heats my face, and I know I must look as red as a stoplight. "What, exactly, is so funny?"

"If the spirit has hidden itself, we cannot access it. Why waste emotion on something you cannot change?" Kintaro asks. "Come inside. My house is a safe space, I promise. Then, at daybreak, you can decide how to proceed."

"How to proceed?" I throw my hands up. "How I'm going to proceed is by finding the Angry Lord of Light. Oni or no oni."

Kintaro looks at me with an expression I've seen on my father's face. As if he's assessing me and approving what he sees. He gives me the slightest smile and nod, and I feel like Inu must when we pet him on the head. I smile back, in spite of myself. No wonder they call him Golden Boy.

We go back inside, and Jinx points to a line of dried beans sprinkled along the doorway. Fuku mame, like at our house. "See?" she says. "That's why it's safe here."

"Safe-ish," I correct her.

"Not a real word."

"I make up words all the time. English is an evolving language."

"Me talk pretty," we hear from nearby. Peyton is sitting up and spooning rice into his mouth while holding a bowl against his lips. He's now the color of a glacier, somewhere between white and blue, but I'm just glad to see him awake.

I run over to him. "Peyton!"

"Unnnh," he grunts. He squints at me without focusing. "Ice cream?" Peyton reminds me of my father when he got his appendix out. When Dad woke up from the anesthesia, he had no idea who we were, and he kept babbling about squirrels attacking the doctor.

I sink down next to my friend. "No. Sorry, dude. We'll get you some as soon as we get home. Your favorite: mango."

Peyton lets the rice bowl fall out of his hands. I catch it before it hits the floor. "Go home now," he slurs. Then he slumps over, and I gently lay him down. Peyton will just have to sleep by the table all night if that's what needs to happen.

"At least he ate something." Jinx kneels on the other side of the table.

I eye his nearly full rice bowl. "Not enough." Maybe we should let Peyton stay here.

But Peyton is my responsibility, not Kintaro's. What if somebody else needed saving and Kintaro ran off and left Peyton alone? And what about that vengeful spirit? This place might not be any safer than the rest of the mountain.

My brain feels like a dried-out old sponge. I can't think about this any longer. I'll decide by morning. At least we have a place to rest for the night. I tuck a jacket under Peyton's head.

"Wait a moment, Xander, and I will move Peyton into a bed." Kintaro moves the small table into a corner. He slides open a *shoji*-screen closet and removes a stack of futons—basically sleeping pads—dragging them out into the center of the room. I leap up to help him.

Jinx gets a pile of sheets from a shelf. "So, Kintaro, how did you come to be up here in the mountains all by yourself?"

"He's not alone," Kuma growls from his place near the hearth. "He has me."

"So I do." Kintaro smiles. He and I unfold the first futon, and Jinx tucks a sheet over it. "It is the most interesting story you'll ever hear in your lives."

Ugh. I'm sure it won't be. Has there ever been anyone as full of himself as Kintaro?

"Really?" Jinx and I both say at the same time. In completely different tones, of course.

"Is it a long one?" I help Jinx with the sheet. "Maybe it'll help put me to sleep."

She shoots me a murderous look. "I'd love to hear it." She flutters her lashes at Kintaro again.

"All right." Kintaro starts talking. "A long time ago—"

"In a galaxy far, far away?" I lie down on the futon. "Let me get comfortable."

Kintaro nods, and then begins again.

"A long time ago, there was a princess named Yaegiri. She lived in Miyako, or what is now Kyoto, in Japan. This was once the capital, a place of the greatest beauty and culture. Yaegiri was not only a princess but the most beautiful and brave princess who ever lived.

"A samurai named Kintoki fell in love with her, and soon they married. But this made Kintoki's enemies jealous. They convinced the emperor that Kintoki was trying to overthrow him, and Kintoki was killed. His enemies took over the court, and Yaegiri had to flee into the mountains. She was with child, unable to move fast, and very scared indeed.

"A group of woodcutters, feeling sorry for her, let her live in a hut, hidden and far away from her enemies. Soon after, she gave birth to a little boy: me.

"With my first breath, I outcrowed the rooster. My first bath was in the freezing mountain waterfall, so cold it would have killed most newborns. Even the woodcutters told my mother not to bathe me there. But her doing so just made me stronger.

"I talked when I was only three months old. I walked at six months. The woodcutters were amazed, but my mother wasn't. She took me with her when she worked in the forest, leaving me in a basket as she cut down trees. I listened to the language of the animals and plants. Children absorb more than you know.

"One day, when I was but a year old, my mother and I came across a bear cub and his mother. Now, mother bears tend to be extremely protective when you come between them and their cubs, which we had done. My mother screamed at me to run away, but I was not afraid. Neither was the cub. The mother bear was not angry as much as cautious, much like my mother.

"The cub and I circled and sniffed each other as our mothers watched carefully. Little did the mothers know that I could understand the language of bears. 'Let's have a wrestling match,' the bear cub suggested.

"'All right,' I agreed.

"I did not know it, but I was speaking in growls.

"I leaped into the air, and so did the cub. We wrestled and my mother shouted, afraid I was getting mauled, but soon I pinned the cub to the ground, panting."

"And that cub was me," Kuma interjects.

Kintaro smiles. "Yes. The cub was Kuma. From that day on, he and I were inseparable.

"As I grew, I learned all the animal languages. The woodcutters gave me an ax, and I chopped down trees, always careful to avoid the ones with bird nests.

"One day, when I had just turned thirteen, a famous samurai

came through the woods and saw me wrestling with Kuma. He asked my mother if he could train me. She did not want me to grow up to be a woodcutter and knew that my father would have wanted me to be a warrior. So I went with him. He became the shogun, the military leader of Japan, who was just as powerful as the emperor. I served him as a samurai for a long time."

Here Kintaro looks at me. "I knew your forefather, Musashi Miyamoto."

"Really?" I think maybe he means he knew *of* my forefather. "Is that why you use the two swords?"

"Indeed." Kintaro's eyes crinkle. "You know your history, Xander-san. I am impressed."

"I'm the one who told him that," Jinx mutters.

Kintaro continues. "And then I became tired of court life. I missed my mother and the solitude of the forest. So I returned."

"And you built yourself a golden house for fun?" I ask.

"No. The people I saved from a monster built me a golden house." Kintaro smiles briefly.

"That *is* the most interesting story I've ever heard!" Jinx flops down on a futon.

Kintaro takes four fluffy comforters out of the closet. "I thought it might be." He makes a bed for Peyton, then picks him up as though my friend is a toddler and tucks him in.

Watching him do all that for Peyton makes me even more aware of how incapable I am. I should feel really grateful, but instead I feel annoyed and guilty.

I grunt. "It's not as interesting as if you were born a weakling and became strong." I make up my bed and climb in with all my clothes on. Not that I brought pajamas or anything. I look up at the ceiling and sigh.

"Like you?" Kintaro asks.

"Yeah, like me."

Kintaro produces a small pillow that's filled with something that crunches softly. He tucks it under my head. "This is buckwheat," he says. "It's good for your neck."

I move my head back and forth, feeling the small kernels. "If you say so."

"Xander." Kintaro's eyes crinkle at the corners as he smiles down at me. "There can be more than one hero."

I adjust the pillow again. The buckwheat's actually not as bad as it sounds, except for the crinkly noises it makes when I move. "I know."

Kintaro puts the comforter up around my neck as though I'm his child. He sits down on the edge of the futon. And, like he really is my dad, I can feel a lecture coming on. "Me being here doesn't make you less brave or worthy. You do not have to compete with me. I am your ally."

I draw in a long breath. Now, that sounds like the kind of thing people say when they actually *are* competing with you. "You think you're better than me, though, don't you?"

He pats my shoulder. "I am not. But I hope that whatever I say spurs you on to greatness rather than crushes your spirit."

I shut my eyes. "I guess you just know all sorts of things I don't," I say, not even attempting to keep the bitterness out of my voice.

"Of course I do," Kintaro says.

I snort.

"I know more," Kintaro goes on, "because I've lived for hundreds of years longer than you, Xander."

Hundreds of years? I open my eyes and regard this Golden Boy superhero person. He's hundreds of years old, but I'm the one with the gray hair. "I'm not even going to question that," I say. Not in this world and this golden house, with its talking bear.

"Of course you never thought about it from Kintaro's point of view," Jinx interjects, her voice scratchy with fatigue. "You're too stubborn."

"Yeah, right. Look who's talking."

"Enough." Kintaro stands and nods to me and then to Jinx. "Sleep well, you three. You will need all your strength tomorrow."

"Thank you, Kintaro," Jinx says. She sounds like she's halfway to sleep.

"Yeah, thanks," I say, too, but I might say it only in my head.

Kintaro turns off the lanterns.

CHAPTER TWENTY-ONE

S ome stupid rooster crows before it's even officially dawn. I yawn and turn over on my futon, reaching for the blanket.

Which isn't there.

Dirt moves beneath my fingernails. No blanket, no tatami.

I wake up all the way, blinking, trying to get oriented. This has got to be a dream, right?

A bright yellow bird perches on top of Peyton's sleeping head, trilling a high-pitched song. It looks down its orange beak at me before it flies away. Jinx snores beyond him, undisturbed.

The house is gone.

I look around, rubbing my eyes. A stack of rocks lies where the chimney was. A curvy indentation where the pond was now sits dry;

the floor is a cracked red clay, encircling the small mound where we are.

Alone in the landscape, the willow's dusty green branches still flutter softly in the breeze.

I get up and walk around, thinking that somehow we were moved in the middle of the night. My foot kicks some dried beans near where the doorway was. I reach down and put a few into my pocket.

"Jinx?" I whisper. I lean over, shake her.

"Ugh. Why's it so bright?" She rolls over, covering her face with her arm. "Just a few more minutes, 'kay?"

A pile of gray grass stirs. I reach for my sword.

"Stay your hand, Momotaro," I hear, in a vaguely familiar growl. The gray mound trembles as it stands on four legs. It shakes off what seems like a thousand years' worth of twigs and dirt, showering me with debris.

It is a thin, old bear. His teeth are yellow and dull, his claws broken and brown.

"Kuma?" I almost fall forward, scrambling to get to him. "What happened? Where's Kintaro?"

The ancient bear seems to smile sadly. Most of its teeth are missing. "Oh, long gone, I'm afraid."

I look around wildly. "But how? . . . The house was here . . . I saw it!"

"Must you really ask *how* anymore?" the bear says. He sits back on his haunches. "Kintaro does not appear often. Only to those who need assistance, and not to everyone." Kuma chuckles. "As those skulls inside the cave will tell you."

"So why did he help us?" I ask.

Kuma blinks. "He *saw* you. That is all I know."

"Well, how are we supposed to leave Peyton with him?" Jinx is alert and listening now.

Kuma lifts his upper lip. "Peyton would have gone into the other world with Kintaro until you returned. *If* you returned."

"That doesn't sound much better than this situation." I glance over at Peyton.

Kuma moves his once-massive shoulders in a shrug. "Impossible to know." He lumbers over to the fireplace rubble and digs around with his broken claws. "Kintaro wanted you to have this."

From the ashes he unearths a package wrapped in brittle paper, tied up with ancient-looking string. The bear dangles it toward me on one claw.

I take it. Then, unsure of what I need to do, I bow. *"Arigato."*

"What's in it?" Jinx peers over my shoulder.

The string crumbles into dust when I touch it. Inside the package there's a set of kimono clothes, exactly like what Kintaro was wearing. The blue-silver jacket, the wide-legged gray pants, and a silver sash, or obi.

"These are the clothes of a true samurai," Kuma says.

I hold up the jacket. "Thank you." It should be too big—Kintaro is (was) so much taller than me. But it looks like it's my size.

"And, Jinx"—Kuma turns—"this, he left for you." He hands her a smaller brown-paper package. "Be careful," he advises as she tears off the wrapping.

Jinx yelps with excitement the way I do when I get a new video game. "A *tantō*!" Her eyes light up like a church full of candles as she shows us a thick, slightly curved dagger. It looks like a miniature version of my sword, with a carved ivory handle. "Oh boy!" She holds it out on her palms, the blade facing toward her. "Arigato gozaimasu." *Thank you very, very much*. Then she leaps up and hugs the bear around his great neck. He closes his eyes briefly.

She lets go of him. "So Kintaro is really gone? Really truly gone?" Disappointment colors her voice like food coloring dropped into milk.

Now I feel kind of bad for giving Kintaro a hard time. When he wasn't even really there. Or there only temporarily.

Kuma nods his great head once, then shakes his fur as though he's tossing off water. He blinks at us and goes off into the rubble once again. "One more item for you, Xander." Kuma noses a ball across the ground toward me, about the size of a basketball. Um, okay. I'm not going to be playing much basketball on my quest, but maybe Kintaro thought I'd be bored.

I pick it up. It's not a ball at all, but a rounded helmet made of some kind of silver material. It comes up to a point on the top and its curves remind me of something natural. Like a piece of fruit. Like . . .

"This is shaped like a peach!" I exclaim.

"And look at this." Jinx points to the emblem on the front. It is definitely a peach, the shape sticking out in relief, with crosshatched lines giving it depth.

"Is this silver?" I tap the helmet experimentally. It rings out with a hollow sound.

"Nah. Silver's too soft and heavy—not good for armor." Jinx taps it, too.

Kuma noses the helmet. "This was a gift to your forefather from the Moon King. It is made of a mineral from the moon." He tosses it from paw to paw. "It is as light as a feather, but as hard as iron." He holds it out to me.

Moon King? Cool. That particular story wasn't in my unofficial Momotaro handbook (the comic book about him), but nothing surprises me. I take the helmet in both hands and place it on my head. I totally expect it to be heavy, but it's really not any worse than wearing a baseball cap. A little visor sticks out above my eyebrows to shield my eyes from the sun—and maybe swords, too. And the inside is lined with something silky. I bow. "Arigato gozaimasu."

Kuma nods.

I think about Kintaro's last words to me. *There can be more than one hero.* Just because Kintaro is (was) a great warrior doesn't mean that I, too, can't be one.

And if Peyton is a good artist, that doesn't mean I can't also be a good artist. Or if one person is good-looking, that doesn't mean everyone else in the world is ugly.

I feel lighter, like something heavy has been lifted off my chest. Or at least off my mind.

Jinx puts her hand on Kuma's ruff. "You must be terribly lonely. Why don't you come with us? You could help with Peyton." She gestures to him, still sleeping, slack-jawed and oblivious to our chatter.

I'm not too sure about that suggestion. Kuma's so old he can barely get around this small site. I don't think he could walk up the mountain, much less carry Peyton. But what *are* we going to do now that Kintaro is definitely out of the picture? I should have taken the Golden Boy up on his offer. How was I supposed to know that he was going to disappear at dawn? Why didn't he wake me? Instead, he just left it up to me, like I'm a responsible person or something.

Kuma takes a step away from Jinx. "My place is here." He nods toward an obelisk made of solid gray stone, about the same height as me, covered with Japanese characters. A grave marker. "I am waiting for the moment when my master and I will reunite."

Jinx and I bow our heads toward the stone. Then Jinx puts her hand on it. "Good-bye, Kintaro."

I steal a look at her face, afraid she's crying, but she just gives me a placid nod.

Kuma points at a path going up the mountain. "Fudō's shrine is on one of the peaks. I don't know which. That trail is the closest and will take you to the southernmost peak. Good luck."

The clothes Kintaro gave me seem too fancy to wear on a quest, but then again, they brought him luck, so why not? I go behind a tree to change, putting the jacket on over my T-shirt and trading my jeans for the new pants. Just like I thought, they fit perfectly. They're a stiff sort of silk, substantial but light.

When I emerge, Jinx raises her eyebrows. "Snazzy!" She waves her fingers at my head. "Really brings out the silver."

"That's what I'm going for," I reply. Jinx and I each put one of Peyton's arms around our shoulders. "Bye, Kuma," I call. "Thanks for everything!"

The bear smiles—or smiles as much as a bear can. *"Iie,"* he replies. *It was nothing.*

Slowly, we walk up the trail, heading southeast to the peak, Peyton between us, his weight divided between Jinx and me. Somehow he's managing to hold on enough for us to support him. His head lolls on his chest like a sleeping airline traveler as his feet shuffle forward. I don't know how he's moving at all, to tell you the truth. All I know is that every muscle in my body aches like it's about to pop.

Suddenly I'm glad that Dad made us do those workouts, running up the mountain with heavy packs and weights on. If not for that, there's no way we'd be able to help Peyton now. I don't want to tell Dad that, though, in case he goes crazy with even more training and is all *I told you so!*

Are he and Mom and Obāchan and Inu as bad off as Peyton? I

speed up as much as I can, which isn't much. We have to finish this quest today, no matter what.

The sky turns dark and gloomy with roiling thunderheads in the distance. I don't love how it looks, but I figure we'll be okay if there's a storm. The trail we're on has two steep banks on either side, so it's like we're walking in a long ditch. If lightning strikes, it'll hit one of the trees high above, not us. I hope. Besides, we have no choice. We have to get to Fudō-Myōō, even if a hurricane blasts up.

Stupid Fudō-Myōō. How does he expect people to find his shrine if he doesn't have a sign? I mean, what's the point of a secret shrine? You won't get any offerings or pilgrims that way, that's for sure.

Jinx walks with her gaze cast down. *Trudge, trudge, trudge*. She's the embodiment of the word. I trip over a tree root, and she doesn't even make a snarky comment about my lack of coordination.

Okay, something's wrong. "What's up, Jinx?"

"Nothing." The sad look gets wiped off her face. "Just thinking about Kintaro."

"'Cause you're in love with someone who's a ghost?" I say sympathetically. I thought so. I pat her awkwardly on the shoulder.

Her eyes spark fire—figurative, not literal. "No! I just think it's sad that he only appears every once in a while, and the bear has to wait there, watching for him." She wipes at her nose. "Isn't that the most awful thing you ever heard?"

"Jinx." I tighten my grip on Peyton as we navigate across a long swatch of round rocks. "In case you haven't noticed, there's a lot of stuff like that going on around here. Like those people who got eaten and turned into orb bait. If you want my advice, don't think about that too much. We can't do a single thing to help him."

"Well, I don't want your advice. It's not going to help." She slips, and we stop so she can get readjusted.

"Of course it will. You just won't listen." I adjust my sweaty grip around Peyton's shoulder, and we crawl on, one big blobby moist creature.

I sigh at her as loud as I can. My not-particularly-minty-fresh breath ruffles her bangs. She makes a face and sighs back toward me. Her breath smells like week-old rotting trash. One thing we forgot: toothbrushes.

Peyton jerks awake with a gasp, his face creased with disgust.

"Now we've done it. Our bad breath woke up Peyton." I stop and examine him. His skin is still an unhealthy color, more blue now than it was at Kintaro's house. An uneasy knot forms in my gut. Not good. Not good at all.

"Where am I?" His eyes dart around.

"In the middle of the wilderness. But no worries." I keep my tone cheerful. "We've got it under control."

We've arrived at a small clearing, where there is a thin covering of snow with a few patches of grass sticking out of it.

"Rest," Peyton says, managing to nod toward a group of boulders.

"Sure, dude." I could use a rest, too.

Jinx and I help him sit against a rock, bending his legs and waist as if he's a Ken doll we're seating on doll furniture. Immediately his spine melts and his head sinks between his knees.

I pat his back. "You okay?"

"Urgh." His voice is muffled.

Jinx and I exchange a look of concern. "How are we ever going to get him to stand up again?" I ask.

"We shouldn't stop at all." Jinx arches her back as if it hurts. "We'll never reach the peak before sunset."

I know this, too. A day-old baby would know it. We need to get this done—yesterday. Maybe Fudō can come here. "Fudō-Myōō! Come out, come out wherever you are!" My voice echoes across the valley.

No response except the not-too-distant rumble of thunder from the black clouds studding the sky. I sniff the air. Rain's coming. Just what we need.

"Fudō!" I shout again, louder. "Fudō-Myōō!"

Nothing, nothing, nothing. And a little more nothing.

I sigh and reach into the backpack for a can of green tea for Peyton. I pop it open and hold it under his nose. "Drink this. Maybe the caffeine will help."

His arms move like slow windmills from his doubled-over position. "Help."

Jinx and I each take a shoulder and heave him upright. I place my pack between him and another rock, and he leans back against it. I hold the can up to his mouth, and he takes a tiny sip. Then he looks at me, focusing for the first time since yesterday. "Sorry," he breathes.

"Shut up. There's nothing to be sorry about." I offer him the tea again.

Peyton blinks rapidly, but there's no emotion in his eyes. They're as blank as a doll's eyes. I look away. "I shoulda stayed home," he says dully.

"I hate to say it, but he's probably right." Jinx kicks a rock like a soccer ball, pinging it far up the trail.

I suppress the urge to snarl at her. Instead, I say through clenched teeth, "Remember what Dad said? *Is it helpful? Is it kind? Is it necessary? If not, don't say it.*"

Jinx laughs. "Like you ever take that advice."

"At least I remember it." I turn to Peyton. "She's just cranky because her boyfriend was a ghost."

"I DO NOT LIKE KINTARO!" Jinx shouts. "Not in that way."

I ignore her. "Anyway, Peyton, you'd do the same for me."

"Yeah," Peyton says softly. "But if you can't take me, then leave me."

"Yeah," I repeat, holding up the can of tea again. "And I'll cut off my left foot for no reason while I'm at it. Nobody's leaving anybody. So just do what you can and we'll do the rest, okay?"

"Hey." Jinx points to the ground ahead of us. "It's going to be tough to get Peyton across this, with all these rocks."

The path is completely covered with loose stones. It will be quite a Slip'N Slide situation. "We'll just go slow."

I pick up a round rock, and it triggers a memory. A lesson—okay, lecture—from Dad. During our last hike, when I was bitten by the oni scorpion. Naturally, I'd tuned him out then. But he'd said something about the rocks. . . . What was it?

I look around, at the rocks, and the steep banks on either side of us.

Dots of water sprinkle my face and the clouds rumble. "Let's find some shelter."

"Good idea." Jinx throws Peyton's arm around her shoulder, and he rises like an animatronic robot.

Rocks. Water. Now the information nudges its way out of my brain like a piece of new grass. "We're in a riverbed!"

A flash of lightning temporarily blinds me. Then thunder shakes us and the ground we're standing on. The clouds open and pour water as if someone's standing above us with a bucket.

Rivulets of liquid and gravel start trickling down the path toward us.

I hear a rumbling sound. *Get out of the riverbed!* I can hear Dad yell. *Flash flood!*

"Get out!" I shout. "Get up the bank!"

"Come on!" Jinx grabs Peyton's arm and begins pulling him up, grabbing bushes for support. "Hurry." Peyton stumbles backward, and Jinx catches him by his collar. Despite the rain and the noise, Peyton's barely responsive, like someone waking up from a coma.

"Get up there. I'll push." I go behind Peyton. "Can you crawl?" I ask him. "Just crawl up to Jinx."

"Ungh." His hands automatically splay, seeking grips among the vegetation. I guess he can only grunt because all his energy's going toward his physical activity. A good thing.

"Attaboy!" Jinx gets a grip under his armpits.

"Come on, Peyton!" I push on his bottom, but it's like trying to urge an earthworm to win a race. "Little farther!" I yell encouragingly to him, though I'm not sure he can understand me in his half-sleep state. "You can do it!" I shove my shoulder against the seat of his jeans. Now would be a really bad time for him to toot, I think fleetingly. My helmet's uncomfortable now, pressing on Peyton and against my head, and I take it off and toss it onto the bank.

The rumbling gets louder, as if a fleet of trucks is about to drive by too fast. "Xander!" Jinx screeches, and points.

I look up just in time to see a wall of water and boulders and rocks and debris hurtling down the mountain straight toward us.

CHAPTER TWENTY-TWO

I have just enough time to give Peyton a good shove upward before the cold water hits me and I go horizontal. I scrabble for something to cling on to, but my hands find nothing. I ricochet off the riverbank with an *oof*, and my backpack with all its supplies is wrenched off of me.

"Xander!" Jinx screams again, from farther away, and I look up to see her and Peyton on the edge of the embankment. Good. Peyton's safe.

"I'll meet you downstream!" I try to call to her, but I doubt she hears me because water fills my mouth.

The flash flood carries me off, jostling me like a tennis ball in a washing machine. Something sharp hits my rib cage, and a *crack* like a wishbone snapping comes from inside my chest. I yelp in pain, but there's nothing I can do except try to keep my chin above water and take lifesaving gulps of air.

"Xander!" I hear again and again, but I think it's my imagination because I'm going too fast for Jinx to follow and I know I'm zigzagging all over the place, as though this river is a pinball machine.

Then I run into something—a sodden tree branch, hanging over the water. I grab hold and try to catch my breath.

To my surprise, Jinx is waiting for me on the other end of it, her face as tense as a bowstring. "Come on, Xander! Climb up to me!" she hollers.

I try to pull myself up the branch, but my rib hurts and my arms quiver too much. "I can't."

"You *can*." She shakes the branch gently. "Xander, don't you *dare* give up on me now. I will never forgive you, do you hear? I'll play my emo music all day and night unless you get over here."

I laugh a little, despite the pain. "How are you going to play emo music at me if I'm dead?"

"I'll find a way to reach you beyond the grave." Jinx sounds so ferocious, I believe her. "Now get up here."

Forcing my arms to move, I slither up the branch. I hug it, pressing my cheek against the bark. The water's trying to pull me back in. I'm so tired it's hard to keep my balance. I'm in real trouble now.

Then Jinx crouches above me, holding the nylon rope that we'd packed what seems like a million years ago. "Let go so I can slip this over you."

If I let go, I'll drown. But I'm too tired to disobey her.

Instantly, she throws the loop over me and tightens it as expertly as a cowhand lassoing a calf. The other end is tied around her waist. I grab the branch again, and she bends to help me get on my hands and knees.

"Now follow me." She crawls nimbly across the branch, holding on with her fingers and bare feet. I slip a couple times, but the rope keeps me steady and finally we make it to the bank.

We flop onto the ground, breathing heavily. "How'd you find me?" My voice is weak. It feels like someone is stabbing me in the side every time I inhale.

"I followed you, of course." Jinx's hands and arms are covered in red scratches. She holds up her forearm, grimaces, then plucks out a large brown splinter. "Monkeys can move pretty darn fast when they want to." She's covered in mud from head to toe. She gives me a brief smile. "Come on. Let's go back and find Peyton."

We pick our way through the mud and the trees, following the river back to where we left Peyton. Annoyance and worry propel my legs. We're losing so much time! Why can't anything go smoothly? If only I'd remembered what Dad said about the rocks earlier! Why am I so slow with stuff like that?

"Almost there," Jinx says over her shoulder because, of course, no matter how fast I go, she is faster.

"I'm going as quick as I can. Sheesh."

"All right." She shoots me a look of mild annoyance. "I know."

But when we arrive back at the spot where Peyton should be, there's nothing except a boy-size indent in the mud, and my helmet. Thank goodness I didn't lose it—I don't even know what it can do yet. Maybe if I'd kept it on my thick skull, I wouldn't have gotten swept away. I pick it up and put it on my head.

"Shoot." Jinx kicks a rock straight up into the air. "Peyton!" she bellows.

"Where is he?" My voice rises in panic and anger.

"I don't know." Jinx's tone matches mine. "I told him to stay put!"

"Dang it! You should have stayed with him!"

"Then you'd be dead!" Jinx yells, and we look at each other in silence, knowing that it's true.

I swallow. "I'm sorry. Look." I point at the mud, where Peyton's size-twelve shoe prints are rapidly washing away. "Let's find him before all his tracks disappear."

We follow the footprints between thick trees and across other trails. Where was he heading? "How could he go so far when he couldn't even move for us?" I wonder aloud.

"Maybe he wanted to find us. Maybe he felt better." Jinx shrugs. "Come on."

When the footprints fade completely, all we can do is keep walking in the same general direction. The sun breaks through the clouds, making the air suddenly summer-hot and instantly drying our clothes. Soon we're sweating.

This search reminds me of one time at Boy Scout camp in second grade. I wasn't the most reliable of kids, always getting separated from the group on class field trips, but my dad figured, hey, it's a fenced-in campsite. How much trouble could I get into?

A lot.

During a campfire session, I'd had to go to the bathroom. I could see where the building was, and I'd slipped away without telling anyone except Peyton.

Except, of course, it wasn't the bathroom.

I got all turned around and ended up in a field on the opposite side of the building. I couldn't even see the smoke from the fire because it was a cloudy night. So I started walking.

And walking and walking and walking.

Pretty soon I found myself sitting on a hollow log, bawling my eyes out. Then Peyton's shiny eyes and shock of hair popped out from between the trees, followed by a flashlight beam—his dad, our Scout leader, was with him. "There he is!" Peyton had shouted.

"How'd you find me?" I'd asked him.

He shrugged. "You have melted marshmallow and chocolate all over your shirt," Peyton had said. "I could smell you from a mile away."

At the time, I hadn't thought much of Peyton finding me. Or connected it to his birdlike nature. But now I remember what we read about monkeys and birds the day when everyone lost their dreams. Both have a strong sense of smell. Birds have to follow scents in the air.

"What do we do if we can't find him?" Jinx bursts out.

"We're going to find him." I'm the optimist now. I guess it's the law—someone always has to keep acting brave so the group doesn't fall apart.

"But what if we don't?"

"We're going to!" I snarl because I'm scared, too. "Jinx! How's your sense of smell?"

Her nose crinkles. Then her eyes light up. "Oh!"

She gets on the ground, her palms flat against the dirt, and inhales deeply. "Ew! Dirt went up my nostrils." Jinx raises her head, sniffs the air, and points. "That way."

CHAPTER TWENTY-THREE

We follow Peyton's scent down into a vast valley that's crowned by foliage in glorious Technicolor, as though packets of Kool-Aid had been sprinkled over everything.

Jinx puts her face right into the dirt. "BO, soda, unwashed socks," she reports with a shake of her head. "Basically, he smells exactly like you."

I snort. "I'd rather smell like unwashed socks than like a monkey."

She raises an eyebrow. "And how does a monkey smell?"

"Like poop," I say, and she gets all mock indignant and gives me a little shove. I shove her back, and we're giggling like two little kids who have to be separated by the teacher. It's such a relief to laugh that I start laugh-crying, and I have to turn my head away so Jinx can't see it. Because she'd either think I'm unstable or feel bad for me, and I couldn't stand either.

We walk along the path, still scuffling with each other. Suddenly it gets frigid-cold. There are patches of frozen stuff that looks like pink Slurpee between the rocks and the trees and on the sides of the path. "What is that?"

"Beats me." Jinx scoops up a handful and puts it to her lips.

I gasp involuntarily. "What if it's pink snow because some monster pees pink? Or it's blood?"

Jinx grins at me, wiggling her eyebrows up and down. "It's not like I haven't tasted blood before." She smacks her lips. "Yum. Cherry blossom."

"Cherry blossom?" I repeat dumbly, looking around the decidedly wintery landscape for a blooming tree. "What cherry blossom?"

"The flavor." She holds her hand out to me, proffering the snow.

I taste it. Pistachio and vanilla with an undercurrent of cherry. "Not bad." I grip her wrist and take a bigger bite. Ugh. I spit. Twigs and dirt in that one.

Jinx lets the pink snow fall out of her hands and wipes her palms on her pants. "This bit may not be so fresh. But I have an idea." She takes out a plastic bag and packs some snow into it, then presses it against my rib. I wince. "You have to ice that. It might be broken."

"Thanks." I clamp it to my side.

Just then, I hear the faint sound of a whinny in the distance, followed by a low murmur in a deep-ish voice.

"Peyton?" I shout and run up over the small ridge.

"Xander, wait a second!" Jinx calls as she follows.

I stop, and she thuds into me.

On the other side of the ridge, there's a small gully. A herd of horses, about a dozen, mills about. They're not as big as regular horses but not as small as ponies. They're stocky, with short legs, and spotted in black and white and soft pink, maybe so they'll be camouflaged in this environment, in the dappled pattern of shadows and light falling on the mountain.

The horses nicker and whinny softly at one another.

Sitting on his bottom in the middle of the herd, as if these wild horses don't concern him at all, is Peyton, his backpack next to him.

His eyes are half-closed, and he's scratching the head of a horse while talking to it in soft tones.

"Peyton?" I say, quieter this time.

The smallest horse sees me and lets out a high-pitched squeal, its eyes rolling back in its head until I can see the whites. It jostles the other horses, who now spot me and similarly start freaking out, trying to get away, all going in the same direction but getting caught on one another's hooves.

Great. Stampede time.

The biggest one rears, pedaling its shiny hooves through the air. Sharp hooves.

Oh no.

I take as many steps back as I can, but there's nowhere for me to hide, really, just behind trees. The stallion's nostrils flare, and it stomps the ground hard. Its hooves leave deep indentations in the soil, as if to say, *Yeah, look what I did to the ground! That's gonna be your skull!*

There's no way I'm going to use my sword on these animals. I kneel, trying to think of what to do, how to act.

The biggest one, who is as tall as my shoulder, looks at me with alarm. It neighs and stamps its front hooves. It nudges its way through the other horses until it's face-to-face with me, blowing hot breaths of steam through its nose. Great orange-black eyes survey me with suspicion.

I freeze. I've only had one interaction with a horse: a fat lazy one named Dodge that I rode at Boy Scout camp. It kept stopping to eat grass as I yanked pitifully at its reins.

Well, what would I do if I were meeting a dog? One, let it smell me. Two, give it a treat. Inu, I could bribe with bacon. Or a Cheeto. Or anything, basically. What do horses like?

I hold out my left hand in a fist, allowing the horse to get my scent. Then I slowly take a granola bar out of Jinx's backpack and rip the wrapper open. Its big nostrils sniff the bar, and its lips curl away from its large white teeth, which remind me of those windup plastic teeth from a joke store. It slobbers all over my hand as it sucks up the bar.

Jinx appears beside me, as silent as smoke. "What are you doing?"

"Trying to make friends," I whisper.

The horse turns away, as though I'd never offered it a treat at all, and makes its way back to Peyton.

"Peyton!" I follow the stallion and try to go through the horses, but it seems like they're standing shoulder to shoulder to block my path. They snort and glare at me like huge burly bouncers at a night-club door.

Then Jinx is in front of me, firmly pushing one and then the other out of the way, as though she's some kind of Secret Service agent. To my amazement, the horses docilely step aside.

"How'd you do that?" I ask her, trying not to look dumbstruck.

"When you live among demons and animals, you pick up a few things." She shrugs, patting the smooth forehead of the largest horse. "Show them you're the leader." She barges through the throng to where Peyton sits—thankfully not trampled.

He's still petting the foal, whispering soothing words into its ear. His backpack's open, and granola bar wrappers are strewn about.

"Peyton!" I kneel by my friend, weak with relief. His color is still that odd blue-green shade, not normal. He's shivering but doesn't seem to care. I dig in his pack for the down jacket, the kind that packs into the size of a folding umbrella, shake it out, and help him put it on. "Hey, buddy. Let's get going."

Peyton focuses on me. It seems to take him as much effort to do this as it does for me to walk to social studies class on a warm spring day. "I can't."

"What do you mean, you can't? *Can't* isn't in the vocabulary of Peyton Phasis. Not the Peyton Phasis I know." This is the kind of pep talk he usually has to give me, when I don't want to finish my math homework, or go to school, or do my social studies project. Why, Peyton must have given me seven hundred pep talks, a hundred for each year of school. I put my hand on his shoulder. "You can do it."

The stallion comes over and blows at my hair, no doubt looking for another granola bar. Jinx cups his muzzle, and he pushes it against her stomach.

Peyton turns his face away. "Nope."

I put on his backpack. "Quit talking crazy." I stand up, taking him under the shoulders and using every bit of my strength to force him to stand. The movement makes my rib ache, but I don't care anymore. "We are going. Now."

Peyton reluctantly gets to his feet with my extreme assistance. He leans across the stallion's back. The stallion nickers sympathetically, turning his head to gaze at Peyton.

Jinx and I look at each other.

"Are you thinking what I'm thinking?" I ask.

"I don't know. Are you thinking about climbing that tree over there?" Jinx asks with a mischievous grin.

I have to snort. "No. That we use this horse to get us to the peak."

"Good." Jinx gives me a funny look. "Which peak?"

What?

She points over my shoulder, to the left and then to the right, and I slowly turn, not wanting to see what I think I'm going to see.

Yep. There are two peaks, each capped with pink-white snow. Two directions.

And we have no idea which one we were just on.

yell as loud as I can, "I HATE THIS MOUNTAIN!"

"Yeah," Jinx says, "that's definitely going to help." She squints against the sun, looking at the peaks.

"Well." I wipe at my running nose. Cold always does that to me. "Yelling helps me keep my sanity. That's something."

"We need to think this through." Jinx squeezes her eyes shut, crosses her arms. "Step-by-step."

The horse neighs and stamps.

"Do you know what we're talking about?" Jinx pats his flank. "Can you understand?"

He pushes his nose into her backpack.

"He doesn't understand. He just wants a treat." I sit down where I am, ready to give up.

"Stand up, Xander." Jinx steps toward the peaks. "Which one should we choose?"

"Who knows? We have no idea which direction we came from." I look back in despair. Between the flash flood and the search for Peyton, we are good and lost.

"Picking the right one is a fifty-fifty shot." Jinx gives me a curious look. "You'll have to choose."

"Me?" The last thing I want is to be responsible for yet another thing going wrong. "Why me?"

"Because you're Momotaro," Jinx says, as if this explains everything.

"Powerless Momotaro, you mean." I get up, regarding Peyton, who's still using the horse as a stand to prevent him from falling over.

"I mean Momotaro." Jinx grabs my shoulders and turns me to face her. "Don't think. Just hold up a hand and point."

"That doesn't make any sense."

"You're thinking," Jinx says, and she spins me in a circle. "Hand!" she yells, and I throw up my left hand automatically.

But I'm not left-handed. Could this have actually worked?

"Don't stop and second-guess yourself." Jinx glares into my face.

"Okay," I say, with about a million times more confidence than I feel. "Let's go."

We push Peyton on top of the horse and strap him on with bungee cords. The stallion paces nervously, but Jinx produces an apple for him.

"A face apple? Jinx!" I shudder. "You've had that thing in your backpack this whole time?"

"It's no different than eating an apple with a bruise on it." She tightens the cords around the horse. "Really, Xander. This isn't our world. We have to do what works."

"I guess." As I watch the horse gobble up the apple, I want to barf. "Just hang on and try not to fall," I tell Peyton.

I peer up at the mountaintop. Thankfully, I've chosen the peak that's closer to us. "It's not far. We're practically there," I say to Jinx and Peyton, trying to inspire them—and me.

We start moving. The trail takes us through dozens of switchbacks and hidden places. It reminds me of waiting for a ride at an amusement park, where you think, *Hey, the line's pretty short*, and then it winds around into a back room and through an underground tunnel and behind some stuff until you see there's, like, five hundred people waiting. I hope I picked the right way.

Jinx and I look at each other, and we both know what the other one's thinking. She shrugs. "Well, we might as well keep going and see what's up here before we try the other peak."

"Yup," I say. So this is what it's like when both of us lose hope. Not good.

Finally, in late afternoon, we round a corner and enter a flat snowy clearing. I look around, huffing and puffing.

I don't know what I expected to see—neon lights proclaiming

WELCOME TO FUDŌ'S SHRINE! would have been nice—but there's nothing here except a few trees and a cliff with a steep drop-off.

Wait.

Behind a tree at the far end of the clearing, by the cliff, is some kind of structure. No big lacquered pieces or nicely wrought statues there. It's small, wooden, and leaning to one side, but it's a structure nonetheless.

Fudō-Myōō. It's got to be.

I can't believe our luck. I race forward. Maybe we actually have a chance of finishing this mission. "Come on!"

Jinx unties Peyton from the horse and helps him down. "Be careful, Xander."

"It's fine." The shrine looks like it's been here for a thousand years. The wood is weathered, and I can see splinters from a distance.

At its entrance, dozens of small wooden signs, each a bit larger than a Popsicle stick, dangle from ancient rusty nails. I examine one. It's covered in Japanese writing.

"They're prayers or wishes. Same thing, really." Jinx has her arm around Peyton, who barely looks awake. His legs wobble so much that Jinx starts to topple backward. "A little help here!"

"Peyton?" I rush forward to catch him. "Peyton, time to wake up!"

His eyes open. He sways back and forth on his unsteady legs, which then give out. Jinx and I lay him on his side as gently as we can. I grit my teeth. We had better find Fudō here, or else Peyton's a goner. There's no Kintaro to help us.

I peer into the shrine. It looks like a small horse stall with shallow shelves built inside against the back wall. On the top shelf is a dented green bronze statue, about two feet tall, of a man sitting cross-legged. The frown on his face is still apparent. He holds a sword in one hand and a rope in the other.

I take off my helmet and run my hand over my hair, making it stand up from my sweaty scalp. "Is that you, Fudō?"

The statue doesn't answer. Just sits.

On the ground behind me, Peyton coughs painfully, as if he's suddenly caught the worst case of whooping cough in history. I turn to see him curl into a ball. He hacks until it sounds like he's about to barf.

Jinx and I exchange a worried look. Jinx whips out a water bottle, props up Peyton's head, and tries to get him to take a drink. "Just a sip," she urges, and he manages to take one.

Fudō *has* to show up. If he doesn't, my best friend is going to die right in front of us. My pulse pounds in my ears. I put my helmet back on and climb into the shrine, over the prayer blocks, and up to the statue. I look into its sightless eyes. "Fudō-Myōō, appear!" I bellow.

Nothing happens.

I take down the statue and carry it over to Jinx and Peyton. I don't know why, exactly. To bring us luck?

"Maybe you need to meditate again." Jinx kneels on the ground by Peyton, putting her hand on his forehead. "Oh my gosh, Xander, he's so cold." From the backpack she pulls out a space blanket, the kind with a shiny side.

The stallion nickers and folds his legs under him, settling down right next to Peyton. Jinx puts the blanket over both of them. We'll warm him with body heat, the way Dad taught us.

"Fudō-Myōō!" I am howling. Tears sting my eyes. "Appear!" Come on, work!

A gust of wind blows up, drowning out my words.

This has all been a big waste of time.

I pick up the statue—hollow and worthless—and heave it over the cliff with a grunt.

Jinx shrieks. "Xander, stop!"

But I don't want to stop. It feels like someone threw a grenade inside my head. White light blinds me, and I don't know if it's a reflection off the snow or an explosion in my brain. I start kicking the outside of the shrine. "He's." I kick. "Not." I shove the walls with my shoulder. "REAL!"

The shrine rocks. I kick it again, aiming for a rotting corner.

The whole thing, this collection of old firewood and ancient lies, falls down with an ear-shattering *whomp!* Some of it slams into my helmet with a gong-like sound, but hey, that's what a helmet is for. It doesn't hurt at all.

I stomp on the pile of debris for good measure. I know I must look like a totally crazy person, but I can't help it. If I don't do this, I *will* lose my mind—and leap off the cliff into the abyss.

It must be all the jumping, but I don't feel the cold anymore. In fact, the snow seems to be melting around the ruined shrine, forming puddles. Did my anger do that?

"Momotaro-san."

A deep voice as smooth as melted chocolate sounds from above me. I stop crushing the ruins into dust and look up.

A man steps out of the sky onto the edge of the cliff.

I gasp.

His skin is the shade of a ripe blueberry. Flames surround his back, leaping and twirling, yet not touching him. He's about six feet tall, with a mop of golden hair. Two long white fangs protrude from his mouth. He wears a red wrap skirt with a green sash over it, and a golden cloak thrown over one shoulder. In his left hand he holds a golden rope. In his right, a sword.

He's frowning. Hard, as though he's the CEO of Frowns Incorporated. Deep furrows run across his forehead like freeway lines, and his angry eyebrows rival an old man's in their bushiness.

Of course, that fire surrounding him adds to the angry effect. There's no way anyone would call him Fudō-Myōō, the Happy Lord of Light.

My jaw unhinges as I stare at him. Seriously, flies are flying in and out of my gaping mouth right now.

Jinx's face mirrors mine. "Fudō-Myōō?" she whispers.

He extends his hand toward her. A flame dances in his palm. "For the sick one."

Jinx stares at the fire as if she's turned into a moth, and then she reaches out and touches it.

"Stop!" I yell. What's wrong with her?

But the flame just dances over to her hand, disappearing into her flesh. Underneath her skin, the red light rolls up her arm to her shoulder, across her throat, and down the other arm to her opposite hand, which rests on Peyton's shoulder.

The flame jumps out of her and disappears into Peyton. His legs jerk once, then go still. His skin starts to turn pink again.

"Your friend is safe for now." Fudō-Myōō turns his red-eyed gaze to me, and I blanch.

Did I mention that his eyes are burning red, redder than Fourth of July firecrackers?

They are. Like they'll explode in my face if I make him mad. Which I think I already did, by annihilating his shrine.

I take a breath, getting ready to explain everything that's happened so far.

He holds up a hand to silence me. "Come."

I step gingerly out of the rubble, trying not to impale my foot on a nail. There're no tetanus shots up here in the other world, right? "Jinx, get Peyton together."

"Leave them. They cannot come where you are going." Fudō's voice leaves no room for argument.

Jinx looks up, her gaze pained. "He's right, Xander. Peyton wouldn't make it."

"But . . . are you sure?" I know this has to be killing Jinx. She is a person of action, not someone who would typically choose to stay behind to take care of other people.

She shrugs. "It's not like I'm the Momotaro. So go on already. Go get everybody's dreams back." She smiles up at me, and I think it's the bravest thing I've ever seen Jinx do, and that includes the time she saved my life.

I nod, unable to trust my voice.

Fudō turns and walks away.

Right off the cliff.

CHAPTER TWENTY-FIVE

O h no, he didn't.

I get on all fours and peer over the edge of the cliff, searching for a blue mishmash on the rocks below.

There's nothing. Not even him waving at me that it's okay to come on down.

No way I'm doing that.

"Xander," Jinx says from behind me, her tone steady, "you have to trust him."

But when I look back at her, her expression is as worried as I feel.

"How do you know?" I ask her. "Maybe he's mad because I smashed his shrine, and now he's getting revenge."

I back up all the way to her and Peyton. The horse blows out through his nostrils, as if distressed that I didn't jump off the cliff.

Peyton is shivering under the blanket. He's still alive, thanks to the flame. But how long will that last?

Jinx surveys him, then me. "Do you have a better plan? You literally have no other option."

I think and think.

Jinx is right.

I hate it when that happens.

I don't tell Jinx to take care of Peyton because I know she will. Instead, I untie the belt with the netsuke on it and hand it to her. They'll need the food and the salt more than I will. If I'm descending into some kind of dream-within-a-dream world with the Angry Lord of Light, I won't need anything, right? Except maybe my sword. "If I don't come back—"

Jinx whomps me in the arm, her eyes bright. "I'll never speak to you again!"

I manage to give her a half grin. I raise my hand in farewell. Then I close my eyes, hold my breath, and run off the ledge.

This may come as a surprise, but I absolutely hate roller coasters. That sickening *oh-no-I-left-my-stomach-behind* feeling when you free-fall.

Peyton's dad took us to Magic Mountain once. It didn't end well.

Mr. Phasis had been willing to let me wait on a bench while he and Peyton went on a crazy roller coaster called the Vortex, but

Peyton had insisted on sitting it out with me. That made me feel so bad, I went on it with him.

My stomach and the corn dog I'd eaten for lunch did not like the Vortex.

After that, both of us skipped the big fast rides. Peyton didn't complain once, but his father grumbled about our wasting his time and money.

Peyton is a true friend.

I'm going to find the baku for him, no matter what it takes.

At least on a roller coaster, you can be sort of sure you're not going to die. Plunging off a cliff is different.

I want to scream, but that won't help. Instead, I shut my eyes, unwilling to look at the cliff face rushing past my body and at the ground coming up to crack my skull.

And then I've landed, tumbling down a grassy hill. My nose gets ready to sneeze, but it doesn't. This grass feels like feathers.

I roll to a stop and get to my knees, waiting for the dizziness to pass. Fudō-Myōō stands there, still holding his weapons, flames crackling and fizzing around his head.

"Where are we?" I struggle to my feet, the world still spinning and my ears buzzing.

We're on a plain that extends as far as I can see in all directions, like an ocean of grass. The sky is a brilliant aqua, but there's a mist of fog above the ground. "Did I leave my body again?"

"You did not." Fudō-Myōō extends his hand to me. "There are things I must teach you before you can move on, Musashi."

How does he expect to teach me anything when I have no powers? I eye his hand warily. I don't see a flame there this time, but still, I don't want to get burned. "I don't have time to be taught stuff, thanks. Just tell me where I can find the baku. I have to save my family and my best friend." My voice cracks at *friend*.

The Angry Lord laughs dismissively. "You don't have a choice in the matter. Now, take my hand!"

I glare at him. How dare he? I am Momotaro. Why does everyone try to boss me around like I'm some kid? First Kintaro and now him. Well, maybe it's time to show people that I'm not a pushover. I steady myself on my shaky feet and, trying to ignore the pain of my broken rib, take out my sword. "No. Show me how to find the baku!"

He bares his teeth, his white fangs shining against the dusky blue skin. Unlike Peyton's blue pallor, Fudō's has a red undertone, indicating that he's full of life.

With one fluid movement, he charges at me, and I barely have time to lift my sword to block. The clang of metal on metal wrenches my shoulders, and I almost drop the sword. I realize belatedly that I've never actually fought someone who was also wielding a sword. Dad was supposed to get to that part of my training later. Whoops.

Fudō-Myōō holds his weapon over his head and brings it swinging down at me. I leap to the side and scurry around to his back.

There are advantages to being small. I chop at his flames, but my blade just whizzes through them.

Now, as if the first part were just a test, Fudō really goes on the attack. He whirls around, his feet moving in a blur, and swings his sword at me. All I can do is react: block, duck, scamper. No time to figure out how to win. And I'm really, really glad I have the helmet now. I think it's saved my skull three times.

Just when I'm sure he's going to finish me—because, really, it would be easy for him—he tosses the lasso around me and yanks it tight, pinning my arms to my sides and making my rib pop in pain. My sword falls, and I move my foot just in time to avoid losing a toe.

"Are you done?" Fudō-Myōō gives the rope another good tug.

I twist my shoulders to loosen the scratchy cord. "I won't be done until I find the baku!" I try to use my Momotaro powers to imagine the rope breaking free of my body, but of course that doesn't happen.

"Xander." The way Fudō-Myōō says my name sounds like a rebuke, as if he's caught me stomping on butterflies or something. "Your anger summoned me. Now I must teach you how to handle it, or you will never be able to capture the baku and overcome her master."

My neck whips around in a double take. "Her *master*? Who's the baku's master?"

Fudō-Myōō sweeps his hand across the plain. "The ruler of this land. The dream land."

He lets the rope slacken now, and it falls around my feet. I step out of it before he changes his crazy angry mind. "Dream land?"

Fudō-Myōō winds up his lasso, securing it at his side. "Did I stutter? Open your ears!" he bellows, this time so loud I clap my hands over my ears. "No, you heard me; you're just repeating."

"Okay, okay!" Dang, Fudō-Myōō is more impatient than Mr. Phasis. I wish Peyton could see this.

Fudō sits on the ground with more grace than you'd expect from a man who's on fire, sinking into a cross-legged position. He encourages me to sit, too, his voice now as soft as a flower pushing up from the soil.

I don't argue. I can't afford to—I need to find out more, as soon as possible. Okay, so there's some kind of dream lord, the baku's master. Does this have anything to do with the scorpion thing that attacked me and made Mom so weak? I rack my brain, reviewing everything that's happened, trying to remember all that Dad has ever told me.

"Xander." Fudō-Myōō looks levelly at me. His eyes are horrible, with golden glowing pupils. I gulp and try my best to hold his gaze. "Your bad dreams were caused by you, not by any oni."

"By me? How?" He seems to know quite a bit about me, this Fudō-Myōō, but then again he's some kind of deity, so maybe that makes sense. . . .

"You carry a great deal of anger within you." He points at my chest, his fingernails like red daggers. He needs to see a manicurist.

I cross my arms. Between my mother coming back, my misuse of my powers, and the whole dream thing, if I had a dollar for every time someone told me I was angry this year, I'd have enough money to buy a pony. "So?" I realize how obnoxious that sounds, and I uncross my arms. "I don't have any more anger than the average person. I mean, have you met Jinx? Maybe she should be here, too."

Fudō-Myōō ignores these comments. He just stares at me, so motionless that he looks like one of those statues of himself. "Have you heard of an *onryō*?"

I shake my head.

"These are demons, ghosts of your own making. Your own anger and sorrow call them to you. And then they haunt you relentlessly." He ties his rope into a lasso and begins twirling it carelessly in his hand.

I blink slowly at him, processing this new info. All those dream images—the wraith dad trying to kill me, the worst version of me trying to kill my best friend, the slinking figure I'd mistaken for Gozu at Kintaro's house—all that came from me?

Huh. So I truly am a horrible person. It wasn't an oni making me think that I'd wanted to do all these things. "That doesn't make me feel better, Fudō."

"Xander," he says, "your father has begun teaching you many important lessons. But I must teach you more. Do you remember how you hurt Lovey?"

Ugh. Fudō-Myōō really does know everything. "She had it

coming." I cross my arms defensively again. "And I was helping Jinx."

"I'm going to show you how to defeat people by using only your presence." He stands up. "How did you feel when you saw me?"

"Freaked out? Scared? Terrified?" I back up just a little bit.

He closes his eyes as if I'm the dumbest person he's ever had to talk to. "What else?"

I try to come up with a better word. "Awestruck?"

His eyes open. "Good. Very good."

We look at each other for a moment.

"What's going to happen now? Are you going to make a flame come out of my head?"

"Your own version of a flame," Fudō-Myōō corrects, "which you can possess only when your anger and sorrow are completely under control. They must work for you. You are their master."

Frustration bubbles up as fast as soda mixed with Mentos. "But I don't have time to learn how to do all that! I need to get to the baku! Can't you just give me the abbreviated version?"

"If your spirit is not strong, your physical self will surely be defeated." Fudō-Myōō brings his hands together in front of him, lacing his fingers and pointing his index fingers.

He nods at me, and I realize he's waiting for me. I get up, my legs stiff and numb, and try to imitate his pose.

"Your knees should be slightly bent." Fudō-Myōō demonstrates, bouncing a little. "Do you feel the earth beneath your feet?"

"Yeah." What kind of question is that? "Of course I do. If I didn't, I'd be floating around."

"No. Do you feel the energy of the earth? The flow?"

"I thought we were in some dream land, not earth." I shuffle my feet. It feels like plain old ground to me. Nothing more, nothing less.

Fudō-Myōō snaps his eyes closed like blinds shutting against the afternoon sun. Apparently he's not that patient, either. "Miyamoto-san, quiet your mind." He points down at my feet. "Remove your shoes."

I kick off my sneakers, then peel off my socks for good measure. My bare toes wiggle against the earth. Be quiet, mind. Quiet, like I'm meditating under the waterfall.

Onamae-wa? Daruma had said to me. *What's your name?*

Xander. Musashi. Miyamoto. Why is that important?

I try to concentrate. Really I do. But I don't feel any mystical energy seeping up through my feet. I don't feel anything except a pure annoyance that flares as though someone flicked a lighter inside of me. I need to get going. I stifle a sigh.

"Point at me." Fudō-Myōō turns his sights on me once more. "Like a gun. Point your fingers at me."

I do, a slightly sick sensation coursing through me. Maybe lightning will come out of my fingers and zap a hole in him.

"Now, take all your energy and blast it through your body, from your toes to your fingers. Point it all at me, and yell."

"Yell?" This is, without a doubt, the weirdest exercise I've ever had to do in all my training as Momotaro. But then again, this is the weirdest teacher I've ever had.

"AHHHHHHH!" Fudō-Myōō howls, the sound coming from deep within his belly. His navel disappears as his abdomen is sucked inward.

A surge of energy, invisible but as real as a brick wall, hits me. I'm knocked five steps back, and it takes my breath away.

"You have the same kind of force. That is how you call it up. Soon, you won't have to make the gesture. You'll do it automatically." Fudō-Myōō nods. "Try it."

The energy dissipates. I inhale to refill my lungs. I definitely felt his blast, but . . . "I can't do this."

"The anger. The sorrow," Fudō-Myōō prompts.

I close my eyes again, trying to imagine the same kind of power coursing through me. But nothing happens.

"Master it!" Fudō urges. "Make it work for you! It is in your service, not the other way around."

"It's not working!" I open my eyes, suddenly furious again. Okay, I've got the anger. Now how do I direct it at him? I point at Fudō-Myōō and scream.

My scream doesn't sound like his did. It doesn't come from my belly but from my chest. It's high, strangled, and wailing, like the worst winter storm shrieking through trees.

The ground between us stirs, and a cloud of dirt and grass swirls up.

The cloud dissipates to reveal a dark figure. Gozu?

No, it's the figure from my dreams. The wraith with my face.

It's not Jinx's father at all. I made this. It is me.

I pull out my sword and swing. I miss, the blade whistling through air. The creature hisses, turns away from me, and springs on Fudō-Myōō with its claws raised.

He stumbles backward, clearly not expecting this. He fumbles with his rope, then throws it at the onryo.

The creature bats it aside.

"Xander," Fudō-Myōō shouts, "catch!"

He throws me the rope.

My anger has been replaced by extreme fear. I manage to catch the rope, barely. I try to lasso the onryo.

I miss.

The creature overtakes Fudō-Myōō, growing into a great black noxious cloud that billows up and over him.

I cover my mouth, gagging, my eyes stinging. "Fudō!" I shout.

The cloud swallows him whole.

I point both fingers and yell at the creature. This time the bellow comes from my gut, and it's as low as a foghorn. My own voice rattles my teeth. It has the impact of a boxer's knockout punch, a live grenade thrown into a foxhole, a china plate dropped onto cement.

The wraith collapses and evaporates.

So does Fudō-Myōō.

I'm alone on this empty field.

CHAPTER TWENTY-SIX

S o much for that lesson.

"Fudō!" I yell, turning around in a circle. "Fudō-Myōō!"

The only answer is the rustling of the grass that stretches out to its endless golden horizon.

My puny lungs struggle to draw breath through the knot choking my throat. An irregular *thumpity thump thump* sounds in my ears, like my heart is some crazy rock drummer. My mouth is as dry as a handful of gravel.

"Fudō!" I cry hoarsely once more, but I know he won't answer.

My anger's all gone. There's no shrine to kick over. Nothing to fight. How, then, can I call him back?

How in the world am I ever going to find the baku and her master thing?

I sink down onto my shaking knees. I need a moment to think. I take off my helmet and put it down in front of me, noticing that my hands are quivering, too.

Okay, Xander, calm down.

What about that demon that came out of me? The onryō? Did I, like in my nightmares, create a monster that destroyed something I desperately needed?

Did I, Xander Miyamoto, Momotaro-without-powers, just kill the one and only Angry Lord of Light?

I bend the top half of my torso to the ground, my hands in the dirt. I think I'm going to cry and barf at the same time. But nothing happens, not even a dry sob or heave.

"I'm going to die, basically," I say aloud, my forehead against the earth. My voice sounds wrong in the silent air, like a shout during a church service.

I shake my head. "I'm going to be fine." This makes me feel a little better. I stretch my arms outward.

My fingers touch something twisted. The rope.

I close my hand around it and sit up. The rope! I hold it in front of me. It's gold in color—or maybe *actual* gold, mixed with a few threads of red and green and blue that are soft enough to be silk. I trace the colored strands with my fingers.

Maybe my anger was attached to the onryo. Maybe I got rid of it with the second scream.

Or maybe I merely sent it away temporarily and now it's back inside of me.

I shiver. Well, I may not be angry anymore, but I'm sure feeling a lot of sorrow. I gather the lasso in a loop and tie it to my belt. You never know when you'll need a rope. I smooth my silvery old man's hair out of my eyes and tuck the helmet on top. I place my sword in its sheath. I put my shoes and socks back on.

I really want to head straight back to Jinx and Peyton, but I have absolutely no idea which direction I'm supposed to go in. The baku could be anywhere, right? So I go straight ahead.

Maybe Fudō's lesson will guide me, somehow. I have to believe that, hold on to it like it's a boogie board in the open ocean.

After a while, what had seemed like endless horizon actually dips down steeply, as though I've started descending some invisible stairs.

I walk for a long time, until it feels like it should be nighttime, but the sky is still as light as in early afternoon. I wonder how my friends are doing. Did Fudō's flame of healing go out in Peyton when Fudō disappeared?

No. They're okay. They've got to be.

I stop for a second.

What if time moves even faster in this subworld of the first dream world, and when I get back my parents and Obāchan are gone, Jinx is an old lady, and Peyton is . . .

I grit my teeth and start walking again, faster. I won't think about it. I can't do anything now but find the baku.

A hollow opens up below me. The ground is shrouded by a layer of thick fog. I hesitate, watching the mist.

Guess I have to go into it.

I stick one foot through the mist, and hit solid ground underneath.

The fog feels kind of substantial, like steam in a sauna. I put my other foot down cautiously. I can't see the lower half of my body, that's how thick the mist is.

When we're at the beach, Dad always warns me to shuffle my feet through the shallow water. "Stingrays like to lie underneath the sand," he says every single time we go, so I've heard it at least five hundred times. And I always say, "Okay, Dad, okay," and I shuffle. Only once did I see a stingray leap up, startled, the stinger at the end of its tail quivering, and swim away. I have to admit, I was grateful for Dad's advice that day.

I shuffle my feet now, just in case I need to scare off any critters. Who knows what could be in there?

Then I hear something that reminds me of whinnying, except it sounds more like flutes than horses. Almost as if the animals, whatever they are, are humming a song. Through the mist ahead, I can barely make out a band of four-legged animals frolicking. At first I think they're the horses we met before, but then I see they're taller, with long necks and delicate legs.

As I get closer, I notice that their bodies are covered in scales the color of spring grass, like dragons, but they are shaped more like deer. Their tails look like an ox's, long and hairless, with a broom of lavender fur sprouting out of the end. They have manes, also lavender, wrapping all the way around their jaws. Two sharp horns—antlers, really—protrude from their foreheads, pointing backward.

I slog through the mist, moving as quietly as I can so I don't scare them off. They barely notice me, dipping their heads into the clouds and nibbling on something.

Oh. They're walking *on top* of the fog. Not through it. Their hooves hover, as though the creatures are hummingbirds. They can probably even fly. One bends its giraffe-like neck and delicately takes a bite of mist, the cloud trailing out of its mouth like a piece of cotton candy. I inch closer.

Abruptly it looks up with the calmest eyes I've ever seen. I guess it makes sense that it wouldn't be scared of me—it has probably never seen a human before. Its irises are as dark as its pupils, like wet pieces of onyx.

I stop and hold my breath. The last thing I want to do is accidentally alarm them so they run me over. Because, after all, they can walk on mist. They ignore me, though, so I keep walking.

I break through the other side of the mist and find myself standing at the top of the foggy hollow. Oh no. My stomach drops. Did I just walk in a circle? I should feel frustrated right now, angry at my own stupidity, but I don't. Being mad would take too much energy.

Good, Xander, I swear I hear Fudō say in my head.

I start hiking again, back the way I came, slogging past the frol-icking creatures. I'm definitely going uphill this time. At least I think I am. I don't have any landmarks guiding me—just mist on all sides. I emerge from the fog again.

And, right in front of me, is the same hollow.

Since I'm alone, I mutter a bad word I'm not allowed to say, and leap back into the mist, not bothering to shuffle my feet.

This time I stop at the dragon-deer creatures, watching them chew. As they dip their heads, some of the cloud disappears, and now I notice there are blank spots where the animals have grazed the fog away.

Huh.

If I could somehow encourage them to eat enough cloud, then maybe I could see a way out of here.

I cautiously approach one of the creatures. "Hi," I say in the super-soothing voice I use whenever I talk to a scared animal, like the kitten that Inu once found stuck under our house. I hold up my hand so the dragon-deer can sniff it.

Something nuzzles my side, wet through my shirt, and I jump in surprise. Another one of the creatures. I shouldn't be surprised that it moves quieter than a cat.

Soon all of them are gathered around me, nosing into my pockets, testing the edibleness of my sword with long black tongues, licking my hair. I wish I had some food to offer them. I wonder absently if they'd like face apples. I pet one of the creatures on the neck,

cautiously, and it doesn't flinch. Its scales are sparsely covered with fine fur, softer than a bunny's. "You're pretty."

It blinks its large eyes as if it's saying, *Yeah, I know.*

I scratch it under the chin, and it closes its eyes and emits a purr. "You wouldn't happen to know how to get out of here, would you?"

It doesn't answer. Of course. That would be too easy.

I walk forward, and they follow. I go to the left, and then the right, in a zigzag pattern, and they stick near me but go back to grazing. Eventually they lose interest in me altogether and wander off. But they've left behind a maze where they ate away the mist. All I have to do is go through it to get to the other side of the foggy pasture.

I follow the path until I come to the edge of the cloud valley, where the land rises up again. At the top of the rise, I see sunlight and a different kind of forest. I know I haven't been there before.

Phew. "Thanks, mysterious dragon-deer creatures!" I call back.

No response.

Of course.

CHAPTER TWENTY-SEVEN

I continue toward the brightly lit rise and the new forest, no longer hesitating as I make my way through the rest of the fog. The ground is as sticky as a kitchen floor with pancake syrup dripped all over it. I try to get through it as quickly as possible. My feet make a suction cup sound as I lift them.

Then, just as I'm about to begin my climb up the hill, my left foot steps down into nothing. A hole. I try to catch myself, but my right foot is snagged by the stickiness. My knees buckle and I fall face-first into the opening.

I don't even have time to scream or think before my feet hit a new ground, a squishy landscape slightly firmer than a trampoline. I land with a bounce, putting my hands on the ground to steady myself.

I look up to where the hole was, but instead of mist, I see tree roots above me.

What?

Yup. I'm underneath a bunch of trees. It's not dark—I can see light between them, so I'm not belowground.

I shake my head. Well, nobody ever said a dream world would follow any of our rules of physics, right?

I seem to be in some kind of tunnel, with the trees as the ceiling and the ground rising up in curves on both sides. Luckily the ceiling—or the ground, or the sky, or whatever it is—is at least eight feet above me. So I have plenty of room.

There are only two ways to go: straight ahead, or turn around. I check behind me. I can't see what's at that end. There's nothing visible in front of me, either.

"Eeny meeny miney moe." I point in both directions. "Catch a tiger by the toe. If he hollers, let him go." When Peyton and I were younger, we figured out that this rhyme always ends on the second of two people or objects. So, at school, if we ever had to choose between one of us and another kid for a team or something, we always made sure to start the rhyme on the person we didn't want.

But when we wanted the choice to be random, we'd add, "My mother told me to pick the very best one and you are not it," because we always forgot which one it would land on.

I end up pointing in front of me. "That direction it is."

I begin to walk, gingerly, because the ground's still kind of bouncy. As far as I can tell, it isn't rubber or anything, just regular dirt covered by small, multicolored pebbles.

Maybe the trampoline surface will help me go faster. I take an experimental leap, and the bounce propels me up and forward. I start running.

Rocks and twigs hit me as I stir them up. A pebble lands in my mouth, and I accidentally crunch down on it.

Chocolate oozes out. Delicious super-milky chocolate that tastes like the Cadbury bars my dad once bought me in an English import shop.

I stop and pick up another small pebble. Cautiously, I bite into it.

It, too, is chocolate with a candy coating. I grin. Maybe this place isn't so bad. I wonder what the twigs taste like—licorice?

I break into a jog, the candy stones bouncing all around me. Soon the ground grows squishier, and debris falls down from the tree roots that dangle overhead. A big clod of dirt hits my face and I catch a whiff of it. The best-smelling chocolate. Like that box of See's Candies my grandmother buys every Christmas. My mouth waters.

Is it safe to eat, I wonder? My stomach growls inhumanly.

I keep running, and more chocolate chunks fall down. There are worse things in the world to be attacked with, I suppose. As the pieces hit, they melt down my face and arms. I lick my cheek. Sweet.

Then I hear a buzzing from somewhere above.

I skid to a halt. Bees? All my jostling must've woken them up. I can't see them, but the humming gets louder and louder, and it seems to be coming from the base of one of the trees.

I'd better keep on moving.

A flock of birds appears. They are the size of crows but striped yellow and black, with great flapping wings and . . .

Those are not birds. They have stingers. They're not bees, either.

Hornets.

I back away until my shoulder blades are pressed into the curved wall, sinking into the chocolate dirt. Now it seems sickeningly sweet. I remember sitting outside with Peyton on summer days, Big Gulps at our sides, hornets trying to get into our drinks.

They're attracted to sugar.

The hornets swoop down and up, like a cresting wave. The leader stops right in front of my face, hovering there. It's the size of a Chihuahua. Its enormous head, as big as a navel orange, has black mandibles that clack audibly. Its antennae swivel toward me. Its black faceted eyes are seeing hundreds of Xanders right now.

I can't help it; I scream like a toddler lost in a haunted house. Spinning on my heel, I sprint back the way I came.

The hornets rear back, like a slingshot, and then zoom forward after me.

It's no contest. The insects surround me in a great cloud, halting my progress. Their buzzing is overwhelmingly loud. They beat me with their wings; it's like thousands of paper fans hitting me, except I'm not cooling off. It's the opposite—they're *heating* me. I'm dripping with sweat, as though I'm trapped in a sauna.

"Stop!" I shout. I take out my sword and swing it around, hoping to hit at least a couple of them.

They seem to hesitate then, their wings stopping all at once, like an orchestra that has reached a rest in the music. Then one lands on my hand, and I see its lower region stab the flesh.

I don't scream this time. I just turn back the way I originally came and run, clutching my sword in my unhurt hand. There's no pain yet—just a slight burning sensation.

I run faster than ever before. Maybe I can find water to jump into. Or shelter from the rest of the swarm.

The hornets buzz all around me and begin fanning their wings even harder. The air heats up. I try to increase my speed, but I can't get enough oxygen. I slow down, my hands on my thighs, gasping for air.

They close in tight, their wings slapping my face and body, banging against my helmet, and it feels as though I'm being smacked with dozens of rulers, over and over again. The air is so hot, hotter than when we visited Death Valley in August. I sink to the ground, draw my knees to my chest, and tuck my head, shielding my already sore hand and praying I don't get stung again. The organs inside my torso churn and wiggle, and my heart beats so erratically I'm afraid I'll pass out. I can't breathe; I'm choking. I squeeze my eyes shut and know without a doubt that, somehow, this wing flapping is killing me.

A quote from one of the books Dad assigned us springs into my head. *To become the enemy, see yourself as the enemy of the enemy.* Musashi Miyamoto, my namesake. I grimace. That's about as helpful as thinking of a line of Shakespeare in response to a math question.

What *would* the enemy of these hornets be?

Then a breeze kicks up. The insects get tossed around a little, but their buzzing never stops, and they quickly regroup. The breeze grows stronger and faster until it is serious wind. I can feel it flapping my cheeks and trying to rip off my clothes as it increases into the kind of Category 5 hurricane force that rips trees out of the ground.

Yet, for some reason, the wind doesn't move me.

The blast smacks the hornets, though. It's like they've been hit with a giant fly swatter. They tumble willy-nilly back into the tunnel, some sticking to the chocolate, others blowing out of sight.

When the wind dies down, I sit up and stare numbly ahead. I'm not more than twenty feet from the end of the tunnel.

CHAPTER TWENTY-EIGHT

I stumble out into a pine forest—with the trees right side up. The air smells sweet and green. My hand is now swelling up nicely, as puffy as an extra-large marshmallow held over an open flame. Perfect. I hope I'm not allergic to hornet stings. I've never been stung by one before. Bees, yes. Poisonous oni scorpion, yes. But never a hornet.

I sit down right in the middle of the path again and take a swig of water, feeling my lungs open up and my heart begin to beat normally. Thank goodness that's over.

And that wind—where did it come from? I felt it, yet I wasn't blown away. How was that possible?

The wind was the hornets' enemy. But I guess it didn't have anything against me.

I wipe the sweat off my face with my shirt and take in my surroundings. This looks a lot like the forest by my house. A *lot* like it.

"Hello?" I call experimentally, half expecting to hear Inu's answering bark and to feel his big paws clap against my chest. I wouldn't even mind his breath, which normally smells like old tuna, or his slobber all over me. My throat tightens.

Nothing. Not even an echo.

I examine my wound. Do hornets leave their stingers behind, or is that just bees? I guess there was a reason Dad wanted us to learn all this stuff.

No stinger, just a red mound. Too bad there's no snow around here. Some of that cold stuff would feel so good about now. I'll just have to deal with it. I hold my hand above my head, remembering that, at least. Swollen limbs need to be higher than your heart so the blood can drain out. The wound throbs, but hey, at least now I'm not worried about my rib.

I walk forward slowly, my head spinning. Oh no. This stinger has some kind of poison, doesn't it? I don't know what to do. Or if there's anything I *can* do.

A movement amid the trees catches my eye. An animal?

"Inu?" I call. "Is that you? Come here, boy!" My voice cracks, and I fall to my knees, even dizzier. "Inu, come!" All I want is to feel his soft fur under my fingers. "Inu, please!" My words fade to a whisper. "Inu."

Nobody's here. I'll never see my friends again. Never step

through my front door, or hug my grandmother, or pet my dog.

My hand throbs hotly as I cradle it against my stomach. There's no Mom here to draw the poison away. No Dad to teach me what to do. I'm alone. More alone than I've ever been. I bow my head, and tears drip off the end of my nose into the dirt.

I stay like that for who knows how long.

A form emerges from the trees. I barely manage to lift my swimming noggin. "Inu?" No, not my dog. A man. "Who—?"

"Hello, my grandson." Ojīchan, in his young, strong form, stands before me, wearing loose brown pants and a cream-colored kimono top. His silver hair is tied back, and his eyes, the same blue as mine and my father's, gaze down with concern.

I blink hazily, wondering if this is another mirage. "Are you really here?"

"I'm as real as the sun when it's on the other side of the earth." My grandfather holds out his hand.

I take it and he pulls me to my feet. "But I'm not asleep." I pat his steel-cable-like arm.

"Does it matter?" Ojīchan grabs my wrist, examines my palm. "Giant hornet venom. Very painful."

"Tell me about it."

I wince as he prods my swollen flesh with his fingertip. Abruptly, he brings my hand to his lips and blows on the wound. The pain disappears immediately.

"Thanks." I breathe out in relief, thinking, *Where have you been all this time? I could have used your help before this. . . .*

Hmm. Maybe he *did* help me. I tilt my head at him. "Did you send the wind that blew away the hornets?"

His mouth twitches. "I do still have some special powers, here in this world. And when you thought of *the enemy of the enemy*, I decided to assist."

"Well, thank you. What were those things doing to me?" I clutch my stomach. "It felt like my insides were being turned into goop."

"They were." Ojīchan removes my helmet and dabs my sweaty forehead with a handkerchief. "Their fanning wings heat up their prey's internal organs, turning them into sludge so they're easier to eat."

"Oh, I see." My voice sounds faint and faraway. "They were turning me into a Xander smoothie." I knuckle a water drop out of my eye. "But why didn't the wind blow me away, too?"

He gently replaces the helmet. "This."

"The helmet?"

He nods. "It protects you from the earth elements. You know what those are, don't you?"

I shrug. "Ojīchan, I don't want a quiz. I want a nap."

He chuckles. "Come on, Musashi-chan."

Musashi. Ojīchan has called me that in other dreams, too. He's the only one who uses my middle name. I like being associated with the great warrior. I hide my pleased smile and flip through my memories. Did Dad teach me about the elements? If he did, I don't remember. "Just tell me."

Ojīchan crosses his arms and waits, looking so much like my father that my throat closes all over again. "It's important that you use your own brain to make these connections."

"Of course it is," I mutter. At last, I pick the answer out. Earth elements. "Fire, air, wind, water?" I hold my breath, watching Ojīchan's face.

"Excellent!" He slaps me on the shoulder, almost knocking me off my feet.

"So when I'm wearing the helmet, those elements can't affect me?" I think about the events before this. "I definitely should've worn it in the flood, then. Man, you should've appeared earlier!"

He shrugs. "I'm not clairvoyant, Musashi." Ojīchan glances over my head. I turn, but nothing's there. Nothing I can see, anyway. "And you have Fudō-Myōō's rope? Guard it well."

I clap my hand to the rope, and Ojīchan takes a step back, as if he's afraid of it. "Does the rope do special stuff, too?" I'd almost forgotten about it.

"That and your helmet are the only things that will help while your powers are gone," Ojīchan says.

"I also have my sword."

"While you are powerless, the sword is useful as a regular weapon, but that's all. Its special powers come from you." Ojīchan taps my helmet gently. "The rope's powers come from Fudō."

I reach up to palm the helmet's cold metal. "And the helmet's powers come from Kintaro. . . ."

"No, Musashi. This is a Momotaro helmet. Passed from generation to generation."

"This was yours? And my father's?"

His expression darkens momentarily. "No. Only mine." Then he smiles proudly. "But now it is yours."

Interesting that he didn't leave it to my father. "Ojīchan," I say, "is it true what Dad says? That he was a weak Momotaro?"

I almost don't want to hear his answer. I've always thought my father was pretty much perfect.

Ojīchan's smile fades, but he still looks kindly. He puts his hand on my arm. "Xander, there's no use dwelling on the past. We are warriors, not time travelers. All of us do the best we can. We learn, and we teach others. He has been a very good teacher. . . . Tell him I said so."

I nod mutely. I hope Dad is still alive when I'm done with this quest. And everyone else, too.

With that thought, my malaise is shaken off. "I have to get going. Do you know how to find the baku?"

But Ojīchan is fading away. "Good luck, Xander Musashi!"

It's only after he's gone that I remember he never told me what the rope can do.

CHAPTER TWENTY-NINE

This trail is completely uneventful. And not in an entirely good
way. I pay little attention to the landscape and reach the sum-
mit of this mountain peak in five minutes. But the instant I
step onto it, yet another peak comes into view. My heart drops. If my
life had chapter titles, this one would be *No Hope*.

Stop and think, Xander. Assess the situation. I look around and
listen. I hear frogs (maybe) and crickets (probably) and birds cawing.
Or maybe not. The birds sound like they're gargling gasoline. Probably oni birds, then. Not great.

Night is falling quickly. One second ago, I could see my shadow,
and now it has melted into the ground. Luckily, the moon is rising,
one of those moons that looks like it's close enough to touch, bathing
everything in a silvery light.

ARROOOOOOO, some creature howls, and branches snap. Then I hear the high-pitched squeal of prey trapped by a predator.

Okay, then. Time to find shelter. I push my way through a copse of bushes off to the right of the path. "Ouch!" The plants have thorns. Of course they do. I'm Xander Musashi Miyamoto, and I'm here to find the least favorable conditions possible, always. Well, hopefully no hunting creatures will follow me here because animals don't like to be scratched up, either.

I wish I'd brought Peyton's backpack. How was I supposed to know this would be more like an actual world than a dream world? As I push branches out of my way, my fingers touch something soft. A berry. I pick it and raise it to the light. Gotta make sure there's no face on it.

I take a tiny bite, and it's sweet and raspberry-ish. Yes! I pick a bunch by feel, using my shirttail as a bucket, then sit cross-legged in my little den to eat.

Something short crashes into my campsite on two legs. Before I can react, the thing sprints over to me and punches me in the stomach. *"Ooof!"* I huff. "Hey!"

It steals most of my berries, then keeps running. Monkey? my brain thinks. "Wait!" I yell. Maybe it'll be my friend, like Jinx. The thing pauses, looking back at me as it stuffs berries into its mouth.

It's a baby. Like a human baby, but not quite. It's got glowing red eyes, and it bares little sharp fangs in a hiss when the moonlight hits its face. Then it turns and jumps for a tree, clambering up and away.

As I watch the monster, I see something else in a tree—a long, sinewy, furry tail. I also hear the low chuffing of a very large cat passing nearby. And another high-pitched squeal and a growl that makes all my hair stand on end.

I'm so out of here.

I crash through the bushes back to the path, heading up the trail to the next peak. I don't know where I should go, but anyplace would be better than here, with a huge cat or feral monkey baby.

Then I detect a very different noise. At first it's so faint I'm not sure whether I'm imagining it. As I walk closer, the sound of music floats to my ears. Voices, singing in unison.

> *"Momotaro-san*
> *Momotaro-san*
> *o-koshi ni tsuketa kibidango*
> *hitotsu watashi ni kudasai na."*

Momotaro-san? They're singing about me. That's not the least bit creepy. Too bad I don't understand the rest of the words.

They must know I'm here. Does that mean they're a welcoming committee?

Yeah, right, my suspicious mind thinks. I'm never lucky like that.

The sound's coming from the left, off the path. I creep toward the source, peeking through the trees and bushes.

In a clearing ahead, a group of five people sits around a blazing fire, singing. They're dressed in dusty kimonos, as if they've been traveling a long way. A cooking pot hangs over the flames.

There's a small house behind them. No gold on this thing, just super-old-looking, weathered wood. A cabin or shack, really.

They appear to be camping. Somebody must have said, *Hey, I've got an idea. Let's go to Weird and Treacherous Dream World for a relaxing weekend!* And then four others said, *Yes, let's!* Super strange.

It's also strange that I don't smell any smoke. And it doesn't seem any warmer here, despite the large flames.

The person nearest to me turns with a welcoming smile, as if she totally expected some boy to come crashing out of the woods. I was right after all.

It's a woman. She has medium brown hair, medium brown skin, and is generally of medium build. Average, like me. "Hello, weary traveler!" the woman calls, her voice as merry as an elf's. Not that I've ever heard an actual elf, mind you, but it's what I presume an elf would sound like.

I walk forward, looking in all directions for any sign of trouble. Weapons, sneers, even a stray burp and I'm vamoosing.

But I don't detect anything dangerous. They're just people, with nothing that seems unusual about them. Other than their choice of vacation destination, that is.

The woman rises, extending her hands. The rest turn toward

me, smiling. Two women and three men. They seem to be college age. But then, all adults under thirty pretty much look the same age to me. When they're over thirty, they're just old.

"Hi." I keep my distance, just in case.

"Warmest greetings!" they chorus, each of them waving. They sound like an animated e-card.

The smell of the stew finally wafts over to me. It reminds me of one rainy day when I was sick with the flu. I'd slept for hours, feverish and achy under a pile of blankets, and when I finally woke up feeling better, the scent had made its way up to me. I just lay in bed, snug and warm, waiting for Obāchan to bring me my bowl of food, comforted by the fact that someone was taking care of me.

I'm overcome by homesickness now. Tears spring to my eyes, and I blink them away. This is no way for a warrior to act, I scold myself. I should keep going all night long. Everyone's depending on me.

The woman takes my hand in both of her warm ones. She looks totally normal. Black hair. Japanese. Not a monster. Not a ghost. "Come sit with us and have some food. You must restore your strength."

"Yes, come sit," the others chime in.

She pulls me toward the campfire circle. Still wary, I resist, removing my hand from hers. "What's that you were singing just now?"

She blinks at me with her medium-toned brown eyes. "An old folk song."

"Oh." I want to ask her if she knows I'm Momotaro, but that sounds impossibly egotistical, like I'm a Hollywood actor marching in and demanding special treatment at a restaurant. Dad and I saw that happen once.

"Come on. The stew will get mushy." She tugs at me again, and her friends gesture for me to sit. There's a glint in her eye that tells me she already knows my name but doesn't want to say.

My stomach growls. I am hungry, I admit. I haven't eaten properly since Kintaro's house, and that was at least twenty-four hours ago, though my sense of time is all screwed up here. "Thank you, that would be wonderful," I say politely (Obāchan would be so proud!), and let myself fall into a cross-legged position next to a very tall, very thin man with a protruding Adam's apple.

The lady who'd helped me kneels opposite. She picks up a brown lacquered bowl from a stack and uses an iron ladle to spoon out some stew. It bubbles merrily, sending its deliciousness into the air. I hold out my hands to accept the bowl, but she puts it down on the ground in front of me, then hands me a pair of black chopsticks. "Best to let it cool down first. I'm Marigold, by the way."

"Marigold?" I echo. I'd expected her to have some kind of Japanese name. "I'm Xander." I sniff the stew appreciatively. The meat in it seems both familiar and unfamiliar, but it's not beef or chicken. I consider asking her what it is, but Obāchan has taught me that it's rude to ask about things like that unless you have food allergies. *If you are invited to dinner, you are coming for the company, not the food,* she always says. *The food is secondary.*

Marigold nods, touching the black velvet choker ribbon around her neck. The other woman in the group has a matching choker. The three men all have huge Adam's apples, and I wonder if they're related. "Nice to meet you, Xander." Marigold looks at the others and they burst into giggles.

"Momotaro-chan," the second woman whispers.

There it is. "How did you know who I am?" I blow on my soup.

"We follow the news," Marigold says.

I narrow my eyes. "What news?"

She gestures at the moon. "We have our ways."

A corner of my mouth turns up. "You get a newspaper here?"

They all laugh again. "We hear gossip." Marigold touches my arm. "Don't worry. Very flattering gossip."

"I'll bet." Obviously they're laughing at me, thinking Momotaro is some kind of clown. Oh well, at least I'm getting fed. I touch my steaming soup with my finger. Ow. What'd they cook it with, lava?

The man to my right shakes my hand. "I'm Kai."

His grasp is a bit too firm, like he's trying to prove he's stronger than me. I shake back, pressing his fingers together as hard as I can, which is harder than I could a few months ago but only about as hard as a broken clothespin. Then the others in the circle take turns saying their names. I nod, trying to pay attention, but something moving in the soup catches my eye.

At first, I think it's a stray noodle. I pull it out with my chopsticks.

A little wriggling worm with an eyeball at one end stares up at me.

I drop it back in, somehow managing not to barf. Maybe because there's nothing in my stomach. I push the bowl away.

"What's the matter?" Marigold uses hashi to secure her own noodle worm, which she slurps into her mouth without flinching.

My stomach tries to escape through my mouth and run back down the mountain. I swallow firmly. "You know, I'd really better be on my way." I get up.

All five of them rise at the same time. Boy, are they tall. "You are too tired, and it is dangerous out there." The man named Kai stares me down. "We were just about to retire for the night. We have an extra bed you can sleep in." The way he says it makes it clear that this is not a polite offer. It's a command.

"I know our ways—and our food—must seem strange to you," Marigold says, "but we are harmless." She bows her head.

"Please." Kai grips my arm, not too tight this time. He smiles down at me kindly. "We would be honored to serve the Momotaro during his quest."

I look at their eager faces, the night sky, the little shack thing, and consider my options. I really wanted to find the baku today, but I don't want to get attacked by some monster in the dark. And I might not find a safer place to sleep.

Like Dad always says, the enemy you know is better than the one you don't know. I mean, he didn't make that up, but he does always say it.

"Okay," I say.

CHAPTER THIRTY

arigold leads me into the shack. It's dim, lit by just one lantern, but I see there are two rooms. In the first, five futons are arranged on the floor. The other four people follow me in, still humming the Momotaro song, laughing softly. "Time for bed!" someone says, and they all lie down on their futons.

In the second room, which seems about the size of my bedroom closet, is another futon. Marigold smiles at me as though she's showing me to the throne room of the Taj Mahal. "Please sleep well, Momotaro-san." She presses her palms together and bows low.

I bow back. "*Arigato*, Marigold-san."

The others titter. "He called you Marigold-san!" someone says, and they all laugh again. I wonder why. *San* is what you add to

Japanese names to show respect. These people are more than a little bit strange.

Marigold bows yet again, then quickly shuts the door.

I put my backpack and sword down on the floor and remove my kimono jacket. The futon is thick and padded. I should be able to sleep in here, even though the walls are so close I can touch them with each hand.

I lie down and my rib throbs a little, though it's mostly better. I turn onto my other side. My nerves thrum with electricity. My stomach growls. "Too bad," I tell it. "We're not eating any stinking eyeball worms, that's for sure!"

I crawl to the end of the mattress to open the door and peer through. There they are, dimly illuminated by the window, all of them already asleep and snoring like a bunch of buzz saws. Well, if my nerves weren't already keeping me awake, that snoring sure would.

I close the door and lie back down, feeling hot and sweaty and restless. I stare at the raw wood ceiling, trying to remember the advice Daruma gave me what seems like three hundred years ago. *Remember your name.* Whatever.

Then the idea hits me. I sit bolt upright. Why not call the baku for these slumbering people? She'll show up, right? Then I can capture her!

"Baku, come take their dreams away," I say into the stillness of my room. "Baku, come take their dreams away."

I flop down again. The air is still and it's hard to breathe, as though I'm inside a coffin. I have to stay awake, for the baku. . . .

I must have drifted off. I wake up wiping sleep drool from my chin. I sit up. Did I miss the baku?

I hear voices. I put my ear against the door to listen.

"I don't care if we showed him hospitality. He accepted, and we have a right to do it!" A deep voice. Kai's voice.

It sounds like they're farther away than in the next room. Are they outside? I try to open the door again.

The operative word here being *try*. Because it only opens a sliver. The door is barred somehow.

I knew I should have run as soon as I saw those worms. I pick up my sword and stick the blade into the crack. It hits something solid, like steel, but it's not steelier than the Sword of Dreamers. I jam the blade upward and a padlock pops off the old wood. Success!

The door creaks open slowly. I crouch, ready to fight, but all I see are five figures sleeping on their mattresses. So why were their voices coming from outside?

I peer around the room. Nobody stirs. There's no more snoring. When I hear the voices again, from the yard, I step closer to the sleeping forms.

And realize these bodies have no heads.

I suck in a breath. Are they dead? Has someone crept in and

killed them all? I stick my fist into my mouth so I don't scream. I want to run, but the voices are still out there.

"He doesn't deserve to live," a female voice argues. "And Momotaro is the tastiest meat. Like a peach! I read it on the Internet."

Marigold snorts. "So that's supposed to make it true?"

What kind of Internet do they have in this weirdo alternate universe? I kind of want to see what it says about me.

I huff. It doesn't matter if these bodies are alive or dead or what. I'm getting myself out of here, pronto. I tie my kimono jacket closed and put on my sword. Then I peer out the window overlooking the courtyard.

Five floating heads bob around the smokeless campfire. "If we do this, we should take him now, while he sleeps!" Marigold says in a low voice. "It's easiest when they're asleep."

"I don't know if he's really asleep yet," Kai's head whispers. "You should have made him eat the soup."

Marigold's head opens its eyes wide. "What was I supposed to do, pour it down his throat? That wouldn't have made him suspicious. You have no sense of nuance, Kai."

"I told you to leave out the eye worm!" the other woman says. "The humans always freak out about the eye worm."

"Well, if you think you know so much, then *you* be in charge next time," Marigold retorts. "You'll be begging me to handle things again."

"I doubt that very much," mutters another man.

Marigold bares her teeth. So does the man. They erupt into a loud whisper argument, the kind adults have when they don't want kids to hear, but you totally can.

I sink to the floor. It all makes a strange kind of sense. Headless bodies. That ribbon around the girl's neck. The absurdly large Adam's apples in their pencil-thin necks. They've got detachable heads.

What do I do? I can't sneak out without them seeing.

I eavesdrop some more.

"If it was up to you," Kai says, no longer bothering to whisper, "you'd wait until our bodies got moved before you took any action."

The others gasp.

"How could you say such a hurtful thing?" Tears run down Marigold's face. "I would never."

"Too far, Kai," the other woman head says. "Too far."

Kai flushes angrily. "It's true, Marigold."

I duck out of sight. *Bodies moved?*

This reminds me of something. Daruma had told me to keep my body near my head. Of course! And here I'd thought he was just another babbling Looney Tune.

The forms lie there, their chests moving up and down as they breathe. Are they really alive separate from their heads? Will they fight back like zombies? Only one way to find out.

I grab Marigold's feet and pull.

No resistance.

Okay . . . now what? Where can I put the bodies without the heads seeing? I have no other option but to move them into my small room. It's not very far from where they were sleeping, but hopefully it is far enough to confuse the heads and buy me some time.

Luckily, these aren't the biggest of people—their bones are small. I wonder if they're hollow, like chicken bones. I drag one after another inside until they're all crammed into the small room, and then I shut that door. I wish I could put the padlock back on. I quickly stack the futons in front of the door.

Those monsters are *still* arguing outside. I swear, they're worse than Peyton and Jinx. A knot immediately forms in my stomach, and it's not from hunger. I have to leave, and there's only one way out. Through the yard.

I hold my sword and swing open the door.

The heads pause in their jabbering, and they all swivel in the air to stare at me. For a second, I think they must be holograms—this can't be real—but then I remember where I am.

I address them in the firmest voice I can muster. "I have two things to say. One, you guys are terrible team players. You should get along better. And two"—the heads float closer, and I ready my sword—"you'll never get your bodies back now!"

Marigold shrieks and zooms past me into the shack. "They're gone!" she wails from inside.

The heads follow her, bopping against each other like bowling balls. I slam the door shut behind them and take off running into the forest. The moon is glowing above the next mountain peak, and with its light, I find my way to the path that leads to it. My thighs burn with the effort, but there's no way I'm stopping.

"You will not leave without moving our bodies back!" Kai growls from somewhere near my waist. Oops. I didn't know he had glommed onto me by biting my kimono belt. His head is lighter than Fudō's rope.

"Guess again, you eyeball-eating jerk!" I pant, trying to double my speed.

He clamps his teeth tighter.

Ewwww. "Get off me!" I yell.

"Never!" he says around a mouthful of silk.

Oh man. I make a fist and bash him in the temple, my knuckles connecting hard.

That does the trick. His mouth opens, and he falls to the ground, tumbling down the path like a bad apple.

"I'll never talk to a stranger again," I say as I wipe his saliva from my belt. "It's so not worth it."

The low moon looks like a giant coin. Silvery beams stretch out from it, like staircases to the horizon. And in front of the moon, silhouetted in inky blue-black, stands the baku.

inhale so sharply I'm sure the baku must have heard it. The last thing I want to do is scare her off. I approach her gently as she stands there, swinging her trunk nervously, looking at me with large, doleful brown eyes. *Behhh*, she bleats.

I reach out my left hand to let her smell me. She raises her trunk and sniffs loudly. "Hi, there," I say softly. Very slowly, my right hand takes the lasso off my hip, palm sweating. I hope I've guessed correctly about what the rope can do, and I hope I'm skillful enough to make it happen.

Up close, the baku is beautiful. The muscular trunk waves like a dandelion dancing in the wind. Her green fur seems to be tipped with moonlight, all silvery white. The golden mane cascading around her head is something straight out of a fairy tale.

I crouch down. "I won't hurt you." And this is true. All I want to do is capture her and take the dreams back. Where are the dreams, anyway? Inside her? Or does she take them somewhere else?

I think of the demon scorpion that bit me during the hike.

Is that who the baku works for?

Proceed with caution, Xander. I swallow. "Here," I say breathlessly. "Come here." I pat my thigh encouragingly, like I do with Inu.

The baku shuffles forward uncertainly. She touches my hand with her trunk, the prehensile end grasping my skin, pinching it gently, and assessing my hand with sniffs. Through it all, the baku never breaks eye contact with me.

I drop my left hand. At the same time, with my right, I throw the lasso up and over the baku's trunk. Once it is around her neck, I tighten it.

The baku screams, a terrible noise like a chorus of frightened children, as if it's saved up all the fear from all the nightmares it has ever eaten. It hits me with the physical force of a brick wall, and my ears ring in protest.

I fall backward and let go of the rope. The baku turns and runs, the golden cord dragging behind her like a dropped leash.

"No!" I get up and launch myself at the rope, scrabbling in the dirt. It slips through my fingers. I tackle it, grab the end, and hold it tight against my body so it can't get away. Phew.

I don't even have time to catch my breath, when I feel something on my face. I look up. Pearly white robes swish against my forehead like a cool breeze on a hot day.

"What business, pray tell, do you have with my baku?" A young woman glares down at me. Her head is triangle shaped, like a cat's, and her skin is dusky, like a black pearl with pale highlights, glinting in the reflected light of the moon. She wears a crown made of pearls, a long string of pearls around her neck, and a white kimono bound with a wide silken obi.

She puts her hands on her hips and thrusts her chin up. "What do you want with my baku?"

I scramble to my knees, still holding on to the rope with both hands. The baku whimpers. I pull her close to me. Her little heart is beating fast, like a bag of hummingbirds. "She stole my dreams."

"She does not take unless you ask," the woman says sharply. "Baku is incapable of thievery!"

"I only wanted the bad dreams gone!" My voice cracks. "Make her give them back, and I'll let her go."

The woman shakes her head. "You want everything. It is like receiving a piece of cake and then getting angry because you can't have the rest!" Her voice rises into fury. "You weren't satisfied with what she did for you, so you asked for more. Well, sometimes you have to be careful what you ask for."

Then, to my surprise, the woman sinks down into a squat and regards me. Her eyes are luminous. They remind me of a

black-bottomed pool I once swam in. My reflection stares back at me. I'm sporting some impressive bags under my eyes.

But I'm not here to gaze into her eyes like some dopey lovesick puppy. I stand up, tightening my grip on the rope. "I will not give her back unless you give me our dreams."

"Xander." Her eyes close halfway, and she straightens with a sigh. "Son of Akira. The Momotaro line. You were misusing your powers."

How does she know all this about me?

"Tell me something not every creature I've met has told me." I recall that buttery French toast, my room makeover, what I did to Lovey . . . it all seems like several lifetimes ago now. "Maybe I did a little. But I won't anymore. I've learned . . ." I think of Fudō-Myōō. "I've learned how to deal with stuff better."

The woman shakes her feline head.

"You don't believe me."

She shrugs. "I have no reason to believe you, Momotaro-san. How can I trust someone who's taken my most precious pet?"

The baku's trembling, and I put my hand on its head to calm her. She's not trying to run from me anymore, and I wonder if that's because of the rope's magical powers. I don't think I would be able to hold the creature otherwise. "Who are you, anyway?"

"I am the dream keeper." She waves her hand carelessly. "You have dreamed about your worries many times, Xander. The onryō? that haunted you. Your mother leaving."

I tighten my jaw. "So?"

"So how did you ever expect to fully become the Momotaro with all these fears plaguing you?" She tightens her mouth. "It was impossible. Now that you don't have the dreams, your head is quiet. You don't need to worry about becoming the Momotaro anymore. You're normal. Average. You should feel good. At peace. It is better for you to feel nothing, is it not?"

"No!" I'd rather face the nightmares again than what I've been going through. "I need them back. But what I really need is the dreams of my family back, because without them they'll just—" My voice chokes, and my eyes fill with tears.

Something like sympathy passes over her beautiful face. She looks up at the sky as if deep in thought, then back at me, a smile playing across her face. "All right. I will make you a bargain."

I gulp. A bargain *never* sounds good. I wind the lasso around my hands. "What kind of bargain?"

She motions to the baku. "You can have the dreams of your family back if, in return, I get the baku."

"Okay! Then we can all—"

"No, not *we*," she says. "Only *their* dreams. Not yours."

"So that means . . . no Momotaro powers for me?" My heart slows and seems to stop. "Or imagination?"

"Correct." Her kimono skirts swish as she stands up. "No drawing. No creativity. Are you willing to trade?"

Yes, I swore off drawing before. That was my choice. But I don't want it to be gone forever, to never have the option of starting up again. Without dreams or creativity, I would just plod along joylessly for years. . . . Or maybe I wouldn't even last that long—look what was happening to Peyton. . . .

I gaze down at the baku. All this trouble—and I have to give up my powers, too? The powers I'd just started learning how to use?

And misuse.

I think of my family back home, and my two friends, still waiting for me in the snow. If they're even still alive, since this quest has taken so long . . . How could I possibly let them all down?

Besides, I've already lost my powers, so there really wouldn't be any difference.

"Do we have an agreement?" she presses.

The decision is a simple one in the end. I nod once.

The woman smiles. She holds out her hand, beckoning with her fingertips, and I hand her the rope. She unwinds it from the baku's neck and tosses it back to me.

"What's your name?" I ask. Just for the sake of knowing.

"Kaguya. *Princess* Kaguya," she adds, as if this will mean something to me.

"Nice to meet you," I say politely, but she doesn't respond. The princess bends over the baku and strokes her fur. Something like dust rises up, only I see it's not dust but fine particles of gold and silver and pearl. They form a cloud that rises into the air like a freed helium balloon. I watch until the cloud reaches the stars, where it suddenly poofs apart.

"Is that it?" I ask, looking back at the princess. She's already walking away, toward the giant moon that's so close it seems to sit on the horizon.

"That's it," she answers without turning. "Their dreams are free, and so are you."

CHAPTER THIRTY-TWO

Here I am, at the end of my quest.

My Momotaro powers are gone forever.

I wait for sadness to hit. For anger.

Instead, a feeling of lightness washes over me, relief flooding my skin like a cool swimming pool on a sweltering day. My powers are history, but at least my family is safe. I wish I could call home just to make sure.

Home. How do I get home from here, anyway?

"Hey!" I yell to the princess. She whirls around, her kimono swishing with a sound of silk. "Is there some kind of magic carpet I can call?"

She wrinkles her long, patrician nose. "Magic carpet? What is that?"

I hold out my hands. "How do I get out of here?"

"Oh, you want to get home." She puts one hand on her waist, thinking. "I suggest you leave the same way you came."

That's helpful. "By jumping off a cliff?" I ask. "Does it matter which one?"

She sighs, suddenly reminding me of Jinx. "It is not far. Let me show you." Kaguya walks toward me. The way she moves reminds me of a large cat, too, with a lot of power under all that grace. She takes my shoulders and spins me forty-five degrees. "Twenty paces that way, you will come across a gully. Turn to your left, and you'll see a cliff. That is it."

"So it *does* involve jumping off a cliff." I knew I wouldn't like it. I turn and shake her hand. It's as chilly as a jewel. "Thank you, Princess." I dip my head, not really knowing what you're supposed to do when speaking to royalty, but I figure that'll suffice. After all, she's not *my* princess, so I don't have to bow, right? She wouldn't even let me keep my dreams.

Her eyes widen a little in surprise. "You're welcome." She pumps my hand uncertainly in return, then more enthusiastically. A sparkling laugh comes out. "This is a funny gesture."

"Not really. It's polite where I come from." I let go of her hand. Kaguya—Princess Kaguya—is only a little bit taller than I am. If I stood on my toes, I'd be looking at her eye to eye. "What do you do where you come from?"

"Do? About what?" She wrinkles her brow.

"When you greet someone. Do you, um, hug? Or bow?"

She laughs again, the sound like small wind chimes. "We do none of those things."

"Oh," I say, and regard her smooth face, wondering how old she is. Or how ageless she is. If she were human, she'd fit in at a high school.

Princess Kaguya smiles at me and touches my face. "You're very young, aren't you?" she says softly.

I clear my throat and frown. "Not that young. I'm no kid, that's for sure."

"You're right. At a certain point in immortality, age becomes meaningless." She gestures. "I will walk you to your cliff." She moves toward the spot she'd pointed out, her kimono swishing and reflecting the moonlight, as if she's a beam gliding over the earth. I follow.

And then, all at once, I remember the moon princess story that Obāchan told me.

A bamboo cutter discovered a miniature baby hidden in a living piece of bamboo. He raised her, and she grew up to be beautiful (naturally, isn't that how the story always goes?). She fell in love with someone on earth, but then duty called, and she had to ditch her whole family and her boyfriend to go live on the moon, where she came from.

"You were found in a piece of bamboo," I tell her. "I know the story."

Her face falls, and I wonder if she's thinking about that lost love. "That was a long time ago."

How long? I wonder. Desperate to change the subject, I add, "My ancestor was found in a peach. So we both come from a plant."

Kaguya's expression smooths over. She raises her perfect eyebrow commas. "Interesting." Which I know means she doesn't find it interesting.

I close into awkward silence. Why did I have to say anything?

We continue walking for a bit before she speaks again. "I must admit, you impress me with your fortitude, young Musashi." Princess Kaguya stops and bends so her face is near mine. Her eyelashes are long and black and appear to be studded with minuscule dark diamonds. "You were braver than I expected on your journey here. I hope you will continue to be courageous on your journey back."

"Thanks, I guess."

Fat lot of good it did me. If she's that impressed, why can't she give me my powers back? I blink. Her face is really close to mine. She's not expecting to do something crazy, like kiss me, is she? I step back.

"So my story is still popular down here on Earth?" Kaguya straightens, leaving me a little . . . what? Disappointed?

"I don't know about popular, but I've heard it."

"Few have dreamed of it in the last couple of decades. I thought it was forgotten." She strokes the baku's head.

"You know what everyone dreams about, then?"

"Only the people I choose to observe." Kaguya meets my gaze commandingly, and for a second, she reminds me of Mr. Phasis. "You can tell a lot about a person from his dreams."

I get the feeling that she knows way more about me and my quest than she's letting on. Well, there's probably not much to do up on the moon, and I *am* the Momotaro. *Was.*

The baku, no longer scared, lifts her trunk to touch my hand. "Hey, girl." I smile at the creature. The more I see her, the more I believe she didn't mean me any harm. She was just doing her job. "How are you?"

Behh, she says, and lets me pet her chick-soft head.

"There is your cliff." Kaguya points at a ledge that looks vaguely familiar.

"Fantastic," I mutter.

"Time to go, baku-chan." Kaguya bends and scoops her up in her arms. "Good luck, Momotaro-san."

At least she didn't call me *chan*. That's what you use with a little kid. "Are you sure you don't want to give me my dreams back?" I ask. "They're not going to do you any good."

Kaguya strokes the baku's shoulders. "Don't worry. Your dreams are safe."

My shoulders droop. *Safe*. I guess I brought that on myself. I wish I could show her that I don't mind not being safe anymore. That I'm responsible enough to control the powers. I bow to her. "Thank you, Your Highness."

"Xander." She reaches for my upper arm as if to stop me, though I'm not moving. "Your dreams are only one part of you. If you truly want to be the Momotaro, you must remember that your words and deeds are important, too."

"My words and deeds," I repeat. Well, I already performed plenty of deeds. "Why are words important? Sticks and stones can break my bones, but words can never hurt me."

A small smile flits across her face. "Words are sounds of the heart, Xander-san. And they can hurt or heal. What you say to others—and yourself—matters a great deal."

Kaguya releases my arm, leaving a cool imprint on my bicep. She takes a step back. I swallow and look over the cliff into blackness. I guess what people say does matter. But what does that have to do with being the Momotaro, which she's not letting me be? Words don't have anything to do with my Momotaro power. That's all contained in my head. Isn't it?

"Kaguya? I still don't understand." I turn, but nobody's there. I search for her in the darkness, and all I see is the glowing white pearl of the moon.

walk to the cliff without looking at the moon again. I kick a large rock off the ledge, watch it spiral down, wait for the *thud* when it hits land. It never comes. Well, that's super.

I lie down on my stomach to peer off the edge. I don't see anything below but darkness, and it might be better that way. Briefly, I put my forehead on the ground and close my eyes, wishing I was already home in bed. But without my imagination, I can't picture it. My wishes are just regrets now. I wish things could have turned out differently. I wish I'd been as strong as my father and grandfather believed I was. The thought that I'll never be able to fight the oni fills me with dread.

Because there is no more Momotaro, thanks to me. Nobody to stand up to them as they wreak the havoc Dad warned me about.

We are warriors, not time travelers, Ojīchan says in my head.

I exhale. "You're right, Ojīchan." When I get back home and tell Dad what happened, he'll figure out something. He'll help me understand what Kaguya meant about words and deeds. He hasn't done all that research for nothing. I stand up and stretch my neck from side to side. "The only path is forward."

I take a deep breath and leap. This time there's no great sensation of falling—it's just a short hop, like stepping off a curb into the street. I land on my hands and knees, with my hands buried in slush. It's still night wherever I am, the moon beginning to sink as dawn approaches.

I blink, trying to get my bearings. A chill wind blows through my hair and my clothes. "Hello?" I try to call, but it's more like a stage whisper.

I'm alone.

Peyton and Jinx must have already gone home. I can't say I blame them. Who knows how long they would have been stranded here, what with the wonky time thing.

But still . . . I kind of want to cry. I won't, but I want to. There's nothing to do but make my way back down, too. I don't even care that it's still dark. I just need to get out of here.

I get ready to stand, but my knee creaks in protest. I groan.

A nervous whinny sounds from behind me.

"Xander?" Peyton's pulling me up, stronger than ever. "Dude!"

His face is healthy looking again, his eyes bright, his hair plumage standing straight.

I grin and clap my hands to his shoulders. "Dude."

Extending eight feet wide from behind his back are his wings. Glorious iridescent green and blue and gold wings. He flexes them, then flaps them in the air, whipping my hair back. Peyton grins from ear to ear. "The bird is back in town!"

"I knew you didn't have those chicken legs for nothing!" We hug, back-slap, fist-bump, the whole nine yards.

"So that didn't take too long. At least not in this world," Jinx says. She's standing behind the pink horse, stroking his mane as he nervously shifts. Apparently, my sudden appearance out of nowhere startled him. "It must've been pretty easy."

"Oh yeah, totally." I brush the snow off my hands. "Except for the fact that I didn't get my dreams back." I begin telling them the whole story.

As I talk, Peyton uses a stick to draw me in the snow. At least I think it's me. The sight makes my heart beat more calmly. He definitely has his dreams back.

Finally, I end the tale with the mysterious Princess Kaguya and how she seemed to believe she was helping me somehow by keeping my dreams.

"Xander, no!" Peyton grips my arm. "You're the most important one."

"No, I'm not." I try to smile at him. I don't want to tell him it was them or me. No use making them feel guilty. "It's fine. I'll be fine. I didn't want to be Momotaro anyway. Guess I couldn't handle it." Deep inside my chest, disappointment wrestles with relief. It's starting to really hit me. I have nothing, and here Peyton is with his wings. I feel like a tree that's been hit by lightning, hollowed out and scarred.

"What about the oni?" Jinx comes out from behind the horse, clenching her fists. "Doesn't she care about them? They're going to take over the world for sure."

"We'll go home. Talk to my father. He'll know what to do." I speak with more confidence than I actually have, but as soon as the words come out of my mouth, I believe them.

She relaxes her hands. "Maybe. But what if he doesn't?"

"He will," I repeat firmly.

We stare at each other for a moment. Then Jinx closes the space between us in two steps, her arms out. "I'm sorry you lost your powers, Xander."

My arms flail, pinned to my sides by her abnormally strong grip. I couldn't hug her back even if I wanted to. I end up patting her spine awkwardly. "It's okay, Jinx."

She releases me, steps back. No tear in her eye, of course, but close. That's good, because if the super-stoic Jinx cried on my behalf, I would definitely start bawling.

Peyton shrugs, the motion unfurling his wings. "So let's make like a tree and leave."

"Hardy har har. I can't believe you left me to listen to his bad jokes, Xander." Jinx punches me gently in the arm. "And you should have heard him crow when he grew his wings back. I'm still half-deaf."

"Wait a second." I stand stock-still. "If I don't have my powers, Peyton, and your powers come through me, then how on earth do you have wings?"

Peyton meets my gaze as we both get the same idea. His mouth drops open, and his index finger pops up. "Maybe . . ."

Jinx hops up and down. "Maybe you *do* have your powers! Try it, try it!"

I attempt to think of something to imagine into existence. Anything at all. I look around the mountaintop. Nothing. "I can't. I can't think of anything." My mind feels like a fuzzy television screen, and pain throbs at my temples and behind my eyes.

"Okay." Jinx holds out her hand. "Glass of water right here, right now."

That's easy. I know what that looks like. A clear cylinder filled with clear liquid. Wait, that's a memory, not imagination. Or are those the same?

Jinx's palm remains aloft.

I sputter out a breath I didn't realize I was holding. "I can't." My head aches, my vision blurs for a minute, and I stagger back.

Jinx lowers her arm. "I guess that would've been too good to be true. Hey, are you all right?"

I double over, pressing my fingers to my head, trying to massage the pain away. "Not exactly." I must be dehydrated. I always get headaches when I don't drink enough water.

"Dude." Peyton pats my back comfortingly. "Maybe we don't understand everything about your powers. Or maybe the princess changed us when she returned our dreams."

His silken feathers shelter me like an umbrella as they ripple in the breeze. It could be that Peyton's wings are permanent now. He'll be flying around San Diego, a glorious mythical bird. Think of all the sports he can do with those. And I'll be Xander, stuck on the ground forever.

This feels even worse than the moment I gave up my Momotaro dreams. I know I said I wanted to be normal, but normal's not all it's cracked up to be, especially when your best friends aren't. It's like the time I lost a twenty-dollar bill—all my spending money—on a field trip to the county fair. I had to watch my friends eat ice cream and fried Twinkies without me, knowing it was my own fault for being careless. This feels like that, multiplied by a thousand.

Peyton continues patting my back. "It'll be all right, Xander."

I'm reminded of Princess Kaguya's parting bit of random wisdom, about words. For a second, I try to believe my friend.

"I hope so." I straighten up. The pain's better now. I need to sleep for a few days, that's all. "Let's just get out of here. I want to check on my parents and Obāchan and Inu."

"At last, a statement I can fully get behind." Jinx picks up her backpack.

We finish packing and take the bridle off the horse. Jinx rests her forehead against the horse's forelock. "Thanks." The stallion closes his eyes, then nuzzles her.

Peyton takes a grain of rice from the monkey netsuke box and holds it under the horse's nose. "You're the best magical horse I ever knew."

The horse sucks up the rice, chews the onigiri, then butts his head softly against Peyton. He turns, whinnying, and runs down the mountain, back to his herd.

"Oh." The corners of Jinx's mouth turn down. "I wanted to keep him."

"Then why did you take off the bridle?" Peyton asks.

"Because. If he wanted to stay, then he would have. I didn't want to *make* him come with me."

"If it's any consolation, Jinx, my parents wouldn't have let you keep a magical pink horse. We don't have a barn or anything." I take her arm. "Come on. Let's go pet Inu." Longing for my family makes my feet move faster.

Jinx's face brightens. "Inu!"

We haven't gone but a hundred feet, when suddenly there's a great crashing through the bushes and a terrified *Beehhhhhhh!* A long greenish trunk, attached to a creature somewhere between an ant-eater and an elephant, bursts into view.

"Baku?" I say.

CHAPTER THIRTY-FOUR

The baku winds its trunk around my hand, pulling hard. *Behhhh!* she bleats. *Beh!*

"Ooh, it's so cute and cuddly!" Peyton bends to pet her, but the baku shies away, staring fearfully at his wings.

Behhh!

"Cool! The baku." Jinx reaches out for her, but the animal shrinks back. "What's the matter with it?"

"I don't know." I try to remove my hand from her trunk, but she won't let go. "What's wrong, girl?"

Behhhh. She pulls at me.

"She wants me to go somewhere." My stomach flips as I consider the possibilities. Well, there's only one real possibility, as far as I can tell. "This must have something to do with the princess."

"The mean princess who wouldn't give you your dreams back?" Jinx raises an eyebrow at me. "Why would you want to help her?"

"Yeah." Peyton flaps his wings. "Forget her. Let's get home while the getting's good."

For once, they're agreeing on something. Too bad I don't agree. Baku yanks at me again, bleating. "I . . . I don't think I can. I have to help her."

"But don't you want to get back to your parents and grandma?" Peyton says. "We've been gone a long time, and they must be worried."

Good point.

Behhhh, the baku insists.

I think of the princess in her white kimono. I can't explain why, but I know I have to go to her. Just like I know I have to get my grandmother her muscle cream when she is aching. My parents would want me to.

I shrug. "It must be important. She's the dream keeper."

"More like dream *hoarder,*" Peyton says. He and Jinx exchange a meaningful glance.

"What, are you in love with her?" Jinx narrows her eyes.

My face gets hot. "No."

Peyton dissolves into giggles, standing on one leg as he covers his mouth with his hand. "Oh snap. Look at his face. Jinx is right."

I press my temples with my fingers. "Guys, it is most definitely one hundred percent *not* like that." I sigh. "If you saw, like, a tiger caught in a trap, wouldn't you help it?"

Peyton cocks his head at me, thinking. "Depends on whether it would eat me after I got it out."

"You'd let it out!" I explode. "You're just being difficult." I've had it. I leave them alone for, like, two days—which apparently is, like, two minutes in this land—and they've turned into some kind of anti-Xander coalition. I turn and start walking away. "I'll go by myself if you guys won't come."

"Okay, then." Jinx speaks first, to my amazement. "Let's do it."

"Wait. You're agreeing with me?" I clutch my heart.

"Let's hurry up before I change my mind." Jinx pats the baku on the back. "Take us, Baku."

Peyton shakes his head. "Well, I can't say this will be the best thing that's happened on this trip. But it beats sitting around on a mountaintop waiting for you."

The baku takes off, and we follow.

She lopes like a miniature raging elephant and goes straight off the cliff again. Before Jinx and Peyton have a chance to think about it, I jump after her, and they follow like lemmings. How completely bizarre we must look, just leaping into the darkness. But we land on our feet and keep running.

The baku's heading up the hill. Back to the peak? No, toward the setting moon. It's so close I can see the craters. Maybe even a little city, with ant-like people moving around.

Unless that's a real city. Which, in this dream world, it might well be.

A thick beam of white light shoots out of the moon like a bridge toward the earth, ending at least two stories above the ground. We stand looking up at it. "How're we going to get up there?" I say. The baku leaps into the sky and lands on the foot of the bridge. She turns to us and bleats.

"Come on!" Jinx does a running jump like the baku's, but she falls about twenty feet short of the bridge. It might as well be an airplane zooming away. "Dang it!"

"We need some pixie dust." I crane my neck, assessing the distance. "And happy thoughts."

"That's definitely not going to work for me," Jinx says.

"Seriously?" Peyton points to his wings. "You think these things are just for show?" Peyton wraps an arm around each of our waists.

"Are you sure you're well enough?" Jinx gives him an alarmed look. "The last thing we need is for you to overexert yourself."

"Only one way to find out." Peyton grins. He flaps his powerful wings, sending leaves and grass flying around us, then does a squat and pushes off the ground, launching himself into the air.

The wind whooshes around us as the ground zooms away. "Guess he's all better!" I shout to Jinx, who has her eyes scrunched closed. I reach over and poke her. "Are you scared?"

"What, are you afraid I'll do something like this?" Peyton loosens his hand so she slips down an inch. She screams and grabs at his chest. But I have my eyes open, so I can see that his bicep is still firmly around her waist.

"Don't do that ever again!" Jinx yells at him when we land on a smooth white dock. She pushes him away and runs over to the baku.

"I was only kidding around," Peyton says, smiling.

"Yeah, and I thought monkeys enjoy swinging through the air," I add.

"You two are children." Jinx sniffs, patting the baku's head. The creature bleats nervously. "Come on, let's get this over with already."

Jinx walks to a set of steep white stairs. It goes up five flights or so to what looks like a medieval Japanese fortress, with swooping rooflines and stone walls, only it's all white. I hope nobody pours boiling oil over the walls to keep us out. I glance back over the stair railing once and immediately regret it—the earth's looking awfully far away.

We don't have time to gawk at our surroundings, because the baku is hurtling up the stairs at top speed. We just follow, our legs and arms pumping, until we reach the fortress's outer wall and its gate, jaws of white wrought iron thirty feet high. Fortunately, the gate is open.

We stop and stand to the left, where we can't be seen by anyone inside the fortress. I look around. The earth (or ground, I guess—should I call it *moon*?) is white, too, like powdered sugar. Grass and low bushes grow here and there, everything looking like it's been coated in a thick layer of white paint.

A figure comes through the fortress opening. It's a man, his skin, hair, and clothes as white as marshmallows, too. He's pushing a huge wheelbarrow full of white flowers that ripple like seaweed in water.

I creep up to the gate opening and peer inside. There's a large town square with a fountain in the middle spouting white water. People are going about their day, pushing wheelbarrows or leading horse-drawn wagons over the cobblestones, chasing screaming children, setting up stalls to sell their goods. It all looks totally normal, except there are no cars and, of course, everything and everyone is the color of chalk.

I wonder if they're actual people, or some kind of dream figments. Well, even if they're not real, I don't want to stand out. The baku bleats at us nervously and starts moving inside, but I hold up my hand. "Wait. We don't know what's in there. Or who. We should sneak in."

"How can we possibly pass when the people are all washed out?" Jinx whispers. "We'd stick out like flies on rice."

"Not to mention the fact that some of us have wings." Peyton peers in over our heads.

They're being such naysayers. "Let's figure it out." I examine the ground again, the powdery substance that's apparently moon dirt, then pick up a handful and rub it over my hand. It covers my skin like face powder. Inspired, I rub it all over me, in my hair, on my face, over my clothes. "How do I look?"

"Like you've got sunblock all over your face." Peyton scoops up some moon dirt. "You missed a spot." He slaps it directly over my eyes and nose.

I cough. "Thanks a lot."

"I couldn't let you leave your eyelids exposed," Peyton says practically.

"It looks lame." Jinx shakes her head, her eyes narrowing. "This is never going to work."

I put my hands on my hips. "I'm open to other ideas."

She sighs, then grabs some dirt and covers herself, too.

"That stuff's not exactly going to solve my problem." Peyton flexes his wings.

He's right. I peer into the fortress again. A man has abandoned his wheelbarrow full of fruit to run after a small white chicken. Perfect! "Wait here," I whisper.

Before anyone can say anything, I dash over to the wheelbarrow and take its handles. Quickly, I push it over to Peyton.

"What're we doing with that?" Jinx picks up a star fruit and sniffs it. "Mmm. Smells like celery."

I start digging a well in the pile of fruit. "Peyton, you're going to hide in here."

Peyton rubs his hands together. "A plan. I like it." He folds his wings flat against his back and contorts his body to burrow under the star fruit. We toss the rest on top of him until he's completely covered. We stick our backpacks and my sword and helmet in there, too. This will put me at a disadvantage, but what else am I supposed to do? With them, I'd be more out of place than a shark in a koi pond. The white stuff won't stick to the metal, and nobody else here has a gleaming weapon. "You okay?" I ask Peyton.

His hand shoots out from the fruit. Thumbs up.

Then Jinx picks up the handles and with a grunt, lifts the wheelbarrow. The baku sighs in relief, walking straight in. We follow, trying to look as casual as possible. I wonder if the baku's going to stick out—she's not powdery white—but the townspeople don't give her a second look.

Beyond the fountain is a large, official-looking, fancy building with a curved roof. I assume this is the princess's palace. The baku makes a beeline toward it.

We pass through the crowds unnoticed. I try not to look anyone in the face, and I also try not to be obvious about not looking anyone in the face. That would also be suspicious. The people chatter away in a language I don't understand. It sounds like *"Glibbedty gibbety gob,"* and I really hope nobody strikes up a conversation with me. "Do you know what they're saying?" I whisper to Jinx.

"No," Jinx says, panting a little. "It's all I can do to schlep this heavy thing."

"I heard that," Peyton says from under the fruit.

"Shut up, guys," I hiss. I take one of the wheelbarrow handles to help Jinx.

Finally, we reach the palace and stop. Fifteen wide stone steps lead up to its front gate.

"Think there's a delivery entrance around back?" I ask Jinx.

"I don't know, and I'm not going to bother to look," she says. "Let's just get this over with."

"Okay," I say, "but this isn't going to be easy. . . ."

I lift the front of the wheelbarrow, and Jinx lifts the back. *Whomp.* *Whomp. Whomp.* It comes down hard on every step. We carefully make our way up. Sweat breaks out on my forehead, and I feel the white dirt streaming down my face. Great. By the time we get all the way up, I'll probably be Xander-colored again.

The palace gates, more white wrought iron, are flanked by twenty-foot-tall white columns topped with ornate carvings of white dragons. When we arrive there, I hesitate, expecting to find guards, but no one is around, and the gates are unlocked.

We push the gate open and enter a courtyard. A single wishing well sits off to the side, along with some white bonsai trees and a white stone bench. Tall sliding doors surround us, as though every room in the palace opens up to this outdoor space. Above those are arched windows with no glass in them. The openings look big enough for Peyton to squeeze through.

It's completely silent and deserted. I've never been in a palace before, but shouldn't there always be people hanging around doing stuff?

My skin prickles. I may not have Momotaro power anymore, but I still have natural instincts. "Something isn't right," I mutter.

The baku presses herself against the wall, her eyes rolling back so the whites show. *Behh,* she bleats. She's scared.

I squat. "Peyton," I say into the star fruit, "we're going to leave you here. I want you to wait, like, five minutes. Then get out and fly into one of the windows. Got it?"

Again his hand appears, this time proffering my sword. I grab the hilt. I'll take that as a yes.

I square my shoulders. "Take us inside, Baku."

CHAPTER THIRTY-FIVE

The baku's breath comes hot and fast on my arms as we creep through the courtyard. *Huuuuu huuuuu huuuu,* she sounds.

"If anything happens, take the baku and run," I whisper to Jinx. No sense in her getting hurt.

Jinx nods, her expression grim, her eyes narrowed. "Act normal." She straightens her shoulders and walks toward the front door of the palace.

How do we know what normal is for people who live on the moon? I want to ask her.

We get to the wishing well, the wall surrounding it about four feet high and made of marble slabs. Above the opening, a large white metal bucket dangles from a rope and a crank. Standing guard on the ledge is a gold dragon statue, with faceted diamond-like eyes.

It's the only non-white thing, besides the baku, in the whole place. Which makes it suspicious. I grip my sword tighter, waiting for the dragon to spring to life.

"Xander!" I hear a voice coming from deep inside the well. "Xander, help me!"

Kaguya? I lean over and peer into the water.

Nothing but my reflection, fifteen feet down. "Princess?" I say as quietly as I can, wondering if her face will poke up through the liquid.

No answer.

As I straighten, something about the size of a large cat falls off the roof onto my head, scratching my scalp. I see a flash of red—a tail? Not wanting to decapitate myself, I drop my sword and reach up with both hands to grab the creature. The oni scorpion! It bites my fingers with its disgusting human teeth, and I punch it, accidentally knocking myself in the skull. "Get off me!"

Then Jinx is there, swiping it off me and stabbing it with her dagger. Yellow blood spurts out, sizzling as it lands on the marble well.

Hissing, the scorpion smacks her in the chest with its stinger, like a battering ram. She's flung backward to the well, and she tips over the side headfirst.

Splash!

"No! Jinx!" I yell, but the scorpion stings me, right in the spine, and suddenly I can't move. Its human face licks its lips, moving its head back and forth as if deciding how it's going to eat me. "Well!" I manage to get out, for Peyton's benefit. I hope he hears me. But maybe he'll just think we're well.

I hear the creaking of a wheelbarrow nearby. Is it Peyton? No. As the scorpion drags me by the collar across the courtyard, I catch sight of a little black imp pushing the cart. The imp looks like a reddish-black monkey with leathery scales and short wings. It's skipping along and singing as it goes, revealing sharp fangs.

The scorpion keeps a tight grip on me with its claw. Luckily I'm so numb I can't feel a thing. Finally, it flings me into a room inside the palace, and I hear it scuttle off. Guess I'm not on the menu after all—for now, at least.

My cheek's lying on a piece of marble so clean Obāchan would approve of my eating off of it. I look around—with my eyeballs only, since the rest of me can't move. A shiny white throne perches atop a platform, with five steps leading up to it.

On this throne sits a man I've never seen before. He's cradling the baku, who hangs in his arms as limply a rag doll, her eyes darting around in terror as the man pets her.

This man looks to be well over six feet tall, with broad shoulders, muscular arms, and the erect posture of a dancer. His black hair shines, and his skin is prettier than my mom's when she has on makeup. With his luminous blue eyes, black open-collared shirt, and tight black jeans, he looks like he stepped off the cover of one of Obāchan's romance novels.

There's nothing overtly evil about his appearance—he's not snorting fire or dripping slime or anything—but when I look at him, I feel like I'm staring into a black hole in outer space, something that will rip me apart from the inside. His gaze is as blank as an empty computer screen.

"At least you're perceptive." The man's sonorous tone rings out across the room, a pleasant baritone, like a radio announcer. He gently moves the baku to an armrest, then crosses his legs languidly and balances a tall silver scepter in the middle of his palm as though he's doing some circus act. "Which is more than I can say for your predecessors." He circles his palm around, his eyes never leaving mine.

Who is he? The king of the moon? That seems wrong. "Where is she?" I croak hoarsely. "Just let the princess go, and I'll be on my way."

"Oh, Momotaro-chan." The man chuckles. Now I see that what he's balancing on his hand is not a scepter at all, but a sword.

My sword.

I swallow. This is not boding well for me. "Who are you?" I ask, but I don't have to. I already know.

The oni king, Ozuno.

At the thought of his name, I feel a quick surge of excitement, as though I've just won a really difficult video game. But the emotion feels wrong, like it did when I was happy about tripping my mother.

Ozuno laughs again, as though he's reading my thoughts. "Like

I said, perceptive. Better than the last Momotaro, who was so weak he was hardly worth challenging."

Is he talking about my father? The excitement fizzles out.

Ozuno puts my sword down on the floor and crosses the room, reaching my head in two quick steps. He leaves the baku on the throne, as still as a statue.

"Baku," I whisper, hoping she's okay. I think I see her blink.

"Don't worry about that creature." Ozuno squats next to me, regarding my face intently. Like how my mother looked at me when she got home. I shudder. He brushes the hair off my forehead, the way Dad might, but this feels like cockroaches are scuttling over my scalp. I want to scream, to run, but I can't. "Precious one," he says softly. "Dear one. I'm so glad you chose to come here."

I jerk my head away. "Stop."

"Relax, Xander. See? I lifted some of your paralysis. I'm your friend." He takes my hand in his, which is as soft and smooth as a leather glove, and helps me sit up.

I force myself to meet his dead eyes. "I'm here to rescue the princess, not because I want to hang out with you."

A thought occurs to me. The baku led me here. Maybe she's in on this. Maybe the princess is actually evil, too.

The king chuckles, leaning back so hard that he almost falls over. "It's so cute that you think you can rescue Kaguya on your own, without your powers. Against me."

My lips burn. "Well, you know how crazy we Momotaro are. You've never won yet, have you?"

A flash of real anger passes over his face, but he quickly suppresses it. "This is true. But you're here to remedy that."

Uh-oh.

A muffled sound comes from under the throne. A pair of frightened eyes peers at me from under the foot.

The princess.

I look back at Ozuno, who is studying my face with the same kind of amused expression I have when Inu's trying to work a piece of meat out of his treat puzzle. "An agreement," Ozuno says. "I help you, and you help me."

Ha. That's a laugh. "I'll never help you."

"Really, Xander?" Ozuno presses his lips together in a pout. "Why, you don't even know me. How can you judge?" He leans forward. "I help you, you help me. Simple." His breath is surprisingly minty fresh. His teeth are so perfect they look fake. "I have your dreams. I have *everyone's* dreams, in fact, because I have the princess." He speaks in the tone of a parent soothing a wailing baby.

"Then why do you need me?" I tense in anticipation of his answer.

"I need you to be my little soldier, Xander." He smiles at me, the sides of his eyes crinkling. "I'll give you your dreams back. Your powers will be restored. I've seen how well you use them. I won't constrain you, like your old father did."

Old father?

I recall the drawing I made before we left, the one with me cowering while my father crawled to his doom, and my grandfather dead. "That's not true!" I say aloud to chase the memory away.

Ozuno smiles again, but it is terrible this time, and I feel my soul shrink like a snail sprinkled with salt. "Your subconscious never lies, Xander. That drawing only revealed what you already knew deep down."

I want to shove him away, but instead I manage a mere whimper. I *am* turning into that stupid drawing, defeated and sad.

All I want is to go home. I should have gone when I had the chance.

"No." Ozuno ruffles my hair. "I always wanted my very own Momotaro, who would work *with* me instead of against me. Think of all we could accomplish together. Can you imagine?"

The palace around us fades, and suddenly we are standing on a stage. There's a microphone in front of me. Thousands of screaming fans are cheering my name. I'm holding an electric guitar, and to my surprise, I know how to play it. A thrill rushes through me, hot and sharp. My heart pounds.

I turn to look at the musicians behind me. Peyton's on bass; Jinx is on keyboard. Ozuno sits behind the drum kit, grinning. "You'd like this, wouldn't you? Fame and fortune. Together with your friends, for always."

"You're crazy!" I yell, barely able to hear myself above the screaming fans. "I don't even care about music that much."

"Then how about this?" He snaps his fingers, and I'm in a luxury jet, strapped into a soft leather seat, the engine humming outside the window. Which is the only way I know it's an airplane because I'm sitting in a conference room, complete with a shiny wooden table. I look down.

On the carpet is a seal that says THE PRESIDENT OF THE UNITED STATES.

The chair next to me swivels. "Welcome to Air Force One." Ozuno steeples his fingers. "You're the leader of the free world. Think of all the good you could do, Xander."

That oh-so-happy feeling returns, swallowing me whole like an enormous but very comfortable boa constrictor. I gulp, trying to fight the sensation. It's hard. Imagine that you're starving and someone offers you your favorite food, but you have to say no.

I shut my eyes. "No!" I shout as loud as I can. "Who wants to be a politician, anyway? Being the president is way too much responsibility."

"Or this." Ozuno claps three times fast.

Now I'm behind a skirted table in a cavernous convention center. In front of me is a line that snakes the length of a football field. People are holding stacks of comic books. "It's him!" one especially pretty girl exclaims. "I can't believe it!"

I have a pen in my hand. A comic book lies on the table in front of me. *By Xander Miyamoto* it reads. I turn around. Lined up on a shelf behind me are action figures based on characters I've drawn. A big banner above it proclaims MIYAMOTO UNIVERSE. There's a map of an amusement park with rides based on my stories, and my grinning picture is plastered all over the place—I see one ride called "Xander Rockets." I turn back around to the crowd standing in front of me.

I'm at Comic-Con, and apparently I'm a cross between Stan Lee and Walt Disney.

And then Clarissa, the girl from school, comes up to the table, smiling shyly. She's older now—in college at least—and she's looking at me in a way that makes me blush and feel really, really awkward inside. "Hi, Xander," she says softly. "I always knew you were talented."

I smile and nod. My vocal cords won't work.

"Think of all you could skip," Clarissa says in her sweetest voice. "All your lame middle school years. High school, where you'll only get bullied more. You could come directly here. Pass Go. Collect . . . millions of dollars." The corners of her mouth turn up. "You could have everything right now, Xander." She touches my face, and it feels like a small, pleasant electric shock.

Don't say no! my gut yells. *Say yes! It'll be so much easier. You'll never have to see Mr. Stedman or Lovey again.*

And my mouth opens, my tongue in the yes position.

CHAPTER THIRTY-SIX

The word yes starts to leave my mouth. But then I think of Kaguya, shivering with fear under the throne, and the baku, petrified on top. I picture Jinx—is she okay, in that well?—and Peyton and my family. What would happen if I suddenly skipped ahead ten years? Would my ancient grandmother be gone, never knowing what had happened to me? My father would be left with no one to carry on his family line (even if I couldn't be Momotaro). I would have abandoned my mother, like she abandoned me.

Clarissa touches my hand softly. "Are you worried about Peyton? Don't be. You don't have to be artists together like he wanted. You can be the best, all by yourself." She waves vaguely toward something off to my side.

I see Peyton standing there, his posture hunched and defeated. His proud plume of bird hair is gone. His eyes have bags under them, and his skin is sallow. He doesn't look much better than he did after he lost all his dreams.

What? Why would I want Peyton to end up like that? What's wrong with her? I jerk my face away, forcing myself to look directly into Clarissa's eyes. "I don't want Peyton to fail."

She blinks at me. "You should. It's the only way to be number one. To kill the dreams of your best competitors."

I blink back at her, thinking of what Kintaro told me. "More than one person can be good at something at the same time, Clarissa." I crook my finger at Peyton. "Come here!" He never looks toward my table, just at his large feet clad in dirty sneakers. I turn back to Clarissa and realize, finally, who she really is.

I stare unblinkingly into those impossibly blue eyes. "No," I say firmly. "No, Ozuno."

Clarissa melts away and Ozuno stands in her place, still smiling. Ew. I can't believe I almost fell for that.

Ozuno nods, looking halfway impressed. "Let me put it another way." Pain lances through my skull as if he's struck me with an anvil. I fall to my knees, shuddering uncontrollably, my teeth chattering. He leans into my face. "You help me, and the pain will stop. If you don't help me, the pain will be constant, every second of every day for the rest of your long, miserable life. And I'll make sure you live to be a very, very old man." Abruptly, the agony cuts off.

Tears stream out of my eyes, and I can't help but sob. I hear the princess making stifled sobs in return.

Ozuno shakes his head. "Oh, princesses. When will they ever learn that their princes can never rescue them?" He wipes the tears from my face with a finger that no longer feels soft, but instead like a splintery board being wiped across my cheek. "There's nothing to be sad about, Xander. There is only joy." He sits and gathers me against his chest. I can't move or resist. "Why not embrace that joy you felt when you used your powers all the time? It's not wrong to feel good."

"It is when you're on the dark side," I spit through gritted teeth.

Ozuno laughs again, rocking me as though I'm an injured little kid, but crushing the breath out of me. "*Dark side?* This isn't a movie; this is real. Can't you see? The oni are already winning. All your wars. Your diseases. Your disasters. You already live in the dark side." Ozuno releases me. "If you join me, Xander, we can conquer the world much more easily. There will be less suffering because people will accept the natural order of things."

I am desperate to push him away, to jump up and retrieve my sword. But I still can't do more than sit and move my neck. I'm completely helpless.

Ozuno pats me on the head. "I'm being nice, giving you a choice. Like a father lets a toddler choose between doing what his daddy says or getting a spanking."

"You might be a good parent—to Hitler." My body shakes

uncontrollably, as if I'm having a weird seizure. Hives rise up all over my skin, hot and round and incredibly itchy. My back sweats while my front goes freezer-cold.

"All these centuries of fighting your family line, and all I really wanted was to be a father. I never realized it until now." He laughs, then breaks into the song those severed-head people were singing around the campfire. "*Momotaro-chan, Momotaro-chan.* You'll be my son, Xander."

Laserlike pain laces through me, convulsing my body into helpless pile of bones.

"*Momotaro-chan, Momotaro-chan,*" he sings.

And he sings. And sings. And sings.

The pain is intolerable. I'll tell him anything. I'll do anything, if only he'll stop singing. I'll be your Momotaro, I'm ready to say, I'll do it, just let me go, just make this stop. . . .

And then the door slides open, and Jinx stands there, holding the imp in one hand, her dagger in the other.

CHAPTER THIRTY-SEVEN

"Release him," Jinx commands. "Or your little buddy gets it."

The imp whimpers and chatters in its oni language. Then it hisses, baring what can only be super-poisonous teeth. It struggles in her hand but can't get out of Jinx's iron grip.

Ozuno stops singing. All is silent for a moment.

Then he laughs like he's at a world-class comedy show. I mean, he laughs so hard that his face turns red and he can't even make a sound, just pounds his kneecap with his palm.

She lifts the imp higher. "What's so funny?"

"Jinx, Jinx, Jinx," Ozuno says reproachfully, when he manages to speak again. "I can't believe that you, a half-oni, would believe that I would care about the fate of one imp. I am disappointed."

She drops the imp and it scurries away, passing directly by my nose. It smells like dog poop, and it giggles as I cringe. The imp scrambles up Ozuno's arm and perches there on his shoulder, waiting.

And Jinx—she seems to be frozen in place, her arm still outstretched, her mouth contorted, her hand gripping an invisible monster. All the color bleeds out of her face, and her skin turns purple then blue, as if something's choking the air out of her.

"Jinx!" I shout.

Without warning, Peyton zooms through a window opening. He throws a handful of salt at Ozuno, who screams when it touches him. It burns him, and he melts into a puddle. The imp shrivels into nothingness.

Immediately, I'm free of pain and paralysis. I know Ozuno's not going to stay melted for long—already the puddle's starting to lump up as if he's reconfiguring himself. I leap forward to Jinx. She's still stunned. Why isn't she released, too?

Peyton reaches under the throne and picks up my helmet. "Did you lose this, Xander?" He tosses it to me. I snag it out of the air and put it on. It feels right on my head.

He drags the princess out from underneath the throne by her feet. Her body's hog-tied by Fudō-Myōō's rope. No wonder she couldn't move.

Peyton unwinds the rope. "Are you okay, lady?"

She sits up, looking dazed, and shakes her head. "Of course I'm not okay—I was just tied up and shoved underneath my own throne!" She wipes at her mouth. "Ugh. It's dusty under there."

"Peyton!" I call, still trying to budge Jinx. "A little help!"

But just then the scorpion, hissing out of its human mouth, scurries out from its hiding place and leaps at the princess and Peyton, swinging its stinger in the air. This time it's the baku who jumps forward, tusks flashing, and skewers the bug right through the middle. Apparently those tusks are not just for show. The scorpion squeals as yellow acid sprays out of it. The princess grabs Peyton and shoves him away from the goop. The stuff makes a crater in the floor, sizzling it and the giant bug away like a flame-eating paper.

Peyton swoops over to me and Jinx, my sword in his hand. I take it from him and Peyton touches her shoulder. "Oh no." He wraps his arms around her and tries to lift. "She's stone cold! Literally, for a change."

"She's just stunned," I say with way more confidence than I actually feel.

A foot kicks me square in the back, and suddenly I'm on the floor.

Ozuno is already reconstituted. "Birds," he says in a voice laced with disdain. "Not the apex predator." He snaps his fingers, and out of the marble floor leaps a tiger. It's way bigger than an ordinary one—it's more like an Ice Age saber-toothed tiger, the size of a rhino, with long fangs and wild yellow eyes. It growls at Peyton.

He takes off, flying over the tiger's head. It swipes at him with its claws, sending a spray of feathers over me. Peyton makes it up to the window ledge. "Xander!" he calls helplessly. "Shoo, kitty!" The giant cat paces beneath him, growling and chuffing. It leaps up and is almost able to reach him.

The princess takes the opportunity to jump onto Ozuno's back, wrapping her pearl necklace around his throat. His eyes bulge as she twists the strand. "Bind me up in my own home, will you?" She twists harder. His tongue sticks out as his face turns red.

"You look just like a dime-store oni mask!" I leap forward, my sword in hand, and run him through the abdomen.

Or I try to run him through the abdomen. It's about as effective as sticking a toothpick into a piece of hardwood. Ozuno smiles down at me, his eyes still bulging.

I kick him in the side of the knee instead.

He flops onto the ground. The necklace breaks, and pearls scatter everywhere. The princess falls backward. "Ahhhh!" she cries, landing headfirst with a sickening crack. Before I can make another move, Ozuno is on his feet. The princess lies motionless.

"Kaguya!" I move toward her, but Ozuno sweep-kicks my shins, and I fall flat on my face, my sword spinning away. He pins me to the marble floor with his huge and presumably stinky foot. "What are you wearing, stilettos?" I gasp.

He snorts. "See how you amuse me, young Xander?"

Before I can take another shallow breath so I can issue a retort, I hear a *whoosh* like a gas BBQ getting turned on, only times one hundred. The tiger yowls, and I see it running out of the throne room, its back aflame. What on earth . . . ?

Then there's another *whoosh*, and heat surrounds me. I press myself down into the marble. The helmet—the helmet's protecting me from the fire. Something's blazing, smelling of burning coal and melting plastic. Where's it coming from?

"Get your gross foot off my friend!" Jinx yells, and suddenly the pressure on my back is released. I roll away.

Jinx plunges her knife into Ozuno's neck with her right hand. Out of her left hand a white flame shoots straight at him.

He screams in rage, the sound like a hundred squawking birds and a building falling down and a fifteen-car highway accident combined into one bone-shattering noise.

All I can do is stare in awe. Holy pyrokinesis, Batman! What the heck?

Engulfed by fire, Ozuno's form drops. The flame subsides, and there's a pile of dark ash where the oni was.

Kaguya stands in the doorway to the courtyard, swaying slightly, holding the baku in her arms. Blood runs down the side of her face. "Hurry! Get out while you can! I'll carry on from here."

"Really? Like you did before?"

She sends me a look so fierce that I blanch. "I never make the same mistake twice."

Like tiny Lego blocks employed by an invisible builder, the ash on the floor begins to take on a shape. I groan. Not again.

The baku bleats and tries to squirm out of Kaguya's arms. "Xander! If you insist on staying, then hurry up and do something!" the princess says.

"Like what? I can't do anything. *You* do something. You're the one with the dreams."

What we really need is a way to contain Ozuno so we can get away. Like a soap bubble, only solid.

Wait. Did I just imagine something?

"Maybe I can," I whisper.

"No maybes!" The baku succeeds in freeing herself, and she starts running in panicked circles around the throne room. Kaguya turns to me. "What does your heart tell you?"

My heart? *Words are sounds of the heart.* What does that mean, really?

I recall every not-nice thing I said to my mom when she got back and how deeply that hurt her. Every mean quip Lovey's ever thrown at me.

And I remember good things, too. The way Jinx's face lit up when my dad told her she was smart, and how she read even more warrior books after that. Peyton's constant coaching, always telling me I can do things I think I can't, like the time we biked up a steep hill—his cheers were invisible forces that somehow pushed me to the top.

Words do have power.

I look at Kaguya. She waits expectantly, her eyes wide, her mouth slightly open.

"I can do it," I say aloud. "I can imagine things."

In that moment, a bubble appears, iridescent in the white light. Inside it, Ozuno's ash rises, then deflates, as if it needed oxygen to complete the rejuvenation.

"Yesss!" I yell. I move to Kaguya, who stands watching me with a smile, despite her messed-up head. "Did you let me? Do I . . . ?" I'm afraid to say the words aloud. Do I have my powers back?

Kaguya smiles. "Xander. At first I thought you were unworthy, a greedy little boy."

I can't help but make a face.

"But then you sacrificed all your powers to help your family and friends. I realized I had misjudged you." She picks up my hand in hers. "So I restored your dreams, too."

That explains why Peyton has wings. "But when I tried using my powers before, I couldn't. . . ."

She squeezes my hand. "Only because you told yourself you could not. The power of words, Xander. What you tell yourself is just as important as what you can do. You needed to understand that."

I nod and squeeze her hand, my throat closing up. "Thank you."

She lets go. "I have to calm down the baku." She moves past me.

"Hey, you." It's Jinx, sidling up to me, grinning from ear to ear. "Maybe now's not the best time for a date. Even if she is a princess."

"Whatever." I guess I deserve this, after teasing her about Kintaro. I change the subject. "That fireball? That was awesome. How'd you do it?"

Jinx holds out her hand, palm up, and a ball of fire appears just above it. "I don't know. It just sort of flicked on when I got frozen. Like a reaction, like a doctor poking at your knee to make it jerk."

"Wow." I stare at the white blaze. "You know, maybe it has to do with that flame the Angry Lord of Light gave you."

"Could be." She closes her fingers around the fireball, extinguishing it. "However I got it, it's mighty handy."

"And here you were, complaining you didn't have a power." I punch her softly in the shoulder.

"Right now I'm just worried about getting out of here." Jinx looks at the oni king's remains and shakes her head. "Who knows how long that bubble will hold him?"

"Guys!" Peyton shouts from the window ledge. He points outside. "We have a problem."

Now I can hear people shouting and yelling near the palace. Over that is a strange cackling sound. With mounting dread, I see that the formerly white sky is dark with creatures. Oni are swarming the courtyard.

My heart drops. Even with my powers back, how can I defeat all of them? I pick up my sword from where it skittered away. I've got to protect the princess.

There's one simple thing I can do for her. I run to the door, take the beans from Kintaro's house out of my pocket, and sprinkle them along the edge of the frame.

Kaguya materializes next to me, the baku safe in her arms again. "Xander . . . that won't hold them off for long."

"But it'll help a little," I say. "Until we figure out what to do."

The princess considers the oni-king bubble. Ozuno is slowly rising, re-forming into a dark shadow of a man. Then she looks out at the oni in the courtyard. "This isn't good."

"Understatement of the year," I mutter.

She races to the far side of the throne room and grabs what I thought was a decorative piece on the wall—a long white pole. At one end is a two-foot-long blade. Kaguya spins the weapon around like a vengeful baton twirler. "Naginata." She holds it out to let me examine it. "I can strike at a distance with this."

"Cool." I try not to sound too impressed, which is hard because she looks very Bruce Lee with it.

She sticks two fingers in her mouth and whistles louder than a football ref. Two short blasts, one long. "Battle signal," Kaguya replies to my questioning glance. "Now my soldiers will know this is not a drill." She gives the pole another twirl. "I can buy us a little time until they come."

Peyton flies down. "There's no way for us to escape on foot," he says. He glances at the sinuous shapes looping through the sky, cawing and roaring. "And maybe not even on wings."

I cast about the throne room for anything else that could help us. Why doesn't this palace have cannons? But there's nothing. The room's basically a big box with only one door, leading to the courtyard.

"We're sitting ducks in here," I say to Kaguya. "Let's go. We'll figure something out along the way!" I gesture at the door.

But the princess shakes her head. She takes a seat on the throne, her weapon in one hand, the baku in the other. She stares sightlessly at the oni gathering outside. "No, Momotaro. I will remain here."

"But you can't!" I point to the courtyard. "Those things will tear you apart! Come on!"

The baku bleats mournfully, her eyes downturned.

Kaguya shakes her head. "No. I will not leave Yumenushi-kyo. I will die with my people."

I recognize the name Yumenushi-kyo: the City of Dreams. This reminds me that her people manufacture the dreams of everyone on earth. Oh jeez. There's even more at stake.

"I understand," I say to her, shrugging helplessly.

The princess beckons me to her. I climb the steps to the throne. She gestures again, as if she wants to tell me a secret, and puts her hand on my forehead. "There is one last thing for you to discover."

"What?" I whisper.

The princess continues, her breath on my face. "You have great untapped power."

"I do? How do I tap it?" She smells like fresh milk and lavender. Her hand grows warm, or maybe my forehead's making it heat up.

"The Angry Lord of Light."

"What about him?" The Angry Lord of Light. What did he teach me? To use my emotions. To conquer my enemies without touching them.

Her hand grows hot. A shudder moves through my body, from my forehead down to my feet. I lose my balance and grab the throne's arm to steady myself.

The princess meets my gaze with her dark eyes, as if willing me to understand how to interpret this.

I straighten, noticing a strange sort of zinging energy moving through my body. Like I was just mildly electrocuted. "What did you do?"

"Nothing."

Jinx gasps.

"What?" I turn to her.

Peyton points to my face. "Dude, your eyes—they're all white. Can you see?"

"Really?" I blink. "Yeah, I can see."

Jinx steps forward. "Your eyes look like my fireballs." She holds out her hand and creates a flame to demonstrate.

I do a quick assessment of my body. "Everything feels perfectly fine." Well, maybe a little amped up . . . My heart is hammering like I've just raced three Ironmans and downed ten Red Bulls. A sensation of readiness pulses through me, as though I'm on the starting line of a race, waiting for the starting whistle.

Peyton swoops up to the ceiling again. "Well, we're not going to be perfectly fine in about thirty seconds, Xander. You have to do something."

I jump down from the throne and face the courtyard packed with oni.

CHAPTER THIRTY-EIGHT

Turns out I have less than thirty seconds.

A bird glides into the window above us. I recognize it instantly as an *itsumade*. Who could forget? First of all, it goes around cawing, *"Itsumade,"* its very own name. Second, I've fought this kind of oni before. They're nasty, fire-breathing killers.

Peyton meets it in midair, dodging the stream of fire it blasts at him. Jinx stands directly under it and shoots a streak of flame up from her palm. She misses, and the bird flies toward the princess.

Kaguya stands on the throne, the naginata in both hands. As the creature comes close, she leaps through the air and swings the weapon in a fast arc. The itsumade's head rolls across the room.

I guess the princess can take care of herself pretty well.

I check the bubble to see if Ozuno's fully re-formed.

The bubble's still there, as solid as ever, but it's . . . empty.

Where did Ozuno go? I can only hope he returned to the underworld and isn't hiding somewhere nearby.

That's it!

The underworld. I know what needs to happen.

The oni are piling up behind the line of fuku mame beans. They're in the perfect position.

To my utter surprise, my pulse slows. I raise my arms as if I've done this a million times before.

They're glowing.

I'm a beacon. A protector of the land.

The shrieking stops as the oni pause in their creation of mayhem. They turn as one to stare at me.

Gulp. This is not exactly what I had in mind.

Again as one, they abandon whatever they had their claws on and come at me instead. The cacophony resumes.

I extend my arms out to the side, and their glow becomes brighter still. I'm acutely aware of every sound: Jinx and Peyton shouting, the oni grunting eagerly, the baku panting nervously, and the princess breathing steadily. Underneath my feet, I feel the hum of the moon's energy. My mind clears, and I remember what the good ol' Angry Lord of Light showed me. How I could send my good or bad stuff out into the world.

Snarling, hissing, and growling, the oni swarm at the doorway like poisonous red ants climbing up a honey-covered piece of meat.

I imagine them all going to the underworld. Ozuno, too.

Then I inhale deeply. When I exhale, I push all my energy outward.

It explodes like a silent firecracker and looks like the birth of a tiny sun.

I stagger backward, blinded as if a million paparazzi had just taken my photo. The silence is deafening.

"Jinx? Peyton?" I yell, turning around and around, my arms groping the air. I'm relieved I can hear my voice.

"Here!" they call, stepping out from behind the throne, Baku in between them. All three of them have black halos.

"Are the oni gone?" I ask.

"Every last one," says Jinx. "And there's no sign of Ozuno anywhere."

I sink to my knees, feeling like I've stayed up for two nights and three days. All I want to do is sleep.

"That was awesome!" Peyton pats me on the back. "Light was shooting out from every pore of your body! Man, you should have seen yourself! It was like a crazy laser show!"

I manage a weak smile. My vision clears. "So I guess that's what I inherited from my mother. That, and her pointy chin." I flex my arms, which are no longer glowing. I try to will the light to come back, but nothing happens. Maybe I need to recharge, or maybe I have to do something else to make it work. I'll experiment later. Carefully.

I look around the room. "Where's the princess?"

Jinx shakes her head. "She disappeared."

"Disappeared?" I repeat. Oh man, I hope I didn't send her to the underworld, too. I go over to the throne, where I last saw her.

Something gleams from the seat. A silver-white chain, with a pearl the size of a large gumdrop attached. I pick it up.

The pearl is not perfectly round, and it's a deep gray-black color on one side, and a pinkish cream on the other. Like the light and dark sides of the moon. A decorative silver piece anchors the pearl to the chain.

"Looks like she likes you back," Jinx observes.

"It's not like that." I put the necklace around my neck, sticking the pearl under my shirt, where it thumps comfortingly against my heart. "She wanted me to have a souvenir is all."

"Yeah. Because she likes you." Peyton caws his laughter.

"You guys don't get it. She's like Kintaro—ancient." I sink into the throne. Suddenly all the adrenaline and energy drain out of me. Maybe doing that thing with my eyes sapped every spare calorie I had. I close my eyelids, my legs feeling like useless rubber.

"Come on." Jinx pulls me up. "You can sleep when you're dead."

"I can carry you if you want," Peyton offers. "Both of you."

Reluctantly, I stand. I take one last look around the throne room to make sure we have everything. I have my sword and helmet; I pick up Fudō's rope and attach it to my belt. The baku jumps up on the throne and bleats, as if she's reassuring me she'll be all right here in the palace. I wish I knew where Kaguya went, and whether she's safe.

"Let's go home," says Peyton.

"You got it, buddy," I say. "There's just one little thing I need to do first."

CHAPTER THIRTY-NINE

Peyton picks up Jinx and me, and we soar directly from the palace window ledge into a silvery cloudy space, where no land at all is visible beneath us.

I look back, and I can already see the moon, like some kind of giant Christmas ornament, getting smaller and smaller as we drop away.

"Hold up for a sec, Peyton," I say.

He hovers, beating his huge wings up and down. Jinx looks at me strangely.

"This won't take long," I say.

I close my eyes and picture the moon covered in Bubble Wrap, a kind that only Princess Kaguya can undo. There, that should protect them. I just hope it lasts until she gets back. If she gets back . . .

"Okay, I'm ready to keep going now," I tell Peyton, who looks amazed by what I just did. And could that actually be admiration on Jinx's face?

He swoops down through the clouds. When we clear them, there's a forest below us, with a welcoming red torii.

We land hard on the ground and run through the gate without stopping. It doesn't hurt this time. "We're alive!" I shout. "We're alive!" We all break out in crazy laughter.

Some passing hikers shake their heads at our rowdiness. "You kids better not litter," the older lady in the group chides us.

At the waterfall, we skid to a halt. Peyton pats his back. "My wings are gone," he says regretfully. "Guess that means we're back in the real world." Then he pats his front. "But I still have all my organs, so that's something."

"Being intact is definitely a bonus." I raise my fist, and he bumps it.

Jinx rolls her eyes. "The bromance is also intact, I see."

"Come on, Jinxie." I raise my fist for her. "I've got one for you, too."

"*Jinxie?*" Reluctantly, she bumps fists with me, then Peyton. She wipes her eyes, looking back toward the gate. "Do you think the princess is okay?"

We all go silent for a moment. "I don't know," I say at last, my stomach twinging. By taking my dreams, Kaguya showed me what nobody else could—that I really do want to be Momotaro. I won't be abusing my powers anymore. "But did you see how she handled that naginata? I think she'll be all right."

I'll talk to Dad about her when we get home. I just hope I won't have to go on a quest to find her. Not for a while, at least. I still have a lot of training to do.

I put my hand on Jinx's shoulder. "Can you still make fire?"

Jinx holds out her palm. A flame shoots up, three feet high. "Whoops! Didn't mean to make it so big." It sizzles out.

"Cool." I recall what Ojīchan said to me about powers coming through different people. "I guess Fudō's powers work in this world, too. Or maybe that power is independent of him because you're half-oni."

Jinx flexes her bicep. "Or maybe it's because I'm a strong, independent woman."

"That's kind of unfair." Peyton wrinkles his nose. "I wish I could fly all the time."

"Well." I shrug. "Like your dad says . . ."

"Life isn't always fair!" we all chorus.

"Check this out!" Jinx blasts from both hands, almost hitting me. "Yeee-hawwww!"

Good thing I'm still wearing the helmet. "Jinx, for cripes sake, stop!"

"Careful." Peyton adjusts his backpack. "Accidentally setting people on fire is not going to make you the homecoming queen."

"Like I'd *want* to be homecoming queen." Jinx takes out her dagger. It's got some gross yellow stuff on it that I don't want to look at too closely. She carefully wipes the blade clean with a leaf. "I'll leave that for Lovey."

Lovey. Just hearing her name makes me wince. But I'll have to do something to show her I'm sorry for breaking her nose. Maybe I could bring her a nice warm bowl of worm stew. . . . Nah. Maybe I'll drop some books off at her house so she has something to do while she heals. Though I'm not entirely sure she can read.

"Now let's go home already," says Jinx.

Peyton takes off down the mountain, his long legs flying almost as well as his wings. "Best plan I've heard in ages!"

Jinx sprints after him, her speedy muscles making up for what she lacks in size. I, of course, am left standing behind, still wearing the samurai gear. For a second, I consider putting some jets on my sneakers again. But that thought melts away almost as soon as I think it.

Instead, I jog slowly behind my now out-of-sight friends. And in a minute, I find Peyton and Jinx stopped under an oak tree, their hands on the trunk like they got there in a tie, waiting for me.

CHAPTER FORTY

usk is settling over the mountain when my house finally
appears in sight. Crickets chirp, and the cooling air evaporates all the sticky sweat on our skin. I slap at a buzzing
insect on my arm. I've never been so glad to see a mosquito.

Mom and Dad are sitting on the back porch with Inu between
their feet. Of course the dog sees us before they do, and he stands
up. *Woof! Woof!* He races toward us, a bullet train heading straight
for Xandertown. Before I can say *Whoa!* I'm flat on my back, and his
tongue is slathering my face. "Stop, Inu!" I say with a laugh. Peyton
pulls him off me, and the dog attacks him with the same gusto, slob-
bering all over him. Then Inu goes for Jinx, who falls to the ground
laughing.

Next Dad and Mom are hugging us. "We got your note." Dad kisses the top of my head. "It's been two weeks."

"*Two weeks?*" Peyton screeches, leaping up and waving his arms. "Please tell me my parents didn't call the police."

"We, ah, had to arrange a bit of a trick there." Dad winks at me. "Your mother had to work her Irish charms."

I cringe. "*Irish charms?* Ew. Dad, that's Peyton's father we're talking about."

Mom giggles. "Nah, it's a fairy trick. A bit of talk and Mr. Phasis was convinced that you and Peyton had gone on a wee trip with Obāchan."

"A trip?"

"To an ice cream factory." Obāchan appears in the door. She looks fantastic—strong and healthy, with glowing skin. We all surround her for a hug. She kisses each of our heads in turn, and I don't even mind it.

"Yum," says Peyton. "Now that's a trip I would enjoy. Much more than boot camp." He wrinkles his beak-like nose, and I know he's thinking about how he's going to have to face his father soon.

"You don't need to go far," says Obāchan. "The good news is, I have homemade ice cream in the freezer." We cheer. "The bad news is, it's red bean–flavored."

Peyton and I pretend to gag, but Jinx looks up, eager. "That's my favorite!"

"Then you're in luck!" Obāchan waves my friends inside.

I linger on the porch with my parents. It's so good to see them again, bright and alive and not zoned out in front of the TV.

"We're eager to hear about your adventures," says Dad. He examines my helmet and rope. "I see you've picked up a few new accessories."

"Uh, yeah. I hope you have nothing else to do for a few hours," I say with a smile. Then, more seriously, "I wish you could have seen me defeat the oni."

"I'm sure I would have been proud." He pats me on the back. His eyes twinkling, he can't help adding, "I guess all that training I forced you to do came in handy."

"Yeah, yeah, yeah. But if you say *I told you so*, I'm running back there!" I grin. "And guess what?" I turn to Mom. "I had another secret weapon."

She gives me an intensely curious look.

"Turns out you're not the only one around here who can glow." I wiggle my eyebrows. Extending my hands, I send energy out through my fingers, wondering if it'll work.

It does, just for a second. The glow fades away, and I shrug apologetically. "I still have to work out the kinks."

My mother's eyes seem to flash for a second, and then one side of her mouth curls up. "So, my son carries the light of the tall folk." She holds her arms out to me.

I step into them and squeeze her tight, as though trying to make up for all of our lost time, breathing in her familiar scent. Home—I am finally home. My father, watching us, wipes away a tear.

When I break away, I say, "I never thought I'd be called one of the tall folk," and we all burst out laughing.

"You know what this means, don't you?" my mother asks.

"What?"

"Double the training!" she says.

I groan.

My father clears his throat. "Come, let's get some ice cream before it's all gone." He opens the screen door. My mom follows right behind.

Before I go in, I turn and look out to the east. A white sliver is just beginning to rise over the horizon. Most of the moon is in shadow. Still, I think I can see a fuzzy halo around it. It looks like a crescent cookie in a plastic bag.

I salute it, a smile stretching across my face. Maybe I will see it up close again someday. For now, though, I plan to enjoy some summer vacation.

PRAISE FOR MOMOTARO BOOK ONE

XANDER AND THE LOST ISLAND OF MONSTERS

"With phantasmagorical environments, flying white rats, a fire-breathing bird, a giant, a snow demon, and other creepy things, there is abundant action. This retelling of a Japanese folktale celebrates courage, friendship, and pride of heritage, while featuring unforgettable characters and leaving readers eager for the next installment in this new series." —*Booklist*

"Dilloway seamlessly weaves necessary background information into the fast-paced, action-filled plot. Xander's candid and straightforward first-person narration will instantly resonate with middle grade readers, as will his story's themes of self-acceptance and friendship. Yoon's comic-style illustrations evoke Xander's talent for drawing and bring welcome visual interest. This fast-paced fantasy adventure with a foundation in Japanese culture is perfect for fans of Percy Jackson."
—*School Library Journal*

"A richly imagined story filled with its own unique blend of magic, mystery, and adventure. Readers will surely be adding Xander to their list of favorite heroes (and wishing they had their own Inu)!" —Shannon Messenger